ANYWHERE THE WEEDS GROW

DANIELLE STEWART

ANYWHERE THE WEEDS GROW

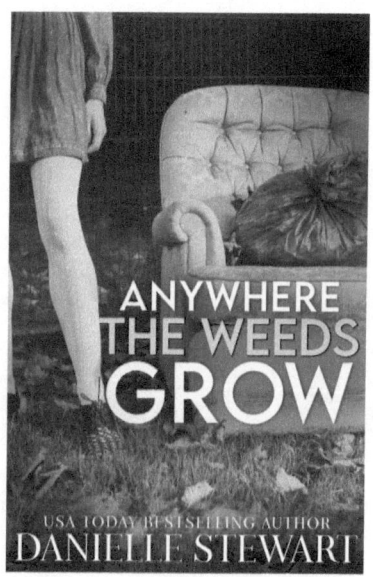

There is a vast difference between having it all and being fulfilled. In the eyes of most onlookers, Carol Burgess couldn't ask for a more gratifying life. She'd climbed the corporate ladder and taken her swipes at the glass ceiling, leaving a few cracks along the way. When she's finally the one in charge, she discovers change is still taboo in the elite literary industry. Faced with the choice of keeping the status quo or starting a revolution of ideas, Carol seeks out a fresh and undiscovered voice in the writing world. Rather than searching the usual universities and conferences, she broadens her pursuit to a less conventional hunting ground. Sending her charming assistant, Terrance, to entice her reluctant prospect, sets in motion a journey none of them expect.

Marta Leduc longs to remember her childhood more vividly. The urge to make sense of the chaos and trauma remains strong even after she accomplishes her lifelong goal of publishing her novel. Generations of her family followed the same trajectory of their New Hampshire town. They thrived on booming millwork and then, upon the downturn, crumbled just as the uninhabited brick buildings did. When success is at her fingertips, Marta is faced with the reality that her past is always nipping at her heels. Like the lingering ache of whiplash, she understands the misfortunes she's endured will always be a part of her. Encouraged by Terrance, Marta begins to imagine a life she never thought possible.

Carol and Marta must unite if they intend to change "what always has been" into "what could be." When their fates intertwine, neither is safe from the forces that wish to hold them back. Will sheer determination be enough to keep them ahead of the next disaster?

CHAPTER ONE

Marta

Memories are gelatinous. Conjuring them, even with great concentration and effort, was like gripping a fish that didn't want to be held. Jerking and pulsing, they always wriggled back to where they'd come from.

Those were thoughts that plagued Marta in recent months. She was exhausted from trying to recall things that seemed hidden behind a soap-scum-like film her mind had created. She wanted to see everything precisely. Technicolor playbacks of what her life had been so far. Wouldn't that make sorting things out easy?

With that type of clarity, blame could be assigned with confidence. Hero and villain could be labeled with conviction. Marta could account for all of her present-day problems and hang-ups by tying them neatly to some distinct moment in her childhood. It would be so tidy and efficient.

But it wasn't working that way. Remembering specific times in her childhood was tenuous. It seemed the harder she tried, the more difficult it became. The best she could do was wait for a trigger. The most peculiar things would transport her back a decade or two. Today it was the strawberry muffin that had been offered to her for breakfast.

The summery sweet smell and the shade of pink brought her back to her seventh birthday. Drawing in a deep breath and pulling the muffin to her nose, she could remember it all. Her strawberry birthday cake. The one that didn't taste at all like strawberry and ended up smashed against the wall.

Birthdays were epic. Turning seven felt monumental. Climbing further up that ladder of years, striving for double digits. Daydreaming of being a teenager. It was important work to grow older, and Marta took it seriously. For a little girl, she took most things seriously.

The party would be tiny, just her cousins on her mother's side. The four of them would be coming over to her house for birthday cake. There was really no room for people in her home. It was bursting at the seams with the five of them who lived there, but somehow, they could throw a party. It was like how she'd seen clowns endlessly pile out of a tiny car. Some kind of magic made it all work.

They'd find space to pin the tail on the donkey. The same set they'd been using for as long as Marta could remember. There would be tiny cups of watered-down powdered lemonade and a couple of generic happy birthday napkins they'd bought in bulk years ago.

The sun was shining on the frost-covered trees, and the wind was coming in through her rattling windows. Her mother had cleverly taped plastic wrap over the ones that let the most air in, but eventually it would be blown off or ripped by the kids playing too rough in the house. Marta found it satisfying to poke her little finger through the stretched-tight plastic, which always got her in trouble and left her room freezing.

The cold was a beast. For most kids, the monsters under their beds were fanged and hairy figments of their imagination. For Marta, she was always outrunning the cold and its icy grip or the heat and its scorching touch. Temperature control was a luxury usually out of reach for her family. Air conditioning drove up the utility bill, so strategically placed fans blew hot air at them during heat waves.

When winter set in, their house had an electric oven that blew out heat from vents on the side. It would warm the kitchen and the small living area but nothing else. Her father lugged a few portable heaters around the house on the coldest nights, but even at her age, she knew they were dangerous. Bad dreams didn't keep Marta up at night. Worry and the temperatures did.

Today, on her seventh birthday, the cold wouldn't deter her. She would wear her best dress. Her only dress. No bother that it was a summer sundress, and this was the dead of winter in New Hampshire. It didn't matter that it had once belonged to someone else. Like all of her clothes, it arrived in a garbage bag of hand-me-downs and smelled of an unfamiliar laundry detergent.

Women her mother worked with were always passing along what their children outgrew or didn't want. This dress had sent Marta into squeals of excitement when she first pulled it from the black garbage bag. She'd worn it for over a year and a half, and it was just now beginning to fit her properly.

The lace was a bit frayed at the hem, and there was a tiny hole by the straps. But the fabric was still a vibrant purple. There was plenty of life left in that dress, as her mother would always say about the things people gave them. Most importantly, Marta felt beautiful every time she put it on. It was impossible to refrain from a twirl or two in her mother's bedroom mirror.

There was so much to be enthusiastic about. Best of all, this year Marta's cake would finally be her own. Because she and her two brothers were all born in the same month, January, they usually shared one cake with all three of their names written in frosting. Marta, being the youngest, never got to pick the flavor. But this year, her oldest brother, Glenn, had protested this tradition and won.

They'd get their unique cakes on their own special days. It was a wish Marta didn't even know she had until it was granted. Now that her day was here, she requested a strawberry cake with strawberry frosting and maybe even some real berries on the top.

It wasn't until she pranced out of her mother's bedroom with her two-sizes-too-big hand-me-down patent leather shoes that she realized something was off. Freezing in the doorway of the kitchen, she held her breath. Her tummy flipped and her scalp tingled in that precarious warning way. Marta had grown accustomed to these sensations. They protected her from stepping into the wrong room when the arguing was about to shake the walls. A space would grow physically cold just before chaos erupted. But this was her day. A birthday. Surely it wouldn't be marred by fighting.

"The cake is horrible," Glenn snapped, clanking his fork down on the scratched Formica counter. There were worn spots and knife slices all over the pale, vomit green laminate, but Marta loved the uniqueness of it. She'd never seen it in any other house she'd been in. No one else in the house found it quite as charming. But that could be said for many things Marta liked that other people did not appreciate.

"Stop," her mother threatened. There were octaves of her mother's voice she'd learned to heed. Glenn was getting dangerously close to provoking her. Something Marta avoided at all costs. "It's a cake. Kids love cake. It'll be fine."

"What did you make it with?" Glenn bit out angrily. "It tastes like nothing. It's pink, but it's not strawberry."

"We didn't have milk," she replied in a hushed voice. "You are drinking it by the gallon every few days, and I don't get paid again until Friday. I used water. And there wasn't any strawberry flavored cake mix. It's vanilla with some red food coloring."

"She wanted strawberries on top." Glenn was standing now, and everything about him was less familiar to Marta by the day. Twelve-year-old Glenn was her playmate. In the backyard, he built little forts for her dolls. He pushed her on the swing when she begged him enough. Thirteen-year-old Glenn, with his broad shoulders and deepening voice, was something entirely different. Another new development was how he began taking frequent opportunities to fight with their parents. Challenging them at every turn. Marta didn't understand why someone would want to do such a thing. Especially when the house was already full of yelling and anger without his help.

Her mother slapped the frosting-covered spatula down on the counter, clearly making a point to be louder than he was with the fork. "Glenn, what do you want me to do? Should I go foraging in the forest for berries? We don't have the money for it. The kids will like the cake. It'll be fine. Stop making a big deal out of this."

"You should start making a big deal about this. You had the money for cigarettes this week—money to buy nylons. But your daughter can't have the cake she wants? How many times have we hung these stupid streamers? They're colored paper, we really can't get new ones? It doesn't look like you're having a party in here. It looks depressing."

Marta didn't even have time to stiffen her back and bite at the raw part of her cheek the way she did when she was bracing for the worst. Her mother was quick. Her hand contacted Glenn's freckled cheek before Marta could close her eyes and try to block out the image.

Glenn didn't flinch. That was new too. There was no longer any pleading or crying when something like this happened. He just leaned back slightly, trying to make sure she wasn't going to take another swipe.

"You're not helping," her mother whimpered angrily. "You're not making this any easier. Do you think we want it to be this way? Do you think this is the cake I wanted to make?" The cake was high now, barely balanced in her left hand. "I can afford to make one good cake. One cake that everyone will like, but that wasn't good enough for you this year. You had to make a stink about it. You had to have your own cake—chocolate with sprinkles. Well, you got it. Jonah got his. Confetti. But there just isn't enough left two weeks later for your sister. You're the problem. Not me. Not my cigarettes or the damn nylons I need to wear to work. You."

Her finger was in his face. Inches from his eye. The fire in her mother's expression was what made Marta quiver. There was a point, once crossed, that meant there was no going back.

Marta wished she had control. When she felt this afraid, it always happened. As she stood in a puddle of urine, her white shoes sopping wet, a tiny cry escaped her. Enough of a sound to have her mother and her brother snap their heads in her direction. A blast of fury visibly shot through her mother as she flung the cake across the room and splattered it against the dingy, peeling wallpaper. There was a yell. One her mother would do only on the angriest of occasions. Primal and wild. It indicated the complete loss of control. It meant things were too far gone to fix. The wooden spoon would come out next. The drawer would slam open, the silverware tray would shift and clank, and then no one would be safe.

Wetting her pants was not something Marta did spitefully, even though she'd be accused of that over and over. It was not a weapon she wielded to hurt her mother. It was a reflex she couldn't control. It didn't matter though; it was always met with anger and threats of being punished. Labeling her as disgusting and manipulative was more comfortable than admitting they were shocking her half to death.

Fifteen minutes later, her cousins would arrive. There would be cake on the wall and pee on the floor, and a handprint on her brother's cheek. Marta wouldn't be able to sit well from the stinging on her bottom. A wooden spoon was a handy tool. And no one would say anything about any of it. Aunts would sweep in and smile and clean up. Uncles would tell familiar jokes and bounce children on their knees. They'd cram into a space that wasn't fit to hold half of them, and they'd sing happy birthday. Lighting cigarettes and pouring clear alcohol into paper cups, they'd change the space from a little girl's birthday party to a place for playing cards and speaking crassly.

That had been the start of Marta's broken gauge. She couldn't measure the danger or the volatility of a situation accurately because the grown-ups around her wouldn't react appropriately. They'd pretend nothing had happened, and so she couldn't tell if what happened was terrible. As an adult, it made her desire to relive it. To remember with clarity. She wanted to take stock again. To look at her life through the lens of adulthood. To measure its dysfunction more clearly. Clinically.

Marta pushed the strawberry muffin away from her that morning, unable to take a bite. She had never eaten strawberry flavored things after that day. Most of the time, Marta told people she didn't like it. Now she was beginning to remember why.

There was still plenty she couldn't recall well. Her reminiscing was mostly flashes of chipped paint, empty cupboards, and lopsided at-home haircuts. The only time she did get to talk about things was in the company of her family. The problem was those stories were told with laughter. They'd recall everything with an air of amusement no matter how dark the story was.

Weren't we wild? Didn't we have a good time? Other families are so dull. Remember that time Mom threw the cake? Remember when Dad would let us walk alone to the store? How old were we? Eight? Was it six miles?

The reminiscing was always distorted. It made Marta question herself and her sanity. Were they having a good time when they were children? Did that make them unique and quirky? It felt like more than that. Precarious and toxic. No matter how much everyone around her laughed, somewhere in her heart she understood that a cake on the wall wasn't funny. It was frightening. They always left out the slap to her brother's face when they retold the story.

Even now, her brother Glenn would tease her about wetting her pants until she was nearly a teen. No one ever asked, *why is she still doing that? What is she feeling? Is she okay?*

If she pressed further into her memories, the yelling would dominate and that wasn't her goal. Most days she tried to remember something positive. She didn't want to cut short the thoughts of their family days at the beach with sun-soaked skin and giant sandcastles made without buckets or shovels. But Marta would remember the sunburns and hunger pangs. The jealousy she felt as other children stood in line for soft pretzels and sandwiches. How she coveted the pretty pink buckets and sturdy shovels other kids brought with them. How she watched other kids being slathered with sunscreen—looking impatient and irritated—and longed for someone to show her that level of care. If she dug too deep into the past, she could tarnish the shiny parts the people in her family had been polishing for years. But still, she longed to know. The truth was something she was hungry for but could also be poison.

"Can you sign that for me?"

The words cut short the memory, and Marta felt anger swell in her. She'd been close to something—a foggy outline of recalling what was always out of reach. Like the snapping back of the bungee cord after a jump, she was quickly yanked upward and away from the thing she was trying to remember.

Just as quickly as it had formed, the anger melted into a puddle of guilt. Marta did not like to disturb anyone around her in any way. Other people's discomfort made her squirm.

"Absolutely, I'd love to," Marta hummed happily. For all the longing she'd been doing for the past, she tried hard not to overlook the present. This was not a reality she ever imagined for herself. Not a wish she ever thought would come true.

Marta was sitting behind a smartly decorated folding table and in front of a banner with her name on it. The bookstore in Sullivan, New Hampshire, had been wonderfully accommodating this morning. The novelty of a book signing had not worn off for Marta, even though this was her fourth one. It was still strange to hold it in her hand and realize people wanted to read the book she wrote. It was astounding to her that she'd forged a story in the heat of her mind and shaped it into something people seemed to enjoy.

It was more surprising that they'd want her to sign it. Enough people to form a line at the bookstore this morning, their copies in hand. Though they were still throwing impatient glances her way. The crowd wanted to see her but wasn't willing to wait too long.

She wasn't that important.

It had been precisely as hard as people had said it

would be. Marta had nearly given up the idea of publishing her book. She toiled and edited. Second-guessed and started over. She pitched it and mailed it until, finally, a publishing company responded positively. A few mentions in local magazines turned into a feature on the New England Author Spotlight on public television. Even some unexpected local awards came her way. From there, she was known. Not widely. Not by random people on the street, but an audience connected her name with something they enjoyed. A wild accomplishment she'd doubted she would ever achieve. Yet here it was, right in her hand. Existing despite all the things that tried to stand in her way.

That should have fulfilled her. The vessel that was her soul, the cup that spent most of her life empty or tipped over, should have been made full by the acceptance of what she'd written. People complimented her. Encouraged her. That was how these things worked. You pour yourself into something, people enjoy it, and you are WHOLE. The realization of that broken contract between her and the cosmos was crushing lately. Why wasn't this enough? When would it be?

"It's spelled L-A-R-K. My parents thought it was a cute name. I'm still not sold." The woman was barely twenty. Her brows were painted on in that obvious kind of way that screamed *trying too hard*. Her delicate features didn't seem to need the extra makeup, but Marta didn't judge. People required all kinds of things to be able to face the world.

Leaning in close over the table, Lark watched to make

sure she spelled it right. Marta held her breath and nodded, never good with strong perfumes, hoping the next person in line might be less abrasive to her senses. But Lark wasn't stepping to the side. There was no "handler" here. Her book was successful, but she hadn't risen to the level of fame that would afford such help. She still had to manage people all on her own. A skill she'd yet to master.

Lark took the book back and clutched it to her chest. "The story of Eden and Will changed my life." Her eyes went wide, and her smile was suddenly comically big. A clown who teetered back and forth between jovial and frightening. "The chapter at the waterfall. I was shaking."

Those weren't the parts of the book Marta enjoyed most. Those were the things she had to include to make the book marketable. There had to be moments that made the heart flutter to include parts that made the mind stew and churn. It was a silent contract between readers and writers. Most people didn't want to spend all their time thinking instead of feeling. They wanted to escape. That was something Marta could understand. "Oh, thank you. I'm so glad you liked it."

"Tell me that's based on a true story. I want to believe you've been out there meeting men like that." Lark's eyes were desperate for hope, and Marta was never one to steal that from someone.

"Will is definitely based on someone I know," Marta lied. "He didn't jump headfirst into a waterfall, but he's saved my butt plenty of times."

Lark swooned. "I knew it. You can't write stories like this if you haven't lived it. At least some version of it."

"Have a great rest of your day," Marta offered, hoping it would serve as the period to punctuate this encounter.

Lark saw it more as a comma. "I tried to get my last boyfriend to read this book. It should be a dating manual. Men could learn a thing or two. The way Will showed up for her on her last day at work, reassuring her that it would all be fine. That wrecked me."

"Yeah," Marta replied awkwardly. She waved for the next person in line to step up and gestured for their copy of the book. "It was nice meeting you, Lark."

Fluttering her eyelashes, Lark pressed on. "Tell me more about this guy you based him on. I bet he's even better in real life."

"I'm sorry, Lark. I don't want to keep everyone waiting too long. Some folks are looking a little impatient."

"Right," Lark sighed. "Thanks for signing the book." Her head dropped a bit, and her shoulders sagged. Her wide eyes were suddenly blinking rapidly, and her cheeks flushed.

This was the weapon from which Marta had no defense. The idea that she'd disappointed someone made her palms sweat, her heart race. There were well-worn grooves in her personality, formed by the heavy marching of people she'd let come too close. They treaded over her with a stubborn frequency that left her permanently marked. If a relationship was meant to be *give and take*, she hadn't realized that those were not assigned roles for each person. One was not meant to do all the giving while the other endlessly kept taking.

All those crossed wires were a magnet for dominant people. It was as if the first person had left the trail for the next to follow. And follow they did.

Lark and her suddenly-sad eyes were now Marta's responsibility, and she sputtered out an offer. "If you hang around a little while, maybe we can get a coffee."

Marta felt her skin prickle. Those weren't her words. They weren't tethered to her actual feelings. But her invitation did the job. Lark inflated like a balloon kissing a helium tank, relieving the weight that had slammed down on Marta. Problem solved. Crisis averted.

"Coffee?" The woman now handing over her copy to be signed raised her brows high. "I'd love to sit and have a coffee with you."

Marta had traded one anxiety for another. A quick slide of her hands, and she'd gone from the guilt of disappointing someone to social anxiety territory. The complexities of her personality were nimble. They had no problem taking turns as long as one of them controlled her life.

She cleared her throat and kept her voice very quiet. "Yeah, I saw a coffee shop across the street. But I won't be done here for an hour or so."

Please don't say you'll wait.

· · ·

"I'll wait," Lark replied excitedly. The other woman nodded her agreement.

"Great," Marta mouthed, not even able to put sound to it.

"Can you sign mine to Carol?" her second coffee companion asked, handing over her opened book. "And maybe write something witty in there too."

"Sure thing," Marta answered, sweeping her favorite pen across the paper. Things like that, pens and brushes, those were the things she'd learned to covet and hold on to. People were fickle and unreliable. But her favorite pen, with that heavy flowing dark blue ink and super comfortable grip, was something she could count on. It understood her better than anyone. She gave it a special place in her purse and never lent it out.

"Looks like your pen's out of ink," Carol reported casually as though it were no big deal at all.

"What!" Marta said through a tiny gasp holding it up to get a closer look.

Even her pen was starting trouble today.

CHAPTER TWO

After an hour of signing books, coffee with two strangers was not on the short list of things Marta wished to do. She'd actually started making a list of things she'd rather do. This was a game she and her brothers had played when they were younger and tasked with visiting their great-grandmother in the nursing home. On the car ride over, they'd make a list of things they'd prefer to do. Giggling to herself as she crossed the street toward the coffee shop, she thought back to some of her favorites. She'd rather put out a campfire with her hands. Or fall down a never-ending staircase. Eat moldy cheese. Step on a rusty nail. Have an at-home root canal.

Stifling her laugh, Marta tried to seem normal as she made her way to the door of the coffee shop. Humor had been the healing balm that carried their family through the darkest of times. No joke was too crass, no jab too personal.

Funerals broke out in giggles. Weddings were basically stand-up comedy routines disguised as toasts.

You had to be resilient. But most of all, you had to be quick. The weak or tenderhearted would not survive. On many occasions, her cousins had brought their new significant others to Christmas gatherings that resulted in them leaving in tears.

To be a Leduc, or in their orbit, strength was required —for both the yelling and the joking. For all the flaws and cracks in Marta's personality, for all the damage and the dents, she was durable. Marta could make people laugh.

Perhaps she'd even get a few chuckles out of her coffee dates. It was time to make the best of it since there was no graceful way to bow out now. Luckily, Lark had a class to get to, so after a little chatting and a small latte, she excused herself. She seemed reluctant to leave but sweet in her goodbye. It hadn't been as bad as Marta had predicted.

Carol, who was older and expectedly more adept in social settings, would undoubtedly get the hint. Marta was giving all the body language and clues to show Carol it was time for them to go their separate ways. When Lark made it to the door, Marta attempted to stand up, bumping the table with her knee and nearly spilling what was left of her coffee.

"Wait," Carol said, looking suddenly sheepish. "Forgive me. I feel quite disingenuous now. My name is Carol Burgess. I saw this signing on your webpage and thought perhaps I could come to speak with you in person. I know that meeting for coffee likely wasn't what you had planned, but this is critical. I didn't want to bring it up until Lark left."

"I don't follow . . ." Marta said, looking more closely at Carol now. She was terrible with names but she could usually place faces. Nothing about Carol seemed familiar. Her strawberry blonde hair was thick and cut to shoulder length. Smooth and obedient in a way Marta envied. There was hardly anything she could do to keep her kinky frizz under control. Carol looked like she woke up with spun silk atop her head.

Piercing blue eyes glistened under heavy lids, making Carol look a bit dreamy. As if she was so relaxed by a life well lived that she never needed to be wide-eyed by something shocking. This was a look Marta would have remembered. Carol was a stranger.

"I'm with the Milton Cesar Foundation for the Arts." Carol stuck her hand out as though they were properly meeting finally. "We've been trying to contact you through your literary agent."

Carol adjusted her gold bracelet but not nervously the way Marta would have if she wore jewelry. It was just a slight movement as it clanked against the table. Marta couldn't help but eye Carol's outfit closely. The thick, rich-looking stitching of her pale blue blazer was magnificent. Marta was always mystified to see people in clothes that fit perfectly. The coat and bright white blouse beneath didn't bunch or fall too long in the sleeve. The fabric was pristine as if it had just been purchased and there hadn't been time to dribble coffee down the front or smudge makeup on the collar.

Though her hands showed age, Carol's nails were a playful sage color, the polish unchipped and fresh looking. She wore two rings, neither of which seemed to be a wedding band. An emerald stone surrounded by diamonds glistened as Carol pulled her hand up toward her face.

As usual, Marta felt the undertow of self-doubt yanking at her feet, trying to pull her down. She was wearing a pair of black pants she'd worn while waitressing for the last two years. They were too big and cinched funny under her belt. Her one belt. It was reversible. Black on one side, brown on the other. The buckle swiveled to make this work.

Marta understood that her belt was supposed to match her shoes, so she flipped it around accordingly, depending on what pair of boots she put on that day. Her shirt was a cheap blouse from a discount store. It fit properly, but the pattern was hideous, and it was obviously not made well. But its best feature was being wrinkle resistant. Marta folded her arms over as much of the ugly shirt as she could as she continued to listen.

"Do you hear me, Marta? We've been trying to contact you through your literary agent." Carol kept her expression undeservingly patient.

Marta's brows dove together finally, her confusion growing. Her instinct to joke took over. "Well, if you get in touch with him or her, will you let me know? I'd like to meet them."

Carol's face lit at the sarcasm. She was disarming and maternal. Like a television mother from the old black and white shows Marta had seen reruns of. Pop on a frilly apron and put a tray of warm cookies in her hand, and Marta would listen to whatever Carol had to say for hours.

"You don't have an agent. We know that now. It took a little while, but we figured it out." Carol's laugh was somewhere between a cackle and a high-pitched siren. It was intrusive but seemed beyond her control. The kind of laughter that was as identifying as a fingerprint. Surely she was known for it among her friends. When she regained her breath, she softened her expression. "Once we realized you didn't have representation, we tried to reach you directly, but your information wasn't available anywhere. I sent an email through the contact option on your website but didn't hear back."

"I'm a week or so behind on those," Marta apologized. Since her last interview on a local New Hampshire radio station, the messages had gotten to be more than she could keep up with herself. "Maybe after you find my literary agent, you could start looking for my personal assistant. If you bump into my chef, send him to my house too." This was all so comical that Marta forgot for a moment just what Carol might actually want from her.

Carol giggled again and waved her off as though it was no big deal. "I can't even boil water, so maybe I'll look for two chefs."

Marta leaned in a bit and raised a brow to Carol.

"What is it you were trying to ask my imaginary agent? I don't know if I can answer, but I'll try."

"Well, I have quite a bit to talk to you about, actually. I saw this signing event on your website, and I thought maybe it would be a good way to connect. I have something to review with you."

"Review?" They'd been talking now for several minutes since Lark left, and Marta was still no closer to knowing what this was about. The only thing that kept her from completely freaking out was Carol's bemused expression seemed to hold enough excitement for the both of them.

Surely, she couldn't be about to deliver bad news. Not with that much joy pouring out of her.

"Should my imaginary lawyer be here for this?" Marta shifted nervously in her chair.

Smiling that charming smile again, Carol folded her hands neatly and placed them on the table. She finally looked ready to share what she came here for. "I have some big news for you, Marta. You've been selected as this year's recipient of the Milton Cesar Breakout Writer Award."

"Selected? Here in New Hampshire?" Marta cleared her throat, any more jokes evaporating from her mind.

"It's a national award," Carol corrected. "Are you familiar with it?"

"I know who Milton Cesar was, of course. And I've seen the national award ceremony plenty of times. I just didn't know you did smaller ones." Her cheeks pinked from the ignorance she must have been flashing.

Sympathetic bemusement spread across Carol's face. "We don't do smaller ceremonies. The award is presented to a rising star in the literary world as part of our annual event. This recognition launched Tabitha Saint Barr, Douglas Prince, and Lidia Jane, just to name a few. They were each recipients of the award and obviously now are household names."

Carol waited. Her expectant look only made Marta more nervous. This was where the cloak would usually fall away. Being a poor child who was now a slightly less poor woman left ample opportunities to make a fool of herself, especially with smartly dressed, worldly women like Carol. The distance between them would suddenly become far more expansive than this small café table. They'd be separated by the differences in the price of their purses. By the places they'd traveled. The people they knew. At any moment, their differences would become painfully obvious.

"Are you sure?" Marta asked, certain this was some kind of mistake. "I've only written the one book."

"I'm very sure. It's a brilliant book." Carol held up her recently signed copy. "Worthy of the award. Of many awards, actually. My team and I read thousands of books a year, looking for the right one. This is it."

She put her hand to her heart. "I'm Marta Leduc. I don't know too many people named Marta, but I think this is a mix-up of some kind. Occasionally people think I'm Mary Leblanc. She wrote that great murder mystery series. She's sixty-five, from Texas, and a redhead, but you might have mixed us up. I'm not the person you're looking for."

"I know it's a shock," Carol whispered, putting the book down and leaning in. "It's a lot to take in. But you should know your life is about to change." Carol looked abundantly hopeful. Not Marta's favorite expression. Hope was just the precursor to disappointment.

"Change?" For Marta, it was a word laced with anxiety. A change had never proven to be positive in her experience. The devil she knew was always more comforting than the one she might meet next.

"The ceremony is the launching point. You said you've seen it?"

"Of course," Marta assured her. "I try to catch it every year. The people sitting up in the balcony while everyone goes on stage and raves about their talent. Those medals around their necks. It's iconic."

"Those recipients are what people tune in for. Their performances and the accolades bestowed on them make great entertainment. I, however, always loved the rising star award. You've seen that feature, right?"

"Yes, they do that video. The movie." Marta's mouth felt full and her words clumsy, but she knew sitting silently would make her look like a fool. Saying something was better than nothing, she hoped.

"Right." Carol nodded, looking oddly proud of Marta for getting the answer right. "Each year, the award recipient participates in the *Up Until Yesterday* video. It's your life up until you received the award. Who you are, what you've experienced. It's meant to serve as a roadmap. It answers the question of how exactly one arrives at that stage. That's what people want to know, and we give them a front-row seat."

"Yes," Marta responded, darkness enveloping the excitement she'd begun to feel. She had seen the awards and did remember the videos. Tuning in to the show was a must for her over the years. Marta had loved writing since she was a young girl. It was an escape and a passion. When every other school subject was too hard and her grades imploded, writing remained her niche. It was the one thing that would keep a teacher hanging on, hoping that there was something to salvage in Marta.

The award ceremony was a peek into the lives of successful creative people. Those folks seemed to have harnessed their raw talent and Marta always watched intently. Tabitha Saint Barr, a winner five years ago, had taken the camera crew back to her private school. They walked the campus. Highlighted where she'd made her valedictorian speech. There was another author, his name escaping her, who'd grown up in Germany. His father was a diplomat. The video crew toured his favorite places to play golf and chess.

"The videos are very well done." Marta gulped. She could already see the problems with this opportunity.

"They are really a fun experience." Carol beamed, blinking her heavy eyes and waiting for something more.

Marta envied the idea of memory lane being a street you'd want to stroll down rather than a dark alley to avoid.

Carol continued explaining as though it were all so simple.

"You'll start right away, planning it out with me, and then we'll spend time filming. After that, you just coast until the award ceremony in California."

"I don't know," Marta lifted her now-cold coffee and sipped to hide for a moment. "I think you might want to give some more consideration to someone else. I am so honored to even be considered. It just isn't a good fit for me." She pressed her hand to her collarbone and tried to steady herself.

"Take a breath," Carol suggested, the wrinkles around her eyes deepening as she smiled. "This is your first time being awarded the Milton Cesar award, but know that this is also my first time having the pleasure of informing the recipient. It's all quite overwhelming. I've heard stories from past years of people fainting, others dancing on tables."

"Has anyone ever said no?" Marta asked in a tiny voice, her lips barely moving. Her eyes were unblinking.

Carol was stunned but seemed skilled at righting herself quickly. Stretching her spine out and rolling her shoulders back, she painted on a smile. "You're in shock. I expected as much."

"I think maybe you've made a mistake," Marta apologized. Her intention wasn't to make Carol feel bad. Clearly, this was an essential part of her job. But Carol screwed it up. "Even if my book is worthy of the award, I wouldn't be. Those authors you mentioned are of a pedigree, a background that's very different from mine. I appreciate the consideration. It's flattering, but I think you should reconsider."

"You and I are not so different," Carol explained with a knowing look. Her saggy, sleepy eyes narrowed, and her head nodded affirmatively. "And there is not only one path toward success. People will connect with you; they'll be inspired by you."

There it was.

The piece Marta had been missing. As if the invisible ink had just been held under the correct light and became easy to read. Carol wasn't ignorant about who Marta really was. Instead, she was silly enough to romanticize the little fragments she could find out about Marta. That was worse. The starry-eyed look Carol held was built on the idea of a storybook transformation. She would be the fairy godmother, and when she was finished working her magic Marta would spin before her in a sparkly dress and glass slippers. That was a dangerously disappointing game Carol was sure to lose.

"I don't think you and I have much in common at all," Marta corrected gently. "And that's not a bad thing. You seem lovely. I just think maybe you've got the wrong impression of me."

"Marta," Carol lifted her coffee up and took a long sip. "You have a story. One that people will want to hear. I'm not talking about your book, either. I'm talking about your story."

"You know my story?" Marta asked, suddenly defensive of her secrets. The burden of her life could be heavy, but it was still hers to carry and contain however she liked. No one got to decide what Marta put on display. In a life where she often felt powerless, being guarded was the only control she had.

"Not nearly all of it," Carol admitted, holding a hand up to slow the conversation down. "And I'd be foolish to make assumptions from the little bit I do know. But you have to understand that no path disqualifies you from this award or from the career you were clearly built for. I know this is all quite daunting. Just take some time to think it over. I'll be in touch next week, and we can make a plan."

That word was the only one to compute. Like a bee, plans were little clumps of pollen Marta couldn't buzz by without inspecting. She'd have to slow down and land on the idea. Lists and strategies had buoyed her through the most tumultuous times in her life. Even in this dizzying situation, the word plan still enticed her. "All right," she agreed. "Here's my number." Grabbing an old receipt from her purse, she jotted her phone number down and slid it over to Carol, who was now standing.

It was evident that Carol wouldn't just give up, so it was better to create a line of communication, a way for them to connect. A method for Marta to let her down gently in the future.

"We're going to make something great here," Carol promised, and Marta cringed. That level of blind optimism always made her feel queasy for the other person. Marta knew what it felt like to fall from great heights emotionally. She didn't wish it on other people.

Marta nodded politely as Carol pushed through the coffee shop door and disappeared from view. Stunned and swirling in doubt, she wondered if her vivid imagination was to blame. It had played tricks on her before. Led her toward places she didn't belong. But Carol was undoubtedly real. She hadn't been conjured up by a dull afternoon of daydreaming.

When her phone rang, she looked from it to her now-cold coffee then back again. It was Heather, and she knew better than to let it go to voicemail. Her friend was too persistent to be ignored. A quality Marta sometimes appreciated and occasionally loathed.

"Hey," Marta said, her voice betraying her. There was a quiver of emotion that would give her away.

"What's wrong? Was it a bad signing? I'm sure it went better than you think." Heather was hyper in a way that energized people around her. There was no room left for dwelling on sadness when she was swinging words around like protective charms. Somehow, she'd envelop the people she cared about in bubbles and work hard to make sure all the bad stuff bounced right off. It must have been an exhausting task, yet Heather never seemed weary of it.

"The signing was great, Heather." Marta stood and tossed her coffee in the trash. She was craving the quiet that would come from stepping out onto the street, the chatter of the other patrons suddenly overwhelming her senses.

"The phone rang five times," Heather scolded. "You know you were supposed to call me when you were done so I'd know you're all right. Traveling all over on your own, meeting a ton of new people. I at least want check-ins."

"I had coffee with some people after the signing." Marta had no intention of going into detail over the phone. This was the kind of conversation best suited for sweatpants and copious amounts of wine. That was how things were sorted out properly. "Can I come by tonight?"

"Of course," Heather answered before Marta even had the words out. "Ray's cooking. Come straight here. I have a stellar bottle of wine I swiped from my folks that has our name on it."

A lump grew in Marta's throat. "I'm not going to burst in on your date night. I can catch up with you tomorrow."

"This is not date night," Heather said, a snap in her voice. "Ray knows damn well you and I are a package deal. He adores you. The three of us have always been friends. He'll be happy to have you over for dinner. I want to hear how things went and why you sound kind of wonky."

"I don't," Marta lied. "And let me bring something over for dinner. I'll stop and pick something up."

"Marta," Heather shot back quickly, "come to my house. Bring nothing. Change into my second favorite pair of sweatpants and save me from drinking a whole bottle of wine on my own. You know Ray doesn't drink anymore, and I hate to waste good wine."

"I'm hopping in the car now," Marta said with a smile. "I do have a lot to tell you."

"Knew it." She could hear Heather snapping her fingers in victory. "I can easily cancel on Ray too, if you want a girl's night."

"No," Marta said thoughtfully. "I'd actually like to hear his opinion. He's one of the good ones."

"I don't know about that," Heather sighed, "but he's got fantastic taste in women."

CHAPTER THREE

Carol

Self-confidence and doubt ebbed and flowed at a relentless pace within her. Confidence would sweep doubt away, rise to a new height, and then they'd change places. It was a pitiful dance, steps she'd long since memorized. The swings from *certain she was right* to *convinced she was wrong* were dizzying.

The voice in her mind might not be clinically troublesome by definition. It didn't tell her to try to conquer the world or hurt anyone. But it spoke loudly in a familiar voice. The voice of her mother. Relentless in its push and pull between believing in Carol's greatness and reminding her of all her shortcomings. Living life guided by her mother's voice was the equivalent of trying to navigate a dark forest with only a temperamental and unreliable compass.

When you rise and fall with the mental health of someone else, you're strapped tightly to a ride you can't control or escape. In her mother's old age, there were days when Carol fantasized about the inevitability of death. The time when the shackles of her mother's control would finally be broken. But it didn't happen that way.

When the words "ashes to ashes and dust to dust" were ceremoniously spoken over her mother's casket, there was none of the freedom Carol had anticipated. Just the weight of an unfinished project. The kind you had to step around and see every day, a constant reminder of your inability to get it done. The half-finished wallpaper. The squeaking door that needed to be oiled.

That was all coming to an end now. The nagging reminders and crushing self-doubt were behind her. This was going to be the turning point. Carol had asserted her place in the family industry. Despite all her mental struggles, she ascended to a position that few before her could say they'd reached. She'd taken a couple swipes at the glass ceiling, maybe even put a crack in it—the first female CEO for the Milton Cesar Center for the Arts. Also, the youngest to ever hold the position. Her success was indisputable. Even the echoes of her mother's haunting doubt couldn't take that away.

"Terrance, I got her. I tracked her down at her book signing." Carol had switched her phone to hands-free as she pulled back onto the highway. Her rented BMW was pulsing with energy as she ignored the speed limit. The model was different than hers, but the engine revved just as well. "This is going to be something special."

Her assistant Terrance was multitasking, but he quickly gave her phone call all of his attention. Loyalty was a trait she saw in him from the beginning, and on her own journey, he'd been indispensable. As she transitioned from General Director of Marketing and Sales to Vice President of Artistic Planning, and ultimately to CEO, she implored him to come along.

On paper, Terrance was unqualified for the role. He hadn't spent enough time in the field and didn't know this particular business well enough. But he'd shown her time and again that he could be discrete and trustworthy. Those weren't skills you could train someone to do. The rest, the business side, she could teach him.

When Carol was in marketing, she'd had her eye out for a new assistant. The last few had been disasters for various reasons, and this time she was determined to select her own. Relying on the human resources and recruiting departments had been a disappointment. She knew what she was looking for, and it had nothing to do with how many degrees the person had or who they already knew in the company.

Terrance had been a new web producer for digital content for about six months, and there had been some buzz around his latest project. He'd developed the innovative concept of creating interactive content that could be used in classrooms across the country. He and Carol had never had any real face time, she'd only heard the idea through a digital manager during a lunch meeting. The following day she asked Terrance into her office and knew instantly he was something special. It was a risk, but she wanted to take him on as an executive assistant if he was willing.

Besides being brilliant at his job, Terrance was confident and passionate. When he spoke, he lit up with the same zest and excitement that she did at new ideas and significant challenges. Her favorite thing about Terrance was his ability—no, his insistence—to challenge her. They would grow in their roles together because they both wanted to be better today than yesterday.

After three months as her assistant, she was convinced that having Terrance on her team was paramount to her advancing not only in her career but as a human. He was a strong, kind, young Black man with his eyes on the future. Terrance didn't mince words, and he didn't take the easy way out. More importantly, he didn't let the people around him do that either.

His big ideas and his dark blue suits were sharp. She wouldn't be able to keep him around forever. He'd surpass the position he was in well before she'd be ready to let him go. But she would indeed watch him soar and cheer him on the whole way.

"The meeting went well?" Terrance asked, and she

could hear him settling into his squeaky office chair. She'd offered him an upgrade a dozen times, something new and ergonomic, but he always refused. He preferred familiar over flashy.

"She was shocked," Carol explained, her voice high and excited. "But there is something to her. Some texture, some depth. It's what the last few recipients have been lacking. Hell, the last twenty recipients. We've needed to pump this thing full of new life for years, and Marta is the key. This is going to take the future of the foundation in a whole new direction."

"Have you told Eli yet?" Terrance asked, just the right level of concern in his voice. Not alarmed, but cautious. His specialty. She could practically see his dark eyes narrowing and his brows coming down in concern.

It was good practice for Carol to spar with Terrance over this. "I don't answer to Eli. I'm the CEO. This is my call. You've read the book; Marta is more than qualified to be this year's recipient."

"Eli might not have the title anymore, but he's been pulling strings for the last ten years. Many people are under the impression you're meant to be a puppet, and he's still in control." Terrance wasn't offering some fresh warning; he was actually stoking the fire she loved to keep blazing. He'd learned that in some unspoken way over the years. Carol needed to know she was the underdog. Having him play devil's advocate kept her on her toes and fighting.

"I'm no puppet. That's not me. I'm tasked with the future of the foundation. Eli is part of the past. He's all about outdated thinking and the handcuffs that come with honoring traditions. Marta is a fresh face in the literary world. She's the story young writers need to hear. We are going to be the ones to tell it. You should have seen her today. She's humble. She's warm. A deserving and lovely young woman whose life we can change."

Terrance hummed out wearily. "It was one meeting. She's an unknown commodity. You don't have all the facts about her yet. It's a risk. What if you find out something that doesn't align with the Cesar brand? What if you are wrong?"

"I don't know," Carol admitted. "A cursory look into her past certainly had red flags but not the kind that should stop us, the kind that should inspire us. Wait until you meet her, Terrance. She has no idea how good she is. It's not fake modesty or some kind of act. Marta Leduc is the real deal."

"It's a gamble, but I'll never bet against you." Terrance laughed, that warm, darling rumble that came from his chest. "How can I help?"

"Help me design a compelling pitch." Carol gripped the steering wheel as her mind spun through the possibilities.

Terrance sounded confused. "I thought you weren't pitching this to Eli. It sounds like you've made up your mind. Easier to ask for forgiveness than permission, right?"

"A pitch to Marta," Carol corrected. "That's the person we have to convince."

"To accept the award?" Terrance didn't hold back his concern. "She's not sure she wants the most prestigious literary award in the country? You're telling me she's a crazy person then, right? You were starting to convince me, but now I'm back in the other camp."

Carol could only imagine how this sounded from the outside. Terrance would loosen the knot on his tie a little and unbutton his jacket to lean back in his chair. She smiled as she heard the chair squeak again. They knew each other well. When she stressed him out, he always leaned back in his chair.

No one in their right mind would turn down the life-changing award she was offering. But there was more to Marta, more to be discovered. Carol could feel it. "No, she's got a healthy level of skepticism. She's scrappy. I like that she wasn't just going to take what I said and jump eagerly at some kind of agreement. I told her we'd talk next week. I just need to be ready."

Terrance, still unconvinced, was at least ready to offer some suggestions. "You want to try to woo her? Should we throw a little gala? We could have some big names there. Maybe that would do the trick? It wouldn't be too difficult to pull something together quickly. She'll see we are serious, and the award is prestigious."

"The funny thing is, I don't think we need to convince Marta that we're something special. I think we have to convince her that she is. You wouldn't believe her face when I told her. It was like she thought it was a prank. We've got to assure Marta that we picked her for a reason. You sleep on it tonight, and we'll brainstorm in the morning."

She could hear him tapping on his keyboard. "You'll be back by then? Do you need your flight changed?"

"I already took care of it. I'm taking the red-eye back. Coming out here means I have a pile of work waiting for me back at the office, right?"

"Yes. But that's because you insist on doing it all yourself. It's my job to call the airline and change your flights. You make things too easy for me. Plus, I don't think the CEO usually hunts down the recipients of awards themselves. You're making a lot of waves for your first year. Why can't you ever just fly under the radar?"

Carol snorted. "I wanted to see if what my gut was telling me was right. I knew the book was good. I knew Marta was different. Now I know she's perfect."

"You could have lied to her and said she was in the running. Now you're boxed into this, and if there are any skeletons in her past that you don't like, it could be very messy." Terrance sounded downright paternal now, even though he was barely thirty, and she couldn't help but smile. She was old enough to be his mother, and occasionally she acted as one to him. They tended to switch roles as needed.

She tried to remind him what they were up against. "You worry too much. We have to take risks. You and I are shaking up the literary industry. We're changing

39

things. That requires grit. Determination. We're fearless."

Terrance sighed, and she could practically see him rolling his dark hazel eyes. "Plus, there's a clause in the contract for that. Our lawyers never miss an opportunity to cover the company."

"You bet your ass," she joked. "But we won't need it."

"Boss, you know I've got your back no matter what. If you think Marta is the person we need, we'll get her. There's a lot on the line."

"Don't I know it—the curse of being the first at something. Now women are all counting on me to get this right. To leave some legacy and space for when it's their turn. Trust me, that's not lost on me."

The severe tone didn't last as Terrance offered his usual levity. "I meant I have a lot on the line here. I need this job. My résumé is still pretty pitiful looking. I'm not ready for us to get tossed on our asses."

Carol joined in on the chuckle. "That's why we need to make this work. I'll be back in the morning, and we'll figure out how to make sure Marta is on board. You're going to like her, Terrance. You're going to root for her."

"I'm rooting for you, and that's plenty. Make sure you get some sleep on the flight. You can't keep going at this breakneck pace. If you plan to upend the status quo, you've got to at least get some rest."

After promising to find some time to relax, Carol disconnected their call, and the audiobook she'd been listening to came back to life through the speakers. It was a biography of a high-ranking female military officer. Compellingly written, Carol found refuge in the stories of broken barriers and hard-won opportunities. It fueled her. This was going to work. This was going to change every-thing. All Carol had to do was prove the literary world was open to all. It wasn't elite and exclusive. Or it didn't have to stay that way. Not if she could help it.

CHAPTER FOUR

Marta

Heather's apartment was in one of the six buildings her father owned, and Marta loved visiting. They were all duplexes with quaint exteriors. The one Heather lived in, rent-free, had white clapboard siding and forest green shutters. The front yard was mowed by a company that serviced all of Mr. Longdrew's apartments.

When a pipe froze or the sink clogged, Heather would call her father and someone would come to the rescue. Some hired help who knew how to fix just about anything. From Marta's perspective, it sounded glorious. But Heather often complained about the setup.

The duplex was old. Built-in the fifties, the kitchen was dated and the walls paper-thin. Heather hated the idea of having neighbors. Sharing a wall. Hearing every argument, every thumping beat of someone else's family movie night. The kids next door rode their skateboards down the shared hallway. The mother worked all day, and the kids ran amok all summer.

It was annoying to Heather but familiar to Marta. The idea of being an unaccompanied minor for long periods was something she recognized in her own childhood. Growing up, the summers were long, unstructured, and, frankly, dangerous. Their neighborhood was relatively safe, but their idea of fun was not. Reckless was an understatement. If other families, people with structure and rules, had seen them playing on the large sand dunes the city had made for treating the road, they would have gasped. Didn't Marta know children could quickly be buried alive in those and suffocate? They played on the railroad tracks and jumped from the waterfall in the quarry where no one else would. Didn't she know that playing on the roof or in the unfinished rafters of an abandoned barn would be treacherous?

The simple answer was that she did not know. Her brothers did not seem informed either. The standard stream of information that led to a healthy fear of danger had not flowed freely to the Leduc children. In fact, her father was usually the one to develop the crazy scheme or wild challenge.

Marta and her family were far more like the people on the duplex's left side than they were like Heather. They were the ones being loud, patching holes in the shared wall from a ball thrown too hard. But it made empathizing with Heather easy. Growing up, Marta always felt a little bad for the neighbors below them in the fourth-floor walkup apartment. The Leduc children must have sounded like a herd of elephants. The apartment, still small and run-down, had been an upgrade from the tiny two-bedroom house they'd moved from.

"What took you so long?" Heather groaned as she waved Marta to hurry up and come in. She squinted her ocean-blue eyes and crinkled up her button nose, pretending to be more impatient than she was.

Heather was good-looking, a natural beauty paired with some costly interventions. Costly by Marta's standards. Fresh manicures, usually with crazy sparkles. Blonde highlights in her light brown hair. Waxed eyebrows with actress-level definition. She used some fancy serum on her lashes to make them long and treated herself to a facial monthly.

It didn't seem pretentious to Marta, only foreign. Grooming was still a pain point of hers. Her kinky, frizzy hair was its natural color, a mahogany kind of brown because the expense of a hairdresser felt out of reach. Her nails were bare because she couldn't keep up with home manicures, and chipped nail polish had never gone well with the foodservice industry. Dressing for her body type, sort of hourglass, had proven to be more difficult than she ever imagined.

Even when Marta did have a little extra money for clothes, she couldn't bring herself to buy something that cost more than twenty or thirty dollars. The idea of good clothes costing triple digits turned her stomach. How could she justify a single item of clothing costing more than an entire week of gas in her car or a whole month's electric bill?

Heather flipped her long hair off her shoulder. It was down, which meant she hadn't worked at the veterinarian's office today. They made her keep her nearly waist-length hair pinned up so the animals wouldn't treat it as a toy. Heather preferred it down, but it was well worth it to work in the field she was so passionate about. Well, this week. Heather's passion was a moving target.

In the two years that Marta had known her, there had been many things Heather dreamed of being. Waitressing was always to keep her parents happy while pursuing her next big goal. First, fashion design was good in theory, much harder in execution. Then she'd considered being a teacher, even using her bachelor's degree from the local university to gain a position subbing at her former elementary school. All those roles were short-lived. The moment the commitment outweighed her drive, she would move on to another field of study. Lately, it was animals. Becoming a vet tech was all she wanted now.

"No work today?" Marta asked, pulling her purse over her shoulder and tucking the broken buckle under her arm to camouflage it.

"No, it was slow, so they gave me the day off. I was super bummed, but it worked out because I cleaned out my entire closet. I have a huge bag of clothes for you."

"You know your clothes are always too long for me. I don't have supermodel legs like you."

"I gave you the name of my tailor. Just take them to him, and he will get you all fixed up." Heather waved as if it was the simplest solution.

Marta had never had a piece of clothing altered in her life. When her pants were too long at work, she'd roll them up, and if that didn't do it, she'd been known to staple them in place. She'd tried hot glue a couple times too. Those were the type of solutions her father would have approved.

"Hurry up. We want to hear your news." Heather let Marta pass then closed the front door behind them.

It was hard to hear Heather speak in terms of *we* when referring to her and Ray now. They'd all been friends for over two years, working at the same restaurant when they met. Ray had been the third wheel to Heather and Marta, always tagging along on their girls' nights out. Now he was Heather's evening plan every night of the week. Not working together anymore meant Heather and Marta saw less of each other than ever.

"I had to stop at my place and drop off all the stuff from the book signing. Lugging that junk around in my car is too much."

"You need an entourage," Ray said, slinking in behind Heather and wrapping his arms around her waist. He was taller than Marta by a foot and still had Heather by four or five inches. His dark hair was slicked back with a comical amount of product. And they had spent time laughing about it often. But the look suited his Italian features, and his hot-cocoa-colored eyes always sparkled with mischief. The dimple on his cheek and the tribal tattoo that climbed just above the collar of his shirt made him a hit with the ladies when he worked the bar. He was still slinging drinks but now at a more upscale establishment, which garnered him better tips.

Things were going well for both Heather and Ray, and Marta was happy they'd finally started dating. She didn't begrudge them for their relationship. It was almost inevitable. Ray loved Heather from the moment they first met and everything he did, all the girls' nights he endured, were so that someday they could be right here, spending most nights together, cooking and laughing before he started his shift at the bar.

Marta couldn't deny that she missed the way things had been a year ago when they were all still working together. Ray would tend bar while Marta and Heather waited tables. It was all inside jokes and subtle pranks. No one messed with either of the girls because they understood Ray wouldn't tolerate that. Regular customers and other waitstaff knew better than to give them any trouble. The long hours and late nights were all made better by the friendships she'd built with Heather and Ray.

The restaurant where they'd met as fellow employees was a family-owned place and the night shifts left Marta with ample time to write during the day. Something she hadn't told anyone she was doing. Even after the book was complete, she kept the accomplishment to herself. It wasn't until the book was published that she even mentioned it to her friends. There were members of her extended family who still didn't know.

Marta had no idea how she would frame today's announcement. Heather had taken to searching the internet to hear about the successes associated with Marta's writing most of the time. Then, with her normal dramatic flair, Heather would burst into the bookstore where Marta now worked and give her hell for keeping it all a secret. Today's news couldn't be kept from them. It required their input.

"An entourage isn't necessary. I'd settle for someone to haul all the books and the display banners around for me. I'm getting sick of that."

They stepped in the door to the right, which led to Heather's living room, and Marta was met with the smell of home cooking. She could discern the difference between a boxed meal and one made from scratch. There was a metallic and processed smell to frozen food. She didn't mind it. Some of her favorite childhood meals had come from a box. But there was no substitute for freshly seasoned meat simmering in a hot pan. Or a tray of recently cut veggies roasting in the oven.

Ray could cook. It was what he wanted to do for a living, but he'd never found the discipline to be formally trained. Marta nagged him often, reminding him it was never too late to follow his passion, but Ray was laid back. The kind of relaxed you could afford when you had a safety net: a family who would wire you money when you were short on rent or between jobs.

Ray hadn't talked much about his parents, but a few drunken nights before he gave up drinking, when he did become chatty about them, he told Marta all she needed to know. Like everyone else, his parents were flawed, but they always came through when he was in a bind. They'd helped him with the down payment on his car, and when he wanted to go to school for bartending, they covered the cost.

Marta couldn't wrap her mind around the idea of gifted money. Unaccounted for funds that just show up when she'd need them. Baffling. Every penny she'd ever earned was typically already owed to someone or something else. Paycheck to paycheck was an overly generous way to define her finances.

There was a science to staying afloat in the leanest of times. That knowledge was the only thing handed down from her parents. Rather than one of those family recipe books passed down through the generations, they could have written a handbook called Robbing Peter to Pay Paul.

You could write a check to the utility company, but if it was ripped in just the right place, making the account number illegible, they couldn't process it. They'd be forced to send it back and provide more time before the lights went out or the water was turned off. When times were especially tough, and the winters were frigid, you could tell the utility company that a family member in the home had a medical device requiring electricity. That meant they would endlessly harass for payment but not disconnect your service.

The phone was never answered. Everything was screened through the answering machine to filter out the debt collectors. In-person was more challenging but not impossible to dodge people. If your landlord was looking for the rent, it became a game to pretend you weren't home. Ninja-level hiding in plain sight. There were dozens of ways to stretch every penny and keep ahead of the debt collectors. You just had to know how.

"You better be hungry," Ray warned, a spatula in his hand. "I cooked enough for an army. You like chicken piccata?"

"Yes," Marta replied, having no clue what that might be. She'd worked in restaurants but mostly those that served burgers and greasy appetizers in combinations that all cost under twenty dollars on Wednesday nights. The place they all worked together had been small with a simple menu of bar food. Besides not being qualified for too many other jobs, food service had some undeniable perks. People usually complained about dealing with rude customers or getting stiffed out of a tip. For Marta, none of that mattered more than the fact that her meals were free. You could take home things that had been cooked but not served. Anything just beyond the expiration date was up for grabs. Some staff would grumble that they got sick of eating the food on the menu, but Marta never grew tired of it. There was always a sense of indulgence and excess for her.

What was never on the menu at her workplace was fancy chicken piccata. She could deduce that there was chicken in the meal, and the other word sounded Italian. Marta hadn't met too many Italian dishes she didn't like, so it was easy to hedge her bet that it would be delicious. Everyone had some foods they didn't like, but she wasn't picky. Hunger was a great motivator to try new meals.

"You don't mind the capers?" Ray pressed, pointing a finger at her, making sure she wasn't holding back just to be nice.

"Capers?" Marta asked, stalling. "I love them."

What the hell was a caper?

"Stop grilling her about food. One, she's here for the wine, and two, she's here to dish to me all the unbelievable things that happened today. It's girls' night now, and you are the chef." She jabbed a finger playfully into Ray's chest.

"I know better than to ever try to get between you two. Well, between you two and your wine. I don't get in the way of that either. Pretend I'm not here. I'll just pour the wine and fill the plates and listen in. I might not be one of the girls, but I am one of your biggest fans, Marta." He winked at her and pulled a bottle opener from his pocket. "Getting right down to that good bottle?"

"Yes," Heather said, leaning toward him and kissing his cheek. "And you can do more than just listen. Marta says she wants your opinion."

"Opinion on what?" he asked as they all moved into the kitchen. The green wood paneling and ornate cabinets made the space look old, but Heather's father kept the place immaculate with fresh paint and the occasional deep cleaning from a company he hired.

Heather's kitchen table was glass-topped with metallic legs. More modern than the room but matched nicely to her taste. Anything that wasn't directly part of the house's structure was a similar style. Sleek and contemporary décor adorned the walls and matched in a way Marta loved but could never replicate on her own. Or maybe she'd just never been willing to bite the bullet and buy a full set of something or look at a display and take every matching piece home at once.

"The book signing today was going well. There were far more people there than the last one I did in Clinton." Marta felt a buzz of excitement filling her, and she tried to subdue it.

Heather gasped with excitement. "I told you there would be. Aren't you glad you took all the boxes of books you had?" Pulling two wine glasses down from the cabinet, Heather handed them to Ray for a quick pour, and Ray quickly filled them.

"You were right," Marta said, playing to her friends' ego. She had already planned to take all her books to the signing, but it was nice to have Heather's support too. "I signed all but one box of books. I have to order more tomorrow."

"So what happened?" Ray asked, pulling down three plates and grabbing the silverware from the drawer. He moved around the space with such ease that Marta felt a little pang of something she couldn't name. He was at home here. As it should be for someone in a serious relationship. But it was still strange to see him in a place that had been like a clubhouse for Marta and Heather for the last two years. The place they came to split a pint of ice cream after a bad night or a lousy date. It hadn't been infiltrated by any men until now. Ray always was around. Came out with them plenty, but he didn't frequent this place much until they'd officially started dating. Ray was a good man, but a man all the same.

"She's being coy," Heather teased as she slid a glass of wine over to Marta. "That means it's a big deal."

"It is a big deal," Marta agreed, a layer of caution in her voice. "It just might not turn into much of anything."

"Did you meet a guy?" Ray asked excitedly as he pointed the spatula in her direction. "Someone came to your book signing and swept you off your feet?"

"No," Marta said, swiping a hand in his direction. "That only happens in the books and the movies."

Heather clicked her tongue disappointedly. "I am starting to get worried about your love life. We've been friends for two years, and you've only dated a couple guys. And mostly for like two or three dates before you ditch them."

"I don't ditch people," Marta corrected. "But not everything is a love connection. Some people aren't compatible, and I don't like to waste my time."

Ray and Heather didn't know that Marta had already been married and divorced. Not unheard of for a twenty-five-year-old these days, but still something she preferred to keep to herself. It was the reason she'd moved so suddenly to Franklin Falls and a big part of why she wasn't much into dating.

"I don't want to put you on the spot," Heather said, hiding a bit behind her wine glass, "but I hope you know no matter who you were attracted to, we'd be very supportive. You don't have to say anything, either way, I just want you to know I'm someone you can share that information with safely."

Warmth spread across Marta's chest. It was a sweet thing to say and reminded her why she adored Heather so much. "I wouldn't hide that from you." Marta grinned. "You'd be the best at helping to find the right woman for me. But that's really not it."

Ray clicked the stove off and turned toward them. "I know I'm not supposed to weigh in much, but I agree with Heather. Nothing you tell us could change our minds about you. You're seriously the best person we know. We talk about it all the time."

"You two need more to talk about than me," Marta teased. "I'm not that interesting of a topic."

Heather smirked. "We mostly just talk about how great you are for always helping everyone and never having any drama."

Marta didn't want to correct them. The drama had followed her for decades. But it was flattering to think the people she hung out with didn't associate her with that. It meant moving had done what she'd hoped.

"It wasn't a guy," Marta explained. "I had coffee with

two women. One was a young girl who loved my book, and the other was an older woman who had been trying to get in touch with me."

"I'm still worried you're going to end up with stalkers," Heather hummed. "What was this old lady doing, trying to track you down?"

"Her name is Carol, and she works for the Milton Cesar Foundation for the Arts. Actually, I looked her up after she left. I think she runs it."

"And she was looking for you?" Ray placed the spatula down on the counter and pressed both his hands down to ground himself. "That's a big deal, right?"

"It sounds like it," Marta gulped, her cheeks burning and flushed as Heather and Ray fixed on her.

Heather put her glass down and stood up quickly. "What did she want with you? Is it about the foundation?"

"She came to tell me I won the Breakout Writer Award. She sat across from me at this little café and just blurted it out. She said I'd been selected." Marta gestured animatedly.

"Stop," Heather demanded, slamming her hand on the counter. "Stop it. You won? That's it, right? That's the thing that launches careers and makes it all legit. You'd be legit."

"It's a really prestigious award," Marta edged out over the sound of Heather's squealing. Ray was stunned. His mouth agape, he stood there, looking back and forth between the two of them before he finally spoke.

"Marta, you're serious? You won?" Ray ran his hand

over his hair, and his eyes stayed wide with disbelief. Marta hadn't prepared herself for their reaction. Speaking it out loud was more significant than she'd imagined. It made it real, and for her, real meant frightening.

"I might not accept it," she blurted suddenly. Taking a couple of steps back from the kitchen counter, she felt compelled to create physical distance between herself and their joy. That level of optimism scared her. When people were this happy, it meant they'd crave connection. Both physical and emotional. Ray and Heather would want to hug her. They'd like to know how she was feeling. What she was thinking.

Ray and Heather were her friends. They'd spilled secrets over bottles of alcohol. They'd commiserated about frustrations in their lives. They would give each other a ride to the airport. Deliver soup when one was sick. But there was a reason Ray and Heather had become close and eventually began dating, leaving Marta as the third wheel.

Intimacy.

Something not just reserved for romantic relationships. A closeness is required to truly connect with someone, and Marta didn't venture into that territory.

That designed distance manifested in many ways. The idea of physical contact with people made her gulp and sweat. There were exceptions. She had no problem showing affection to children. Additionally, if she was in a relationship, she actually craved physical contact. But a casual hug from even a close friend made her very uneasy. Her arms never moved the right way. Her spine would stiffen and stretch. She couldn't remember hugging her parents or cuddling with them in any kind of natural way. Her mom and dad were not cold, uncaring monsters and neither was she. There were so many shades of gray between cruel and kind, and their place on the spectrum was fluid.

Marta had done ample reading and had enough self-awareness to understand why she steered clear of these intensely emotional moments. Why were some people drawn through a type of gravity toward closeness, while others were repelled like polar magnets?

There were all sorts of reasons why but for Marta it was merely discomfort. She didn't like the feel of being pressed up against someone with whom she did not have a dating relationship. It didn't make her feel warm and fuzzy. It made her woozy. And explaining that to people was nearly impossible. Huggers took it personally, no matter how she tried to clarify that they were not the issue. So, most times, she didn't explain at all. She just moved away or jutted out a hand for a handshake even when it was apparent open arms were coming her way.

Like slicing a melon with a sharp sword, Marta felt the need to cut her announcement and their excitement wide open. To bare the guts of it. "I may not even accept the award," she blurted out again over the sound of their celebration.

Heather's face fell first, as though part of her was expecting Marta's reaction. "You mean you might not get the award?"

Ray looked suddenly sympathetic as though he'd read the situation wrong. "Well, it's still amazing to be in the running."

"I won the award," Marta corrected. "Or that's what Carol told me today. I just may not accept it. I'm sure there are plenty of other people who would."

"Um," Heather stretched the word out as she placed her wine glass down gingerly on the counter. "I think anyone would accept it. What are you talking about?"

"It's more complicated than it sounds," Marta explained, looking to Ray for some kind of support. He used to be the impartial judge. The one who would settle the arguments between Marta and Heather. Usually, they were silly things, but it still required some kind of judication, and Ray could be relied upon. But now, he was all deer in the headlights. Partial to the woman he loved.

"Girl," Heather proclaimed loudly as she waved a finger in the air, "this is a huge deal. It would more than launch a career for you. There is nothing complicated about it."

That was where their roads diverged. For Heather, it would have been an easy answer. The camera crew could follow her around anywhere, and she would be thrilled to stand in that spotlight. Whatever angst and fear Marta had would make no sense to her.

"You don't understand," Marta uttered the words before she realized what door she had opened. The one she always dreaded. Being called out. Being seen for what she was.

"Of course, we wouldn't understand," Heather snapped. "Because that would require you to actually tell us something. It's like you don't even want to be friends some days. You're so guarded."

Ouch. The G-word.

The problem with that statement was its accuracy. That made debating nearly impossible. Instead, fight or flight kicked in. Storming out was a reliable option, but Heather was the kind of friend who would body block her at the door so they could resolve this. She'd have to argue her way out.

"Not everyone wants to spill their guts after a couple of swigs of tequila." A shot across her dear friend's bow. A mean barb that Marta regretted, but she knew it was necessary. It wasn't about wounding her friend but about deflecting the attention off of herself. A dirty tactic, but the quickest and most effective.

Heather leaned back, her eyes wide and her mouth agape. "Actually, that's a healthy friendship. You're supposed to share things that have happened, talk about how you feel, and lean on each other. It doesn't take any tequila. It's supposed to come naturally. Do you really think we don't notice how you keep everything to yourself?" She gestured to Ray, and the *we* stung even more this time.

"People are all different," Ray said, sounding as if he were giving instructions on which wire to cut so the bomb wouldn't explode. "Not everyone deals with things the same way."

Heather shook her head, shooting him a stern glance. "Who wouldn't take this award? Who wouldn't want to be successful? I wish you would talk to us, Marta. I wish you would explain why you're afraid of success. Why you're afraid of being, like, actually close to us."

Marta ground her teeth together. She didn't want to let anything accidentally escape and start a conversation she was not prepared to have. "I'm not afraid of being successful. But I don't need to have every part of my life on display either."

Ray made some kind of grunting noise as he folded his arms over his chest. "They do a video."

Goosebumps skittered up her arms. He'd begun to pull the thread and unravel the blanket she was hiding under.

"What?" Heather asked, her nostrils flaring.

Ray softened his expression and fixed his eyes on Marta. "They do like a life story. Some kind of movie about the winners. You don't want that?"

Emotion caught in her throat, and she finally lifted her wine glass, taking a long sip to wash it all away. "There is plenty in my life I don't want to be included." Her voice was tiny, the fight gone from it now. "It's not worth it to me."

"Marta," Heather sighed. "Just tell them you don't want everything out there. You can keep some things private."

"It doesn't work that way," Marta replied, rubbing her thumb against her throbbing temple. "Some things are public information. If someone wants to know, they can find it. If this book really takes off, if people start to know who I am, they'll find out anything they want."

"Why is that so bad?" Heather asked, her face pained by the lack of understanding. "Who cares if people know your past? They love your book; that's what they'll focus on."

Marta closed her eyes and laughed humorlessly. "It's trauma porn. People can't help themselves. They'll get a little bit of my story and latch on. They'll want to hear all the gory details."

"What gory details?" Heather asked, her eyes glassing over with the threat of tears. She was wounded at the thought of being in the dark. Marta didn't pry into people's lives, and she didn't ever feel entitled to know what they'd been through. But Heather did expect that out of her friends. "I feel like you've got a whole bunch of secrets. What am I to you if you don't even want to tell me about your life? Are we not friends?" She gestured between the three of them. "Best friends, I thought. But you get weird. It's like the whole temperature in the room changes when we ask you questions about yourself. God help us if we want to hug you. You cancel plans a lot. It's like you find better things to do and just bail."

There were so many things to be corrected there, but Marta wasn't sure she wanted to engage in any of them. She canceled plans because sometimes the social anxiety was so crippling, she couldn't imagine facing anyone. It wasn't something she did lightly, and she knew for a social person like Heather it was hurtful and baffling.

All Marta kept thinking as this unfolded was, *why did you do this again?* Why did you make friends with someone who will never understand you? Someone who needs things you can't give. Heather was craving oxygen, and Marta was like the bottom of the ocean in that regard.

"I should go," Marta said coolly. That natural way she'd learned to speak in moments like this. Retaining control of her emotions was paramount. When people lost that control, they said too much.

"Go?" Ray asked, shaking his head. "Is that how this usually works for you?" He eyed her closely. "Is this when you run?"

"I'm not running," Marta explained, intentionally moving slowly as she placed her glass on the counter and pulled her coat off the back of the chair.

"Let her go," Heather said resignedly. It was music to Marta's ears. Fireworks of emotions and hurtful accusations could start flying from someone as injured as Heather at this moment. The fact that she was willing to let Marta walk out was truly generous.

"Nope," Ray said, too calmly for Marta's liking. He was the wild card. Heather was fun and a loyal friend. But Marta understood that she required closeness. It was apparent that she would, of course, be sad when she finally realized Marta would not be able to provide that connection. Ray was different. Harder to read. He was also loyal and fun to be around. But for some reason, he seemed to be able to see things in Marta she wasn't actively trying to display. And when he did, he called her on it. Not cruelly or to embarrass her but so that they could talk it through.

"Nope, what?" Marta asked, sliding her arms into her coat.

"Nope, you aren't leaving," Ray said through a smile. "We're having dinner. You don't have to tell us anything you don't want to, but you can't just leave."

Marta opened her mouth to protest and paused, searching for the right argument that would get her out of there. "I don't think that's a good idea."

Very compelling.

"I do." Ray countered as he moved behind her and slid her coat back off gently. "We're friends. It doesn't mean we have it all figured out, but it does mean we try. Leaving isn't trying. I cooked, and we should eat together."

Heather looked mortally wounded as she wiped tears from her cheeks. "If she doesn't want to be here, we shouldn't make her stay."

"I think she does want to be here," Ray said in a chipper voice. "Because fifteen minutes ago, she certainly looked like she was happy. I happen to believe we can get back to that."

Marta stood there, needling at her raw cuticles and avoiding Heather's eyes. She got no pleasure from seeing her friend cry. "Dinner smells delicious," Marta offered sheepishly.

"It's going to be delicious." Ray started plating up the food and throwing cute glances over at Heather until she seemed to soften a bit.

Wrapping her fingers back around the stem of her wine glass, Heather finally spoke again. "Did you make that garlic bread?"

"Of course I did," Ray announced proudly. "And if I've learned anything from having three sisters, it's that big feelings require carbs."

The girls both chuckled and finally glanced at each other again. Marta's shoulders dropped. "I'm sorry if I hurt your feelings. I really didn't mean to."

Heather gulped. "I know. I wasn't trying to be mean either. I just want to understand."

Ray grabbed the forks and knives from the counter and gestured for them to come over to the table. "I'm sure when Marta is ready, she'll explain it to us. I won't take it personally until then."

Heather grumbled, "Stop being so level-headed and calm."

"And a good cook, and handsome and smart," Ray said, counting them off on his fingers. "I can't stop being who I am. You're stuck with me this way."

Marta sat and graciously accepted the food as Heather and Ray giggled to each other in that new love kind of way. They'd have been happier if she wasn't there. It seemed painfully obvious, but for some reason, Ray wanted her to stay, and she felt the warmth of that gesture.

"It probably won't make sense anyway, even if I did try to explain it."

Ray refilled the wine glasses and shrugged. "You might be right. I can't think of many reasons why I would turn down an award. But if you're willing to do that, it must be something serious." He was fishing, but she gave him points for doing it gently.

Heather's spirits seemed brighter now as she began cutting up her chicken. "Were your parents in the CIA or something? You never talk about them."

"They were not in the CIA, more like the EBT," Marta joked as she inspected the small, green pebble-looking things on top of her chicken. These were apparently capers —time to find out if she actually liked them.

"What's that?" Heather asked, furrowing her soft, light-colored brows together and turning down her mouth. Marta had made a few comments about growing up poor, but they'd always just swapped stories about what it was like to be around more affluent people. She'd never really gone into detail about exactly how dire her situation was.

This was one of those moments. A crossroads. She could laugh it off and change the subject, or she could expose something Heather and Ray wouldn't be able to just brush off. It would be the start of something. Beginnings always made Marta queasy. She could deal with endings—even abrupt ones. But the unknown and newness of something was frightening.

Luckily Ray answered for her. "Food stamps. EBT is like food stamps, right? So, you were poor. People will probably connect with that and root for you. It might be even more of a reason to accept the award. Maybe your story will inspire someone else."

"Maybe." Marta placated him while she took her first

bite of the chicken. She did not, in fact, like capers. They crunched and were too similar to olives for her liking. But that wouldn't stop her from eating them. She could muscle them down to save face since she'd already declared that she enjoyed them.

"You don't agree," Ray pressed. "I can see it on your face."

He saw her attempt to swallow the capers but wasn't wrong. She disagreed. "It's just not as simple as you're making it. Poor isn't just financial. It's not how much you have in the bank or if you even have a bank account at all. You're picturing some feel-good story about how I rose from the ashes of poverty."

Heather shifted in her chair. "Well, how poor were you?"

"I don't know how to answer that," Marta admitted, feeling frustrated with the question. "Is there like a zero to ten scale you want to use?"

"I just didn't know," Heather cut back quickly. "You've made a couple of jokes over the years, but I wouldn't have known it was a big deal to you. It obviously is."

"It's not a comfortable conversation for me. You both have known me for a couple years. Those years have been the most stable of my life. Anything before that is not a time or place I like to revisit. And if I accept this award, I'll have to. You've seen the ceremony, the video they put together. It's people going back to their colleges." She wanted to say alma mater but wasn't sure that was the right term. Or that she'd pronounce it right. She thought maybe it was alma marter, and so she dodged it. "They go back to the house they grew up in. Teachers talk about what kind of kids they were. Friends chime in about what it was like to know them way back when. I'm not going to do any of that. It would be a disaster if I did."

Ray, in true male fashion, began trying to problem solve. "Maybe you could tell them you don't want to go back to your college. I went in-state to one of the smallest public colleges. I don't think they'd want to see the run-down library and cruddy cafeteria."

Heather perked up a bit. "Yeah, I started out at community college. No one would be knocking down my door to see it either. I'm sure you get some control over the structure of the video they make. They'll want to paint you in a good light."

"I didn't go to any college. I'm supposed to be this award-winning author, and I barely got out of high school. If they went back and spoke with any of my teachers, they would not have glowing reviews of my work or attitude. If someone flipped through the yearbook, they'd see I was literally voted teachers' worst nightmare, and I wasn't pictured there because I probably skipped school that day." Marta shifted in her chair and brought her hand up to her forehead. "No one is going to think I deserve this award. When they see me, who I really am, they won't be happy for me."

Ray and Heather exchanged glances, both hesitating, looking as though they hoped the other would speak. "I didn't know you didn't go to college," Heather said, nibbling her lip. "You are brilliant. Just naturally intelligent."

"I'm not," Marta laughed, planting her palm on the table more firmly than she meant to. "You could fill this room with pretty basic things I never learned. I didn't take the SATs. I honestly think they passed me in most of my classes so they could get me out of there."

"School isn't everything," Ray said, gesturing down to his plate. "I cook, but I never went to school for it. I have something I love that I think I'm pretty good at."

Marta couldn't help but pounce on the false equivalency he was drawing. "And if someone knocked on the door and tried to give you a James Beard award, you might have some concerns about accepting it."

Ray smirked at her rebuttal. He always appreciated a good debate. "Yeah, that makes sense. But I'm not nearly as talented in this field as you are in yours. I didn't open a restaurant, but you did write a book. An amazing one."

"School is only one part of this," Marta explained, finally locking eyes with Heather. "I'm sorry that I haven't told you more about my life before I moved here. It's not that I don't want to be close to you. I just don't want to be close to everything I left behind. Distance is my friend when it comes to my past. That's what makes the idea of people seeing it scary."

Heather still looked unconvinced. "I get that you wouldn't want the whole world knowing, but why not us? There isn't anything you could tell us that would change our minds about you."

This was the element of friendship people overlooked. The part where someone meant precisely what they said. They were genuine and heartfelt in their intent, but the execution would be impossible. Marta understood that Heather, right now, believed what she was saying about unconditionally loving Marta. But when it came down to it, she wouldn't be able to hold to it.

Ray, seeming to sense the stalemate creeping up on them, handed out some more garlic bread. "You don't have to tell us anything tonight, and you don't have to decide about the award either. We're here. We're not going anywhere."

Marta took another bite of the chicken, the salty capers tasting a little better this time. "Dinner is good. I'm glad I stayed."

Heather leaned in but didn't reach for Marta. "I'm glad you stayed too. You two are the only people I like. I don't want to have to make other friends."

"Same," Marta laughed. "It's so much work."

CHAPTER FIVE

Carol

Terrance would have her covered. There wasn't a doubt in her mind. It was a blessing to have someone like him in her life. He was a great kid. Her flight had landed an hour ago, and she should have gone home. The average person would have. She could shower, get a couple hours of sleep, and head into the office a smidge late. She was the boss. It was no one's business but hers what time she arrived. Especially when she'd spent most of the night on a flight after dealing with delays. There was no time clock in her life. No one looking over her shoulder. No one there should care what time she rolled in.

But one person did care deeply. Carol. She couldn't

stand the thought of passing by all those glass offices filled with people who'd come in before her. They'd be on their second cup of coffee or stepping into their morning meetings. Maybe their stares would only be in her head, but she'd feel them anyway.

The only reason she was in this job was her willingness to be the first one in and the last one out most days of the week. It was her hours of dedication that the people next to her either couldn't or wouldn't give to their jobs. She'd subscribed to the philosophies of the most successful athletes. If you couldn't outplay someone, you had to find a way to outwork them. Carol didn't need to be the smartest in the room. She just needed to be the most committed.

That meant instead of heading home for sleep and a shower this morning, she was dragging her suitcase into the dark offices of the Milton Cesar Building. Nine months ago she'd been named CEO and moved all of her things from her old office to the building's largest one. It had been a laughably sparse space so she'd hastily picked out some additional art and furniture to fill it. It wasn't all to her taste, but her father had taught her an important lesson many years ago that she still took to heart.

Don't be in love with your office or anything in it. One day they'll tell you to leave that space—probably before you're ready to go—and you've got to be willing to walk away from it all. If you care about something that can't fit in a box to be carried to your car, don't put it in your workplace.

The dim overnight lights were just enough to guide her down the long hallway toward her corner office. As she got closer, she saw a beacon of comfort in the distance. Terrance's light was glowing brightly. Of course he was in. Good kid.

"You should have gone home," he scolded without looking up from his computer screen. "You could have slept and come in just before your meeting at eleven."

"I'm not prepared for that meeting," Carol said, flopping down in the chair across from his desk. This was not something she'd ever do if other people were in the office. It was beneath her position to sink into the small leather chair across from her assistant. If she needed to speak with him, it would be more prudent for Terrance to come into her office and take a seat. But with no one watching, Carol bent the unspoken rules.

His office, just off of hers, was cozy and warm. There was only a single, narrow floor-to-ceiling window that gave it a more contained and safe feeling than hers. She much preferred to sit here when she could.

"That's a lie." Terrance finally looked up, rolling his eyes. "You are prepared for every meeting days in advance. But I am prepared for you to be here this morning." He pushed his chair back and stood. "Your bathroom has your red suit from the dry cleaner. Mary is coming in here in about twenty minutes to do your hair. You were out of half of your makeup in the vanity, and I wasn't sure what you'd taken on your trip, so I replaced what you needed. Coffee is on your desk, and you better eat that breakfast wrap. It's only two hundred calories and a lot of protein. You're not going into this day without something in your stomach."

"Thanks, Mom," Carol groaned, shuffling toward her office. She was old enough to be his mother, which made it all the more humorous. "I don't know what I'd do without you."

"You'd be hungry, smelly, and incredibly caffeine deficient." He rounded his desk and shot her a smile. It was a mystery to her how he was single. Or maybe he wasn't single at all. Maybe he just kept his personal life private. They'd had plenty of late nights in the office, chatting about all sorts of things. Life, loss, the way the world worked, but he only occasionally mentioned having a date.

There were times she'd wanted to press. To ask what his deal was. How his date went. If there was anyone special in his life. She wanted that for him. He deserved a nice girl who could appreciate how wonderful he was. Her maternal instinct to pair him off with someone sweet was strong. But that was the fuzzy line drawn between a boss and her employee. She had to tread lightly. There was a power differential created by their job titles, and he might feel obligated to answer any question Carol asked, even if she was just curious.

"You are seriously the best, Terrance." Carol lingered in the doorway of his office, wanting to say more. Her gratitude always sounded hollow and superficial. "I'm serious."

He chuckled. "I know, I know I'm a lifesaver." He

waved her off. "You could find a hundred people to make your coffee and take messages for you. I'm the lucky one."

"No," Carol said, striding back toward him. "Terrance, I've worked with hundreds of people over the years. I've had assistants. I've been an assistant. You are something else. Something different."

"I've been called strange plenty of times but never in this context." His eyes darted away and she regretted putting him on the spot.

"I trust you," Carol replied seriously. "Trust is a commodity hard to come by when you get to this level. It's nearly impossible, actually. You're not here because I'm doing you any favors. You're here because I fully intend to walk into all sorts of firestorms to make changes here, and I know I can count on you. It's not about the coffee or the dry-cleaned suit, even though I greatly appreciate all of those things. It's about knowing that when most everyone in this place questions me and my sanity, you're on my side."

Terrance's face softened, and the uncomfortable look melted away. He blinked slowly as he folded his arms across his chest. "Carol, I've got you. No matter what goes down in this place. No matter what people think, I've got you. Things do need to change in this industry. In most industries. I'm one of those jaded skeptics who usually thinks nothing will ever improve. You make me think that maybe it will. I appreciate your trust in me, and I don't take that lightly."

She wanted him to say he trusted her too. She wanted

him to add that they were real friends. It was a pathetic thought, one she chastised herself for the moment it skittered across her mind. How pitiful was her life that her assistant, half her age, was the closest prospect for a decent friend? When he didn't profess any deep feelings of camaraderie, she just smiled and disappeared into her office.

The best she could do was slip into the bathroom, take a hot shower, and mentally tick off all the things she needed to say and do in her meeting at eleven. That would take up the mental space that was currently being used to inventory the tragedy her social life had devolved into. The more success she'd had in business, the more isolated she'd become.

There had been warnings. Other successful women she knew had laid out the pitfalls clearly. The men in Carol's life would be intimated by her growing résumé. Every rung of the ladder would result in fewer dates. The women in her life would not find much common ground with her.

Carol was childless by choice. A decision that befuddled her old college friends who dedicated their lives and identities to their offspring. Years ago, she'd fallen away from all but one of those women. The nights out had become uncomfortable when the entire conversation centered around motherhood. It always ended the same way. There was some proclamation that life didn't start until a woman was a mother. They'd tell Carol that someday she'd change her mind and finally understand.

But she never did change her mind. There was no

clock ticking in her ear or baby lust clouding her mind. Children were not on her list of goals, and Carol resisted the pressure to follow the most traveled path just because people were convinced she should. It didn't fit her. It wasn't what she wanted.

The friends Carol made at work over the years struggled to transition from buddies to her employees as she was promoted through the ranks and they were not. It became unprofessional to go out for a drink with them once she was in leadership. It was much more appropriate to associate with her peers, but the rest of the leadership were usually men. Married men would only leave her plagued with rumors and drama if she socialized with them. All things she avoided. Which eventually boiled down to isolation. On paper, it made sense to be friends with the other corporate women who warned her about these things. But the truth was they were too damn busy for fun most of the time anyway.

Carol dated when it happened organically and stayed in touch with a few friends who were good for a laugh. Outside of that, it was Carol against the world. Not because she was looking for a fight but because everyone was always swinging at her.

There were plenty of opportunities to talk to someone casually. This morning, Mary would come to do Carol's hair. Not because Carol couldn't do her own, but because she couldn't do it as well as Mary, and it was necessary to look put together. The power suit and the styled hair was all part of the job. She and Mary would gab and laugh, and eventually Mary would leave. They never went out for drinks or talked deeply about their experiences. Really, Carol wasn't even sure what Mary thought of her.

Most likely, the hairdresser was annoyed. Mary had to drag herself in here before the sun came up to primp and press some woman who made more in a month than she did in three years. Or five years. It didn't exactly breed goodwill.

Carol locked the door to her bathroom, spun the knobs on the shower, and drew in a deep breath. This was why CEOs had bathrooms attached to their offices—because the job required long hours. Standing under the hot water, a question kept pulsing at her temples. Nagging at her.

Was Marta the key to everything Carol was pursuing or was she self-sabotage?

Burnout and loneliness nipped at Carol's heels. A menacing cloud of doubt and exhaustion. No matter how fast she ran toward the next level of success, they were always there. Maybe selecting Marta was a way to get herself knocked back down.

Down where the people were. The people she used to know. The ones she used to laugh with until she cried. They'd all commiserate about their bosses and swear they were ready to quit. Now that talk was *about* her instead of with her.

No. Carol rejected that worry. Marta wasn't a show of weakness and defeat. She was strong. She was resilient and represented overdue change. Marta would not be the iceberg that sank Carol's ship. She would be the lighthouse that led other people into the harbor. Marta was the right choice for the right reason, and Carol would fight to make sure she received the award. The gamble was her job. But the win would open doors for so many other people.

CHAPTER SIX

Marta

She didn't sleep over anymore. Heather's house wasn't a slumber party. Now it was a place Ray went back to after he worked his shift at the bar. It would be weird to wake up there with the two of them. The wine had gone to her head, so she left her car and opted instead for a rideshare.

The evening was much less contentious as the hours ticked by. Marta hadn't said any more to Ray or Heather about her worries or her past. They were sweet and, mostly because of Ray, showed restraint. Heather would have obviously preferred to bulldoze her way into Marta's secrets.

Home was the most obvious destination. It was eleven. She had a buzz in her head and a pain in her heart. Her shift at the bookstore didn't start until noon the next day, and the idea of lying awake in her bed, contemplating her future, was too daunting.

"Um, can you drop me off at The Down Easter?" Marta knew rideshare drivers didn't like to change destinations. It wasn't the same as a cab in the city. But this guy just shrugged and took the next left that would take her to the restaurant.

It was the only place she knew she could sit unbothered at a bar this late at night. The bartender wouldn't let anyone give her trouble or make her leave for sipping too long on the same drink.

"How did I know you were going to turn up? I left you two alone an hour ago," Ray asked, snickering at her. "You want more wine or a coffee?"

"Wine," she breathed out heavily. "Heather was nodding off, and I'm not ready to go home."

"I hear you," Ray said, pulling out a wine glass and filling it for her. "It's quiet in here tonight. Hang out as long as you like. If you make it to the end of my shift, I'll give you a lift home."

"I won't be here that long," she said, smiling at his kindness. In reality, she knew as strong as her friendship was with Heather, it probably wouldn't be great to hitch a ride with her boyfriend that late at night. Even if her boyfriend was also Marta's dear friend. The rules were all different now, and Marta wanted to be careful not to break them.

"Sorry we ambushed you like that," Ray said apologetically. "I get it. I really do. I'm not usually big on gushing about my business either. I do it more now that I'm with Heather. She brings it out in me."

"She's good like that," Marta said, sipping her wine and leaning back in the plush bar stool.

"You get enough to eat? Want anything else?"

"I had plenty. You're a great cook, Ray. And a good boyfriend to Heather. I'm so glad you finally got together."

"It's weird, though, right? For you and me. I feel like the whole dynamic is different now, and I don't like that part."

"I know," Marta agreed sadly. "This was the only place I wanted to come, and I was worried it would be weird to show up now. I wouldn't go hang out at any bar this time of night by myself. I just do it because you're here, and I know I can."

"You can come here or any place I work any time. No matter who I date, that won't change. I care a lot about Heather. She's amazing. I liked her the moment I met her."

"I know. I knew right away."

"But you," Ray said, looking suddenly serious. "I got you. I felt like you were different than anyone I'd ever met, and I knew right away I wanted you in my life. Like family. Something better than family."

He'd described it perfectly. She'd felt the same for him. Marta had two brothers of her own, but there was so much baggage there. It made for complexities in their relationships. With Ray, it was like having a brother without any of the history.

"Same," she replied, reaching her hand over and

patting his cheek. "I'm glad you're around. Don't mess things up with Heather, though. I don't want to be in the middle of that mess."

"I'm trying not to." Ray went to help another customer as a jazz band began to play in the other room. The music was wild and controlled all at once. She let her mind wander as she was swept up in the rhythm.

Marta could still remember the day she realized she was poor. Shame nipped at her skin like the tiny sharp teeth of a rambunctious puppy. But without the flappy ears and wagging tail to make it all worthwhile. It was remarkable how many years she'd gone without knowing what her family lacked.

When you're little and uninhibited and dirty, mostly everyone your age looks somewhat unfortunate. The sandbox was full of wild children who seemed better suited for the forest than a house. But eventually, the roads diverge. Some become the people who get clothes from trash bags handed down by neighbors, while others are in line purchasing designer clothes at the mall. Forget the invisible poverty line. The lines drawn between rich kids and poor kids are far starker and impossible to miss. That was a barrier she bumped violently against for years.

It wasn't just poverty that hindered Marta. There was a tragedy in having terribly young parents. They were ill-equipped. How could they be anything else? They hadn't had time to learn. When they started their family, Charlie and Wendy were merely playing house, children themselves. Marta and her brothers were like dolls, occasionally tended to on a whim and then cast aside. However, instead of the bottom of the toy box, they were left in much more precarious places.

On good days, it meant unkempt hair. Dirty sneakers, laces frayed to the point of being fuzzy, paired with a much-too-large hand-me-down dress at church. There was no insistence on brushing teeth or taking vitamins. Hygiene, in general, was inconsistently expected and often neglected. There was a wildness about her childhood. A feral existence that was tamed only by the shame cast on them when they stepped into someone else's world. She didn't know she was doing it all wrong until she saw many people doing it right. The way they leered and hummed their disapproval still loomed in the shadows of her mind. It even shaped the life she tried to build for herself when all the decisions became hers to make.

Even now, a full-grown woman, Marta could sense the canyon between her and those she met in new circles. People knew things she didn't. Those unwritten rules of civilized society. You only know about the things you see. You only learn what you're taught. She was the culmina-tion of all the things her parents did, and conversely, she lacked all the things they didn't know to teach her. Their limitations were now her burdens. How could she possibly be worthy of a prestigious award? She didn't own an iron. She was pretty sure she was sorting her recycling wrong. Her car had had a cracked windshield for the last two years. Forget being an award-winning author. She was hardly a functioning adult.

The movies portrayed the rags to riches scenario as equal parts glamorous and comical. Most people outside of the movies were just rags to reality. The transition from a poor child to a less poor adult was not a storybook dream. It wasn't made up of predictable moments that would make the main character endearing to an audience. There were not many instances where Marta was confounded by which fork to use first at a nice restaurant. It wasn't a lack of manners that made her an uncivilized beast unworthy of good company. The depths of her ignorance about a different way of life were at times debilitating and anything but laughable.

This award would only shine a light on that ignorance. As a child, she hadn't understood that being poor was a relative idea. Even if she was familiar with the notion, she didn't internalize how poverty applied to her. Back then, all she knew was there were people worse off than she was. She'd seen ragged, disheveled panhandlers begging on the corner. There was talk at church about the starving children in far-off countries who needed nickels and pennies to survive. She had coins of her own, so she knew she was luckier than they were. If she was poor, she was not the poorest of the poor.

Even if her family hit rough patches and argued, there had to be people out there worse than they were. People who really fought and hated each other. She knew there was love in her family.

Marta tried to think of a simple way to explain it to her friends. Maybe it was best to just go by the numbers. As a young adult, Marta became aware that measurements for some of these things existed. Metrics to properly divide society. There were ways of quantifying "poor." Phrases like *a living wage*, *working poor*, and *lack of upward mobility*. Politicians could debate it all in this distanced, theoretical way. Argue as "devil's advocates" without ever knowing the sensation of panic that comes with hunger or instability. How easy it was to create and assign a label you'd never have to carry yourself.

There was a poverty line, which always seemed laughable to Marta. A line? Some finite thing that made you poor or not depending on which side you found yourself. How did that line know how much food was in her fridge or how many holes were in her best dress? How did that line's existence help her at all?

Solely by the numbers, she and her family had lived below the line. It was overhead, looming like playground monkey bars she couldn't reach even with her biggest jump. It stood only as a reminder of how low they were; making it to the other side of the line was not a goal they felt would ever be in their reach. Maybe that would be a good enough explanation for Heather.

"You don't have to decide tonight," Ray said, resting one of his elbows on the bar. "Don't look so stressed."

"I don't know what the hell I'm doing," Marta admitted. "I'm going to keep hurting Heather. I can feel it. I don't want that."

"I'll keep reminding her you're worth being patient for. Don't put so much pressure on yourself. I know it's not easy, but for two seconds, can we just toast to the fact that you were selected for this? No strings attached. No worrying about what you choose. Can we just acknowledge how freaking amazing this is?"

Marta smiled and held her wine up. Ray filled himself a glass of soda and clinked it against hers. "I still can't believe it. Of all the books, they liked mine the best."

Marta finally allowed herself to feel downright giddy with Ray's permission. For the first time, it truly hit her.

"How bad will it be if you put yourself out there?" Ray wasn't asking this in some dismissive *how bad could it be* tone. He was genuine.

"Bad," Marta whispered somberly. "I've run away from things. Things I don't really want to catch back up with me. People who I'm glad that they don't know where I am."

Ray nodded. "Maybe this will be an opportunity that helps you put even more space between yourself and what you're running from. It would give you resources to do that."

"Resources," Marta chuckled. "People will come out of the woodwork for those resources. They'll be quick to cut me down and tell whatever juicy story people want to hear. I just don't think I'm ready. I know my life looks pretty pathetic now, but it's the best it's been. Ever. It's calm, and I have enough to get by. I'd be risking that."

Tapping his fingers on the bar, Ray nodded. "I wish I had an answer. I wish I could promise to protect you from your past and make sure no matter what came up, you'd be all right. I wish it was that easy."

"Me too." Marta rubbed at her tired eyes. "I wish it was like scaring off the unwanted advances and unruly customers at the bar."

"My specialty," Ray smirked and moved off again to help another customer. Marta sat for a moment, letting the last few embers of joy fizzle like a sparkler burning down to her fingertips. It was nice while it lasted, but it was time to face reality.

She might be the winner of the Milton Cesar Foundation for the Arts Breakout Writer Award, but she wasn't going to be the recipient of it.

CHAPTER SEVEN

Carol

Eli's cologne was obnoxious. She planned to tell him one day. He wore too much in an effort to cover the cigar smell that lingered on his clothes and breath. It didn't work. Carol tried not to judge people too harshly, but Eli was someone she indeed disdained. When he strolled into a room with his overly long bright blue ties and painfully obvious hair plugs, she internally rolled her eyes. His suits were always padded in the shoulders, an effort to make his frame, shrinking with age, appear more robust than it was. His vanity had him racing toward solutions for all of his physical failings. Botox for his wrinkles had only made him look strange, not younger. His trendy shoes didn't match his suit.

He was everything she'd grown to hate about men in the workplace. There were plenty of good ones. Plenty of mediocre ones who mostly stayed out of the way. But Eli was in the category of men who made her work life miserable and her goals harder to achieve. It was worse now than ever. He had the luxury of hiding behind his age. When he was inappropriate, he would retreat to the excuse that he was a product of his generation and all this newfound tolerance of others was just too hard for an old dog like him to learn.

As if there was a novelty or newness to treating people well regardless of how different they were from you. Eli used terminology that had long since been retired in modern conversations, yet everyone brushed it off and excused it away. He stood too close. Stared too long. And worse than all that, he built and ran a system that welcomed only employees who most closely resembled him in looks and personality. It left no room for new voices and new ideas.

The day the board asked him to step down brought a collective sigh of relief from every person who had been silently cringing in his presence for years. Carol had been positioning herself for his job but never believed it was within reach. There were four other qualified candidates within the company. All men. While more polished than Eli, they all had dominating personalities that resembled his leadership style. She was the outlier. And, apparently, the board wanted change. Real change. She planned to live up to that.

"Darling, are we having a meeting or a social hour?" Eli had plopped into her chair at the head of the conference room table. He could pretend all he wanted that this was some kind of mindless act, but she knew it was a power play. He was always finding ways to assert himself as if he was still in control. It couldn't stand. Not if she truly wanted to lead this company.

"I'd love to start the meeting when you're out of my chair." Carol painted on a brilliant smile and gave him only half of her attention. She went on chatting with Lori, the only other woman in the room. It was as if Lori understood her role in all this, not wavering from their conversation even with the interruption.

"Oh, excuse me," Eli said in an exaggerated sing-song voice. "That happened to be my chair for the last ten years."

Carol didn't offer a reply although plenty of petty ones popped into her head. She waited for him to stand up and then moved to her spot at the head of the table. "I know this is just our monthly meeting, but I want to take the opportunity to fill you in on the status of the Breakout Writer Award for this year." She gestured to the files placed in front of each member of the board.

"This wasn't on the agenda," Robert Riggins said with a mischievous grin. He was one of the good ones. Carol didn't know who on the board supported her promotion to CEO, but she was almost sure Robert had. They'd known each other for nearly a decade, though their paths only crossed professionally. He was always cordial and supportive.

"The agenda isn't written in stone," Carol said light-heartedly as she folded her hands and placed them on the large wood table. "I reserve the right to spring things on you all at any time. But trust me, this will be exciting news."

Eli cleared his throat with a wet cough that made Carol nearly gag. "Good candidates this year," he said. "Mitchel Crowley was a front runner, but something tells me you went for Caryn Westler. You women always stick together."

Carol wanted to laugh and yell all at once. This foolish man had enough hubris to assume she'd even looked at the list of candidates he'd sent her. "I'm certain all members of the board will agree that we need a fresh take."

Eli interrupted her. "Who is this?" His plump face was pinched as he squinted to read the document Carol had prepared for them all.

"Eli." Carol let her stern voice cut across the table. "I appreciate the board inviting you to these meetings, but make no mistake, you're here as an observer. A courtesy for your years of service."

"Pardon me," Eli boomed, shooting glances at each member of the board. "I'm here because my opinion is vital to the future of this company. They may have wanted to appease some feminist squeaky wheels by finding someone in a skirt to take my job, but they still need me here."

She'd had enough. This standoff was years in the making. Carol had no clue if the board would have her back or not. But she wouldn't allow anyone to speak to her this way. "Eli, I'm going to ask you to continue the rest of this meeting as a silent participant. I understand that the tolerance for your inappropriateness has been astronomically high over the years. It makes it hard for you to understand that it won't be acceptable going forward. I think it'll be best if you say nothing else."

The smile on Eli's face was not one of pride. Nor was he impressed with Carol's spunk. His expression was solely rooted in confidence. In his mind, she had no power, and he had it all. "Darling—"

"Carol," she corrected. "And if you have something else to say, please make it quick and final. I have a meeting to conduct here."

"It won't work," Eli chuckled out smugly. "I get it. You're the political correctness police. You want to cancel anyone who makes you feel a little uncomfortable." He made some condescending pouting face before rolling his eyes. "The world is turning into a place full of sniveling unqualified leaders who have gotten there solely because someone has said we better put a so-and-so in the job or we'll look bad."

Carol held up her hand and stood. "Eli, I could stand here and rattle off my résumé and every reason I am more than qualified for this job. But it's beneath me to argue with a man who holds your antiquated views of the world. I don't need to show you how qualified I am for this job because my being here proves I am at least more qualified for it than you. You will not sit in this room and spew misogynistic bullshit and undermine me. I know you feel threatened that the stronghold you've had on the world, just by being you, is loosening. It's unfortunate, really, that your inability to evolve has canceled your value to this company. I don't doubt that there are countless ways your years of experience could strengthen what we have here. But I won't allow it to come at the cost of having to listen to you bulldoze everyone in this room. You don't hold power here anymore."

"Girly, I have more power than you'll ever have, no matter what title they give you. This board invites me here to keep you in check."

"If this board wanted you here that badly, I don't suppose they'd have asked you to leave the CEO role in the first place," Carol cut back. "Now you can sit there quietly while we discuss how to bring the program you nearly ran into the ground back from the dead, or you can leave. The choice is yours."

"Ran into the ground," Eli boomed, now attempting to use his voice to try to intimidate her. "I kept this place afloat. I lobbied for more money than any of my predecessors had ever dreamed of receiving."

"Begging and swapping favors with congressmen for funding isn't a sustainable solution. It also leaves you completely beholden to them." Carol stood and kept her voice level. "We should be making ample funds by driving up viewership to our award ceremonies and attracting more lucrative ad sponsors. It's not about finding money to make the show happen. It's about the show making money. You have no idea what people want to watch, who they want to succeed. You've brought the same candidates for these awards year after year. Boring, affluent academic writers who have faced neither hardship nor challenges. People we want to inspire and develop will never connect with that. Viewership was in the toilet. Our national programs were underutilized and dying. The board knew nine months ago it was time for a change. Get in line with that or get out." Carol pointed at the door and kept her eyes fixed on Eli.

He was not rattled in the least by her ultimatum. Carol had hoped his face would grow red or the vein in his forehead would pulse. But he looked completely calm. "I didn't realize you were such a cold bitch, Carol." He pushed his chair back and stood.

"Lovely," Carol drew in a breath through her teeth. "Glad we're all on the same page now. Goodbye, Eli."

"I'll be in touch," Eli replied coolly, looking to the board members and trying to ice out Carol.

She wasn't sure what to expect. As the CEO, she reported to the board. The shareholders appointed them with the expectation that they would ensure the company was running appropriately. This heated exchange in the boardroom with a long-standing member of the business was not customary and bordered on inappropriate.

"I apologize for the interruption," Carol said with a sigh as she settled back into her chair. "I understand Eli has been a vital part of this business community for years.

That information and your continued invitation to have him join our board meetings are not lost on me." She stopped short of apologizing specifically for the way she spoke to him.

Lori hummed. "I didn't invite him here. That man is repulsive, and the fact that he's survived this long in this business with his attitude is incredible. I applaud you for kicking him out of here."

"I gave him the option to stay if he could act accordingly," Carol corrected. "It appears he could not."

"I'm not excusing his behavior," Larry Mills said, an inevitable *but* on his lips. "But Eli is not expendable. He is the link to most of our funding and has relationships we still very much rely on. That's why he's in this room. It was a miracle we got him to step down, but part of that agreement was that he would still hold some sort of influence in exchange for his networking relationships. This company and the foundation are celebrating sixty years this year. There are just certain things we've always done." Larry had stiff shoulders and rusty red hair that always made him easy to spot in a crowd. He moved like a robot and thought like a cult follower. He was convinced, mostly by Eli, that change was wrong and the company wouldn't survive it.

Carol took back control of the conversation before anyone else could agree with Larry. "The company is celebrating sixty years, Larry. You are right. I can't think of too many things that have avoided evolving in the last sixty years. If they have avoided it, they've crumbled. We have to grow and adapt if we want to stay marketable as we draw in a whole new generation of viewers. You put your faith in me to accomplish that. Please give me the chance to do so."

"It wasn't a unanimous vote," Charles Smith said flatly. "The board was split on you. You must realize that as you make these big sweeping changes." His pockmarked skin looked yellowish under the lights. Charles glanced at Larry and then down at the paper in front of him.

Carol leaned back and crossed her legs. "I think if there was a board that agreed on everything, it would be an ineffective body. Discourse is what makes a group strong. I didn't come here under the illusion that I had everyone's support. I came in here knowing I deserve everyone's respect. If you want Eli's opinion, you can seek it on your own. I have a vision for the future of this company and the foundation. I am ready to implement it and do what you hired me to do. I don't think it's too much to ask that while I do my job, we're not all subjected to his nonsense."

"Cheers to that," Robert announced, clapping his hands together. "Now, maybe we can get through a meeting without a migraine from his cologne. Carol, tell us about this author. Marta Leduc?"

A wash of calm fell over her. She had gotten this job because at least four of the seven board members had confidence in her. She was sure now Robert and Lori were two and Larry and Charles were against her. But she'd defused the current situation for the moment and had gotten Eli out of the room. That was a win. Now it was all about Marta.

"She's perfect," Carol said, leaning in. With the excitement of Eli leaving over, everyone turned their attention back to the document in front of them. "Last spring I laid out a plan to you for my first ninety days. I told you we would increase viewership, energize our current shareholders, and become less dependent on strings-attached funding. Marta is the key to those things."

"What's so special about her?" Lori asked, seeming to skim the bio. "You liked her book?"

"Her book is very compelling. Raw. Nostalgic. Touching. It'll have no problem hitting the top of the charts with our exposure. But the book is just part of the story. I met with her yesterday. People will love her. They'll tune in just to see who she is and what she's about."

"What is she about?" Larry asked, holding up the documents as though they were blank. "I don't see much about her. You've outlined the book well, but who is she? What makes her special?"

"She's real," Carol replied confidently. "She's written this masterpiece, and she doesn't even really understand how good it is yet. Diamond in the rough. Completely untapped brilliance."

Lori grinned. "You're excited about this. Marta must be something special. It sounds like she could be a good part of your strategy."

"Strategy," Larry said coolly. "It seems more like a complete overhaul. The shareholders are concerned that it's too much too soon. You've changed most of the lower-level marketing staff. Burning a bridge with Eli is essentially shutting the valve to government funding and endowments."

Robert groaned. "Eli is not the only avenue we have to sustain government funding. That's certainly what he'd like us to believe. But if you've been listening to Carol's strategy over the last nine months, you'll see it's not just changing lower-level marketing staff. Its fresh, young staff coming in to bring us up to speed on new trends. We should be capitalizing on every social media platform available. That's what the new staff will be doing. We are a foundation for the arts: literature, dance, acting, comedy. Yet we've spent so much time doing the same thing over and over. We're about education and outreach, but we're only reaching out to the same group of elite students and up-and-comers. There is a whole country full of talented people we're overlooking."

Lori piled on. "He's right. The original principles this organization was founded on should still apply. But the process should change. We need to ensure that our various art forms and our audiences are as rich, diverse, and ever-changing as America itself. That means we can't just continue to support, feature, and award the same types of people from the same parts of the country. And we can't reach new audiences in the old ways. The shareholders will be energized to know Carol is ready to implement those changes."

Larry leaned back and folded his arms across his chest. "You'd have to increase viewership by over twenty percent to make up for the possibility of a loss of funding in other areas. If Eli is not out there campaigning and negotiating on our behalf, you're going to have to close the delta on the loss of profit."

Carol nearly called out the mansplaining but instead opted to swallow that down. "I know, Larry. But if we implement the changes I've been laying the groundwork for, not only will we be more profitable but also far more sustainable. We would not be beholden to one man making backroom deals on our behalf. We'd be pulling in a whole new audience."

Larry grimaced. "If it works."

Carol softened her expression. "Your cynicism won't change the outcome. It's going to work. We're going to sit here this time next year with sustainable ticket revenue and private philanthropy. We're going to expand education and outreach programs to all fifty states. The Milton Cesar Foundation for the Arts is about to soar. Buckle up."

Carol closed the file folder in front of her and stood. "Next month, I will bring Marta to town. You'll all have an opportunity to meet her. Until then, I'll settle for your blind faith in me."

A small chuckle broke out around the table as Carol made her way to the door. After she left, they'd be there for another hour at least. They'd look over her latest proposal. They'd pull it apart, and there would undoubtedly be voices in the room ready to dismantle it. That wasn't her concern. She'd done the best she could, and now it was up to them to realize just how brilliant her plan was.

CHAPTER EIGHT

Carol

It was only forty minutes later. In her opinion, record time, but she knew the rumor mill traveled fast. Terrance was in her office, standing with a mischievous grin as he quietly closed the door behind him.

"You badass. You absolute badass. Was Eli crying? Is that part true?" He folded his arms over his chest and looked as though he wouldn't move until he got the juiciest parts of the story.

"How in the world did you hear already?" Carol assumed it would be at least a day before the story of the boardroom battle made its way around.

"I hear everything," Terrance gloated. "What

happened? Is it as good as people are saying? Did you toss him out of the boardroom?"

"Well, not physically. There was no giant hook from stage right or anything. He was acting as absurd as usual, and I knew I'd never be able to make my pitch if he was in there. He's a well poisoner. I'm tired of everyone acting as though we need him in our corner. They pushed him out of the CEO position for a reason."

"Give me something. I have to know what you said to him. Best line. I'm dying here." Terrance looked ready to burst, and she loved him for it. If she had children, she would have been thrilled for them to be like Terrance.

"I might have said I don't need to show you how qualified I am for this job because me being here proves I am at least more qualified for it than you. You will not sit in this room and spew misogynistic bullshit and undermine me. Or something along those lines." She waved her hand as though it were no big deal. But Terrance's reaction was precisely what she expected.

He pumped his fist in the air and quietly cheered. "Yes. Hell yes. Like I said, you are a badass. Eli is an absolute dinosaur. He's a pig. He's a pigosaurus, and you finally booted him."

"Pigosaurus?" Carol asked, choking out a laugh. "I should have called him that instead. I wish you could have been in there with me. The look on his face. It was priceless."

"Well, he deserves far worse than just the door hitting

him in the ass on the way out. I'd love to knock a few of those veneers out of his mouth for all the things he's said to you. The self-control I've had to show is a testament to how much I respect you. If I thought you'd let me, he'd have been knocked on his ass by now." Terrance paced a bit around the office as the adrenaline seemed to fuel him.

"I know that, and I appreciate both your willingness to punch him and your ability to refrain from it. But now the real work begins."

"Begins," Terrance laughed, sitting down across from her. "You've overhauled the entire marketing and tech team with a focus on social media expansion. You've empowered the outreach and education team to expand by ten percent with the direction to hunt for untapped talent in underserved markets. The lineup for next year's award show is exceptional and diverse. You've made inroads with some of the largest private donors and energized them for the foundation's future. Regardless of what a few naysayers on the board are clamoring about, the shareholders are ready for what you've got in store. The last nine months have been nothing short of miraculous, and every bit of that is because of the work you've done." He leaned in and put his hand on her desk. "Carol, you're exactly what this place needed, and everyone is going to see that."

She fought tears. That wouldn't be appropriate and certainly wouldn't play into his idea of the powerhouse boss he was convinced she was. Instead, she straightened her back and smiled. "Terrance, none of that would be possible if you weren't helping me. Half of the donors at the last gala were enamored with you. They were begging me to pair you up with their single daughters. You have helped me work out the kinks in every single pitch I've made to the board. You're right. All of this is going to work. It'll pay off for both of us."

He patted his hand on her desk and stood. "I get a tiny fraction of the credit. I can charm the daughters and stay late to hear your next brilliant idea. But they are your ideas. Keep them coming. If you think Marta is the key, then I say, let's get her on board."

"More like in front of the board. I told them she'd be here next month. We need to make that happen. We might need your charm."

"You got it. Whatever it takes." Terrance slipped out of her office and back to his desk.

The excitement of kicking Eli out of the boardroom left with Terrance. As she sat alone in her office, she realized just how much this upped the ante. Eli would not have left the building, headed off to self-evaluate where he'd gone wrong, and be contemplating an authentic apology. He would have instantly begun working his network and searching for ways to hurt her.

Eli wasn't picky when it came to striking back at someone he felt had slighted him. He was known for his pettiness. Not only would Carol have to prove how obsolete he was to the company, but she'd also need to protect herself against his attacks.

She split her afternoon between meetings with other departments needing her attention and staring off into space every time she retreated back to her office alone. It was still a productive day, but there was a cloud of unease around her as she closed her laptop and told Terrance she'd be heading out soon. He was always reluctant to leave before her, but today she insisted. He'd been in early, and there was nothing left to be done for the day.

"You're positive?" he asked, peeking his head in her office one last time.

"Look, my computer is closed—no more work for me. I'm just going to make a few personal calls before I head out." She waved a hand at him, insisting he take her up on it. Finally, he did.

It was twenty more minutes of wall staring and strategic thinking before she heard a knock on her door.

"Come in," she said, straightening her back.

"I wasn't sure you were still here," Robert said apologetically as he stepped into her office. "But you've got a reputation for never leaving, so I thought I'd take the chance."

"It's usually a good bet that I'm still here," Carol said through a smile as she stood and invited him to take a seat across from her desk. "What can I do for you, Robert?"

"Forgive me," he said sheepishly. "Or at least entertain my apology."

"Apology?" Carol settled back into her seat, and her brows came together as she contemplated what this might be about. Robert had been in her corner throughout the entire transition. After today she was sure he'd voted for her promotion to CEO. So she was puzzled.

Robert took a seat across from her and looked pitiful. His thick, dark head of hair, a splattering of gray at the temples, was a bit unkempt. Not by much but noticeable to her. This wasn't the fresh look she'd usually seen him with at morning meetings. His tie was slightly loosened from his neck.

Robert was a good-looking man with a friendly smile and kind brown eyes. He didn't wear a flashy gold watch or spend time name-dropping. He was sure of himself in a way that didn't seem to require those things. He shifted and cleared his throat. "I don't know why I tolerated Eli in that boardroom for so long. His behavior was completely inappropriate, and I should have taken a stand earlier."

A weight of worry slid off her shoulders. "Robert, I don't need anyone to fight my battles for me. There was no one in that room in a better position than I was to hold him accountable. As a board member, I understand that you answer to the shareholders. Some of them still feel as though—"

"Please don't," Robert said. "Don't let me off the hook. I don't deserve that. The truth is Eli lost his job as CEO because he was incredibly inappropriate and problematic, and the board realized sooner or later it would reflect on the company. Everyone was willing to just deal with it until they realized the world would not anymore. It was cowardly to wait so long to push him out and even more so to invite him back in for any reason."

"I don't imagine you were the one inviting Eli anywhere." Carol leaned back in her chair and softened her posture. Robert was no threat to her now, and she was too tired to pretend to have the upper hand.

"I spoke out against it but backed down. I regret that now." Robert ran a hand over his cheek, showing how exhausted he was. "I wanted to make sure you knew that, going forward, I won't back down again. Eli has no place in that room or in this company. You shouldn't have to make that case alone." Robert perked up a bit as she smiled.

"I appreciate that, Robert. I've always felt as though I had your support. I know I'm proposing quite a bit of change, but it will pay off."

"You do have my support." Robert stood and tucked his hands in his pockets. "Was that hard today? You play it so cool, but those moments have to be tough. And Eli is not just going to back down. He's insatiable when it comes to ego and power."

Carol felt a rush of honesty bubble up in her. "It's not easy," she blurted out. "It is terrifying. I'm not supposed to say that because my number one job is to make sure you have confidence in me. My whole job is to lead with nerves of steel and unshakable confidence."

Robert cut her off. "That is not your job. Those are not requirements. I'd be more worried if you shrugged off Eli. The fact that you understand just how dangerous he can be shows how prepared you are for him."

Her hand shook as she brought it up to her hot cheek. She'd heard all the stories of Eli's vengeance. "I knew what

I was getting into when I called him out. It was necessary." Carol was mostly trying to convince herself now.

"Are you okay?" Robert leaned in, looking concerned.

She felt the color fade away from her face, and a familiar woozy feeling take over. It was happening again. "I just need," Carol gulped and took a few deep breaths. "Sorry, is Terrance still there?"

"No, he was leaving as I was coming in. What do you need?" Robert was bouncing with energy now and coming around toward her side of the desk. She tried to blink the dark spots out of her gaze.

"Food," she said, gripping the desk tightly. "My blood sugar is super low. I didn't eat. And I took the red-eye last night to get back here. I never sleep on those flights."

"Do you have any food in your office?" Robert looked around for anything that might be a cabinet full of snacks.

"Terrance has a drawer full," she said, leaning back in her chair and drawing in another deep breath.

Robert was gone in a flash and then returned with an arm full of protein bars and packaged crackers. "Are these all right?" He spilled them onto her desk like a waterfall of calories.

"Yes," she chuckled. "Any of those are fine. I just need a little something. I'm running on coffee and adrenaline."

Robert pulled open a package of cheese crackers, and though Carol felt painfully self-conscious, she nibbled away at them. He disappeared again into the hallway and came back with a glass of water.

"Here, drink some of this. I thought for a minute you

were having a panic attack." Robert crouched down beside her desk. For all the time they'd been acquaintances, this was as physically close as they'd ever been. His fresh scented cologne and sturdy hands were enough to focus on as she tried to right herself.

"I am so sorry about this," she said between sips of water. "This isn't what I want to portray to a board member. I'm just exhausted, and to be honest, I've been considering all day what kind of retribution I expect from Eli. I was very intentional with how I chose to handle today. But I can't pretend I'm not having some remorse about my choice. And on top of all that, you're the last person in the world I should be expressing that to." She brought her hand to her forehead and slid it down over her eyes.

"I didn't come here this evening as a board member, Carol. I came as a man apologizing for my utter lack of courage and personal responsibility in that board room with Eli over the last nine months. I'm here as Robert, the idiot who should have done more and done it sooner." His warm hand rested for a moment on her arm before he stood and moved back to the other side of the desk.

Carol wanted to believe him. She tried to think that this episode wouldn't paint her as weak and ineffective. "I don't want to change your opinion of me."

"None of this counts," Robert said, holding up his hand as though he were swearing an oath. "The rest of the evening, we're Robert and Carol, and everything is off the record. Deal?"

With a little nod, Carol agreed. "How bad do you think it will be with Eli? Any idea what he'll be plotting?"

"His specialty is blackmail. The man loves lording other people's secrets over their heads. I've heard half the funding he's ever secured for us over the years has been through extortion. I don't know how he's lasted this long. If I were you, I'd be making sure he didn't have anything to use against you."

"I'll be sure to keep my trysts private," Carol laughed. "I don't have skeletons in my closet. It's a luxury a woman in this industry doesn't receive. We've got to be twice as educated, half as demanding, and absolutely scandal-free. All that to just get a shot at leadership." Carol felt the color returning to her face, and her back was sturdy again.

Robert looked fully relaxed as he sank back into the chair across from her desk and spoke again. "My father-in-law, well ex-father-in-law. How does that work when you get divorced? Do they all become your exes?" He shook off the distraction of semantics and continued. "My ex-wife's father was the biggest misogynistic bully I've ever met. I don't know how Rebecca grew up in that environment and turned out to be as successful as she did."

"You and Rebecca divorced?" Carol had met Robert's wife a time or two at social functions. She was a therapist and always spoke glowingly of their children.

"You didn't know?" Robert asked, holding up his hand and showing off the lack of a wedding band. "It was what kept the rumor mill churning most of last year. Rebecca started a relationship with one of her patients. She's a therapist."

Carol put her hand over her heart. "I hadn't heard anything about it. I remember meeting her. She was lovely."

"Love of my life," Robert corrected somberly. "But our kids grew up and left for college. Rebecca and I were high school sweethearts. We dedicated our entire lives to this idea of success in our family and our careers. We worked incredibly hard. I was a good dad. She was a good mom. But neither one of us left much time for our marriage. When the kids left, there was almost nothing keeping us together. We went two years like that, and then Rebecca met someone."

"A patient. That's not even an ethical gray area. It's completely wrong on every level."

"Well, they seem happy," Robert shrugged. "I've stayed civil for the kids. They're adults, but they still depend on us in many ways. I went through the pissed-off stage, but when I stepped back and really looked at the state of our marriage, I couldn't blame her. It had been over for years." He kicked his head to the side and eyed Carol closely. "Are you saying you hadn't heard any of this?"

"I try not to engage in the gossip if I can avoid it. Terrance usually fills me in if he thinks it's going to impact the business. I really hadn't heard at all. I'm sorry you went through that."

"I'm still going through it," Robert said quietly. "I spent my entire career surrounded by men who didn't value their vows and took every business trip as an opportunity to break them. I never wanted to be one of those men."

"That's admirable."

"It's made me about as out of practice as a man can be when it comes to dating. And things are not how they were all those years ago when I'd drive Rebecca home from school, and we'd study at her kitchen table. Online dating, all these apps. It's not for me. How do you do it?"

"Oh, that's easy," Carol said, swiping the air as though she were dismissing his description of the current dating scene. "You work yourself so hard you forget to eat. You find books that keep you up at night with the promise of escapism. A good bottle of wine, and that's it."

"How does that turn into a date?" Robert asked, looking puzzled.

"It doesn't," Carol laughed loudly. "But it's still the best plan I've found so far."

"You've got the greatest laugh," Robert said, joining in. "I always know it's you, even from across a room. It's infectious."

The compliment was probably just an observation, but it still made her blush. "Well, it hasn't snared me the right man yet. Not that a relationship is a focal point in my life right now. I've dated all kinds of men and had various levels of success in those relationships. But ultimately, none of them understood me."

"I'm intrigued. You're a puzzle? A riddle?" Robert leaned in, challenging her to explain. "I'm so good at riddles."

This was over the line. All of it. Socializing wasn't taboo, but this was too cozy. Too intimate. Yet Carol felt compelled to keep chatting. To share more and sit longer. Maybe it was the exhaustion or the intense loneliness she'd been experiencing lately. It felt comfortable to talk to Robert, and she wanted it to continue. "I'm no riddle. It usually goes like this.

"Men: Women are so complex. It's impossible to know what they want.

"Me: Here, let me tell you concisely what I'm looking for.

"Men: It's just so hard to read—mysterious creatures.

"Me: No mystery here, let me lay it out for you again.

"Men: I guess I'll never know what she wanted."

Robert laughed so hard that he grabbed his side and held up a hand for her to stop. "We really are idiots sometimes."

"Most of the time," Carol corrected.

"What exactly were you telling them you wanted?" Robert questioned. "I have to know if I can pass the test."

"It's no test," Carol teased. "It's literally just listening without applying all those random man filters in your brain."

"I will turn them off," Robert promised as he pretended to click something off by his brain. "What do you want in a relationship?"

"I want to be in a relationship that is not dictated by societal norms. I know what the narrative is. I know I was supposed to want children, and even at this phase of my life, I'm expected to take some pre-ordained role when I date someone long enough. Cater to his career or meld into his existing life. I want understanding when it comes to how hard I work. A cheerleader. I want a relationship reimagined. Free of what the world tells me it's supposed to be." Carol was moving her hands animatedly and holding court the way she did anytime she was genuinely passionate about something.

Robert was in awe. He propped his hand thoughtfully under his chin and stared at her for a long beat. "That doesn't sound too bad. And you're telling me men just can't deal with that?"

Carol chuckled. "Can't deal with it? They can't even hear it. The words come out of my mouth and apparently morph into 'I'm a cold workaholic who won't be flexible.'"

"We are absolute idiots," Robert said, slapping a hand jokingly to his head. "How in the world could a man see a woman like you, capable, strong, loyal, and not listen to what you actually want. I love that. A relationship, reimagined. It's brilliant."

"You're in the minority," Carol sighed. "I wish I could reassure you about the dating scene, but it's a jungle out there. It's all ego and games."

"I have always appreciated your blunt advice. It's exactly as bad as I thought it was. Forget online dating. Maybe I'll just apply for the priesthood."

"Don't do that; you're one of the good ones. We can't afford to lose you too. You just need to tread lightly and lower your expectations by about a mile. That's my plan."

"Are you seeing anyone now?" Robert asked, his question sounding somehow both loaded and innocuous.

Far worse than the low blood sugar, Carol was dizzy from the repercussion of this conversation. "What am I doing?" she asked with a breathy sigh as she covered her face with her hands. "This is silly. You are a senior member of the board of directors. I am on the verge of shaking up this business in fundamentally new ways. The last thing we should be doing is blurring the lines and socializing."

Robert looked undeterred. "I feel bad if you think this is socializing. This is far closer to a business meeting than any kind of blurred lines. If you do want to socialize, I know a great Italian place not far from here."

"Robert," Carol said, trying to hold back her smile, "you know damn well that wouldn't be a good idea."

"Do you know how many times I had to sit through dinner with Eli? It was torture. I refuse to believe just because we are a man and a woman, we aren't allowed to enjoy a meal and brainstorm the future of this company. Don't you want to bounce ideas off someone who has their finger on the pulse of the shareholders?"

"It's not that simple," she complained. "You know that. We can try to oversimplify it, but it's all about the optics. What people think matters more than how I frame the narrative. If we go to dinner and then you support me in the boardroom the next day, people will say it has something to do with the bedroom. You can make a case that platonic relationships between men and women should be normalized in the business world. I agree. But it doesn't change a thing for us today."

Robert looked down at his shoes and didn't bother hiding his disappointment. "I enjoy talking with you. It's a shame it can't be over a glass of wine and a nice dinner." He pressed his hands to the back of the chair he had been sitting in. "I wish things were different." It was a simple statement, but it resonated deeply with her.

"I do too." She stood to see him out. "I really appreciate what you said about Eli, and do me a favor."

"Anything."

"If you hear any details about how he plans to retaliate, give me a heads up?" Carol leaned against the frame of her office door as he stepped into the hallway.

"Count on it," Robert promised as he flashed her one more smile before he turned and headed back toward the elevator.

The tug of sadness felt physical. Her heart dropping down to her stomach. Under any other circumstance, Robert would be a wonderful man to date. He was clearly interested in her and she in him. They'd have no shortage of fascinating things to discuss, and he was terribly handsome and historically kind to her.

It was hard not to mourn all the things she'd given up to get what she wanted. Even though she'd made her choices with her eyes wide open, these were the moments that threatened to sink her emotionally.

Robert's cologne lingered in her office, and the crumbs from the crackers he brought her were still sprinkled on her desk. This would likely be the closest thing she'd have to a date this month.

Checking her watch, she knew she should grab some takeout and head home. Judging by the spell she just had, her body required that. To compromise, she'd take home a stack of reports to pore over as a distraction. For another night this year, paperwork would be her companion.

CHAPTER NINE

Marta

There would be no casual way to account for why Marta had driven the three hours this morning. There were plenty of places near her to get her oil changed. But this garage had one thing those others did not. She knew every inch of the shop and front office. For three years it had been her job to keep the place running when the owner, Nick Miller, was fighting cancer.

Marta was the eighteen-year-old office manager. The three mechanics laughed at a kid coming in to keep the shop afloat, but she'd done more than that. By the time she gave her notice a few years later, she'd straightened out their books, streamlined their parts ordering process, and reorganized the shop's whole layout. The one thing she'd left behind was still exactly where she left it.

Her brother.

"Whoa stranger, what are you doing here?" Glenn had a red rag in his oil-stained hand and wore his familiar tough-guy scowl. "What's the matter? Something happen?"

Marta understood that question well. Being ready for bad news was what the one therapist she saw two times called a trauma response. Her big brother Glenn was apparently afflicted with the same thing. But everything else about them was different. This life they had lived—the chaos, and the constant upheaval—had been like fire. Glenn had been forged into something unbreakable. Melted down, changed, and fortified by it all. He was gritty and strong. When challenged, he spoke his mind and stood up for what he believed in. Well-practiced from sparring with his parents over the years, people understood not to cross Glenn. He wasn't cruel or mean, merely unwilling to pander to anyone or betray his beliefs for the sake of peace.

For Marta, the fire had burned, leaving everlasting scars. She had become an emotional slave to the elusive idea of peace. To the goal of maintaining it at all costs. And the price was usually her own mental or physical health. She'd failed miserably as a child to quell the unrest in her house, so she still searched for it, feeling the endless responsibility to keep people chronically happy and habitually comfortable while keeping herself safe from their anger.

It played out in all of her relationships, big and small, work and personal. She agreed to be agreeable rather than making waves and being true to herself. She was a perfect employee, rarely taking her entitled time off and never questioning whoever she reported to. Marta was a rehab center for poorly behaved men. The perfect friend for a drama queen always seeking validation. Rather, those were the traps she'd fallen into before. Now, in her new life, she'd managed to insulate herself from those old habits, so change felt all the more frightening now. It was as if she had more to lose.

The great mystery to Marta was why her friends and family had never questioned that behavior. They didn't know how Marta quivered and crumbled at the thought of conflict. She'd easily and likely unanimously be described as a firecracker. Witty, always quick with a punchy one-liner or a joke. People saw her as brave. Because they measured it solely by how she acted, not by how she felt inside. Marta wasn't afraid of spiders, or heights, or scary movies. But she was terrified when two people started to argue, even if it was pretty tame. Walking home alone at night didn't bother her. Dirty jobs and manual labor never slowed her down, but the idea of making a mistake did. Blood didn't make her queasy, but hugs would. The dichotomy of her fears and her boldness was baffling at times, giving people the impression that she was courageous and sturdy. They saw a log cabin ready to stand up to the elements when really she was hastily-glued-together toothpicks not prepared for a light breeze.

"Nothing happened," Marta lied. "I just need an oil change." The place smelled exactly the same. That was obviously because motor oil and other fluids still flowed freely here. But the smell of pine air freshener that everyone doused the lunchroom with after John heated his fish sandwich in the microwave and the earthy musk of Miguel's liberally applied cologne were both unique to this shop.

"One, you can change your own oil. And two, if you're too good for that now, I am sure there is a shop in your town that can do it. You're three hours away now. It's not a hop, skip, and jump back here. So"—Glenn tucked the rag back in his pocket and closed the hood of the car he was working on—"something must have happened. Do I need to bust some guy's head in or something?"

"Nothing happened," she said, waving for him to follow her. "Nothing major anyway. I just want to ask you a couple of things."

"Oh boy," Glenn groaned as he followed Marta into the quiet breakroom and spun a chair around backward, sitting on it like a cool high school senior about to break some rules. "What can I possibly help you with that all your new friends in your new town can't?"

"It's not a new town. I've been living there for two years now. And my friends are great, but I need to hear from you. You're the only one who gets it the way I do. When I talk to them, I either confuse them or hurt their feelings."

Glenn pounded a hand to his chest. "You know I have

no feelings to hurt. Ice in these veins. It makes me the perfect person to talk to then."

That was a running joke in their family. Having feelings, showing them, was some kind of deficiency. Being strong enough to seem cold and rugged enough to withstand anything was what their family considered normal.

"You know the book I wrote—"

Glenn cut her off, sitting up a little straighter. "I'm reading it. I swear. I'm just a slow reader, but I really like it. It's not just a chick's book."

Marta cringed at his choice of language. Not because she judged him for it, but because if this was an interview with someone at the Cesar Milton foundation, Glenn wouldn't adjust his language at all. "Chicks? Really, aren't you a little old for talking that way?"

"Oh, this town you moved to," Glenn waved a hand through the air. "Hipster and all politically correct. I was trying to pay you a compliment. I like the book."

"He said with an air of astonishment," Marta retorted as though she was narrating this moment. "It is a great book. Apparently so great I've won an award."

"You told me, or Mom did. I always get you two confused." His devilish grin grew. There was nothing worse he could do than joke around about how much Marta and her mother were alike. From the moment he realized it bothered her, he did it as often as possible.

"Very funny," she shot back. "I'm not talking about the award from the New Hampshire library. A big award. A national one that could change everything for me. The Cesar Milton Award launches careers."

"I've heard of that," Glenn said, nodding as he clapped his hands together. "You won it?"

"Well, they came and told me I won it, but I don't know if I should accept it or not. It's complicated."

"Complicated? You're working at a bookstore and waitressing catered events some nights to pay your bills. You busted your ass to write that book and get people to read it. If something is going to make you famous, you better take it. What's the problem?" Glenn fidgeted with the tire gauge in his pocket as he drew his brows in low.

"They'll do a documentary on me. Come back here and talk to my family and go to my school. That's what they usually do. Well, they don't go to high schools. They go to colleges. Everyone is going to want to know how someone like me, someone with no education, won this award."

"Screw 'em," Glenn cut back quickly. That was his go-to answer to everything. An oversimplified solution that basically meant you stopped caring about what other people might do or think. It was impossible for her. "Who cares if they think you deserve it or not? Someone at that foundation thinks you do. Take it. Take whatever you can get."

"They don't want me. They just think they do. Once they dig around and find out how screwed up our lives have been, there is no way they'll still think I should be the recipient. But everything will be out in the world by then, and I'll lose what I have."

"What do you have?" Glenn asked, sounding annoyed. "What do any of us have? Look at my hands, Marta." He held them up for her to see. His pointer finger was permanently crooked from a bad break he never had treated properly. His hands were stained with oil and banged up. "I'm going to be hitting my hands on radiator caps for the rest of my life. My shoulders will go. My knees. Look at Miguel. That's the life I have coming. Stooped over, still trying to work to feed my family. I'm no better than Mom and Dad."

"Don't say that," Marta cried. "You are doing much better than either of them. You and Samantha have a good life."

"It's more than just having to bust my body up to make ends meet. They're a part of who we are. I'm right on the edge of starting a family and I'm supposed to do it different than they did."

"You will," she insisted vehemently. Glenn had spent most of his life being either they buffer or the protector. He absorbed the brunt of most ferocious turmoil. Marta didn't doubt for a second that he would be a great father. "Our parents were a mess at your age. Think about how mom showed up at school and screamed at Mr. Johnson in front of half your friends. Or when Dad would bring us on those 'adventures' where we'd almost fall off a cliff or get swept away in the ocean during a hurricane warning. You are nothing like either of them. I've been trying to figure out for a long time now why they were like that. What made mom so angry and selfish? What made dad so reckless and irresponsible? I don't have the answers but I know that you are nothing like them. You're a great brother, a perfect husband and you'll be the best dad. You were more of a father to me then dad was."

Glenn made a familiar and comical face. "Gross, stop getting mushy. You know I can't deal with that."

He was serious. They could hardly deal with accepting a compliment or diving too deep into the emotions they both obviously shared. "Then stop whining about your life." She gave him the out. Let him off the hook. Shoving his shoulder back playfully she rolled her eyes.

"I'm not whining. I'm explaining why you need to change things for yourself. Sammy works the night shift changing bedpans and mopping up blood. Nursing school is taking her forever because it costs too much, and she's exhausted all the time. Our apartment is falling apart, and our landlord isn't doing anything about it. Sammy wants to get pregnant, and all I can think is how hard it's been to keep enough food on the table for the two of us. The idea of buying diapers makes my head spin. If I had any talent, a fraction of what you have, I'd be taking everything I could get. You have to break this shit cycle. You have to do better than they did."

Marta dropped her head into her hands. "I don't even know how I'll fit in with any of them. A board room? Me?"

"Please," Glenn replied with a huff. "Maybe you sucked in school and you haven't been to a bunch of fancy places but I've seen you with people. Whatever it is in you that makes you this amazing writer, it works in the real world too. You've got a way of talking that people like. You don't sound dumb like me even though we grew up in the same house and went to the same school. I don't know what it is, but you do a really good job of hiding the trashy parts."

"Um, thanks?" she said, twisting her face up like she smelled something terrible suddenly. Marta wondered about this often. Glenn wasn't wrong. For as worried as she always was about her flaws being obvious and her limited experience being clear to everyone, she did mask it well. Her mind liked words. New ones. Odd ones. She read feverishly over the years and while it never made her academic or studious, she had learned ways of speaking that she could apply in many different conversations. Reading books wasn't enough to make her worldly, but it got her by. That didn't solve the real problem still on her mind.

"Nothing will be private. Nothing. Think of all the things we've been through. Think of what they'll find."

"Don't tell them what you don't want them to know," Glenn suggested. "It's no one's business."

"It'll be everyone's business if I take this award. And it's not like we can just keep things a secret. There are court cases and police records. Not to mention that anyone who knew us growing up will be dying to tell whatever stories they can about us. And then there's Keith."

"Forget Keith," Glenn said, pursing his lips. "I see him now and then, and he's not a problem. You guys have been divorced for more than two years. He's with some girl who slings drinks at The Down River Bar. Who cares about him?"

Marta wanted to explain her apprehension. She wanted to finally tell her brother how bad her marriage had been. But the same reason she hid the bruises and plastered on a smile kept her silent now. Glenn would not control himself if he knew what Keith was really like. They crossed paths often enough, and if her brother knew the truth, fists, or maybe worse, would fly.

"Yeah," she sighed, moving her hair away from her face and pretending to be okay. "Maybe I'm overthinking it all."

"You're not," Glenn finally agreed. "Trust me, I had to make this family look halfway normal for my wedding day. It was like threading a needle with your eyes closed, but it worked out. We cleaned Mom up enough to get her through the day without making a scene. Uncle William didn't get kicked out of the reception hall. My in-laws were only slightly freaked out by our family. We'll do the same for this thing."

Glenn was a fixer. That was his way. He'd try to muscle the situation, bend it to his will. He was right. It had worked on his wedding day. Their mother was quiet enough to pass as a normal human being, and there were very few outbursts of crazy from the rest of the Leduc family. But this was going to be on a larger scale. People would be looking for her problems, for their failures.

Marta wasn't sure what she had hoped to hear from her brother. She'd nearly made up her mind already. Was she trying to be talked into or talked out of her choice? Either way, this visit hadn't brought her any clarity.

Debating wouldn't get her any further, and she didn't have the heart to explain any more of her fears. Instead, she decided to take advantage of the time they had together. "You want to grab a grinder next door?"

"Who's going to change your oil?" Glenn asked, pulling the rag from his pocket and wiping at his hands again.

"I got it changed three weeks ago." Marta shrugged. "I just wanted your opinion on this stuff. Come have a sandwich on your break."

"You think we get breaks around here?" He pointed to the cars waiting for service. "It's not like when you used to run the shop. We're a mess most days. But hey, if you turn this award down, maybe you can come and get your old job back."

"I have a job," she said, rolling her eyes. "I'll get sandwiches and come back here. You can take ten minutes to eat with your little sister."

"Better get a sandwich for everyone. You still know their orders?"

"Sadly yes," Marta called from over her shoulder. She did, in fact, remember each of their orders. "I'll be back."

"Kid," Glenn called before she reached the large metal door leading back outside. He hadn't called her that in ages, and it stopped her in her tracks. "You gotta do this. You earned it. It's your shot to get away from this garbage."

Marta nodded and decided not to counter with a

reminder of just how many good things that garbage had stunk up and ruined over the years. She'd get sandwiches from the deli and enjoy the lunch break. She'd missed that part all these years she'd been away—how they'd tease her and she'd fire back relentlessly.

Nothing had been resolved. She was no closer to an answer, but at least for a little while, she could laugh with people who knew who she was but didn't seem to mind.

CHAPTER TEN

Terrance

There were things he'd learned to read and anticipate. The pace at which Carol's heels clanked as she moved down the hallway leading to his office door was always an indication of her level of anxiety. With a practiced eye, he could spot if she'd had one cup of coffee or three by lunchtime. His job wasn't just to answer her office phone and manage her meeting schedule. Terrance took his role of taking care of Carol seriously. Mostly because of how desperately she needed it.

Work swept Carol up like a tidal wave, and Terrance was the only one who could reach in and pull her back before she drowned. It wasn't as if he was the only person in the world who could do it, but Terrance seemed to be the only one she'd allow to. So, he took the responsibility seriously.

This morning, the pace of her steps and the smudge of her mascara told him there was a storm raging. One where he'd have to hold an umbrella for her.

"Boss," Terrance said brightly as he stood. "You've got the first hour of the day clear of meetings. Want me to hold all your calls so you can get through email?"

She'd been crying. He could tell. It wasn't obvious. Indeed, no one else would notice. But he knew.

"I'm screwed," Carol whispered. She stepped fully into his office and closed the door. In the early morning hours, she'd chat with him at his desk but not usually this late when the office was already full of life and judgment.

When the door closed, he relaxed and spoke more freely. The way they talked when he was certain no one else was around. "What's up? Why are you screwed?"

"She's not picking up. Marta is completely radio silent. I put everything on the line, went up against Eli, and now she won't even return my calls. I thought for sure after it sank in, she'd realize this was not something she could walk away from." The words came fast and ran together. Another tell-tale sign that Carol was in a panic. This was the kind of frantic speaking she would never do if the door was open. Terrance had come to learn that he was one of the few people she'd trust showing this much concern.

"What is wrong with this girl?" Terrance asked, folding his arms across his chest. "She's a nut if she's even considering turning this down. Maybe we're dodging a bullet if she bails. There were four other candidates you liked, right?" He made a move to his files. He'd already committed the other options to memory. Their names and backgrounds. He'd gone so far as to read their books. If Carol needed a backup plan, he'd be ready.

"They don't have it," Carol huffed, gesturing to the folder he'd pulled from his drawer. "It's this intangible thing. Something you can't just pluck out of a folder." She waved her hand in his direction. "I understand I sound like an alarmist. It would be foolish of me to think there isn't another candidate who deserves this award. Marta is more than just deserving. She's a catalyst for change."

Terrance nodded as he considered their options. Carol was not going to budge on this. Whether he thought she was right or not didn't matter any longer. What made Carol successful over the years had been this very attribute. Her steadfast belief in things was the differentiator in her journey. Terrance refused to be a roadblock. Instead, he'd be a bridge.

"I'll talk to her," he suggested, uncrossing his arms and pulling out Marta's file for the hundredth time. "Maybe she'll listen to me."

"We have no time to waste, and she's not answering my calls. I need her back here in five days. In front of the board, not begrudgingly but with some real zest and enthusiasm." Carol practically fell into the seat across from Terrance's desk as she lay her face in her hands for a second. When she emerged, the desperation was palpable. "Please don't be confused about my motives. As the CEO,

I'm supposed to be obsessed with retaining my job for as long as possible. That isn't what propels me forward on this."

"You don't owe me an explanation," Terrance said through a smile. "I know why you do the things you do."

"Maybe I'm just practicing for the people who don't know my heart as well as you do. I know this will be an uphill climb, and I'm risking it all, but I believe in the long run it will be worth it."

"You have my support. Always." Terrance checked his watch and sprinted through a list in his mind. "I can grab a flight in a few hours and meet up with her in the morning. If she doesn't take my calls, I'll track her down and get some face-to-face time. I'll do what I can to convince her your intentions are good and she's ready for this award."

Carol lit with excitement. "Are you sure? That's not exactly in your job description."

"I'm positive. It might not be in my job description, but charm and persuasion should be on my résumé. You know I'll do my best."

"You are a good kid, Terrance," Carol sang. "I don't know how I got so lucky to have you on my team, but I thank my stars every day." She began to tick things off on her fingers as she did when she was stressed. "I already tracked down the address for the bookstore where she works. I didn't want to ambush her there last time, but she doesn't have another book signing for two weeks. That's too long. You'll have to find her there. Marta needs to fly back here with you and meet the board. She needs to embrace the idea of being the winner of the award and start thinking about what she'll do going forward. Those are the goals."

"I'll start with making sure she doesn't mace me for turning up unannounced in her hometown." Terrance laughed, but he also could assume exactly how overbearing his arrival would be to Marta. He wasn't expecting it to go smoothly.

"Yes," Carol agreed. "That's step one. You have an expense card. Use it. Book the flight. Get a great hotel. Eat like a king while you're there. You are working well outside of your job description, and I want you to take full advantage. I wouldn't trust another soul with this, and the only way I won't drown in guilt is if I know you're indulging a little."

"You know that's not like me," Terrance said, dropping his head down a bit. "I don't like to take advantage."

"But you do like to follow instructions. So, I'm instructing you to use your company card liberally. Whatever gets Marta here and happy. If that's a shopping spree for a new wardrobe for her or fancy dinners, it'll be well worth it in the end."

Terrance nodded and offered a bashful smile. "I'll do my best."

"I've got the rest of the day covered," she insisted, waving her hands at his coat and bag. "You go home and get what you need. Call me when you find her and keep me posted on how everything is going."

"You've got it."

Carol stood, flattened any wrinkles out of her pants, and drew in a deep breath. She was about to step back into the real world. The one where she needed to be perfect and guarded. There was no room out there for weakness or fear. Terrance liked that she could escape into his office and be imperfect and worried. Carol was a good woman. Though he never met his own mother, he wondered if she was at all like Carol. He hoped maybe she was.

CHAPTER ELEVEN

Marta

If not for Heather, Marta would have kept her phone off completely. But her dear friend would have a search party organized by lunch and missing persons fliers posted all over town by dinner. Marta couldn't go off the radar or slip into hibernation like she used to before she'd moved to Franklin Falls and met her new friends. Heather insisted, lovingly, that they stay connected. It was scary to Marta to feel beholden to someone in that way, but she smiled every time she thought of Heather's reactions to her spells of hiding out. At least someone would notice if she fell off the face of the earth.

The downside was she couldn't completely keep out any attempted contact from Carol. She didn't have the heart to block the number, so every time it rang, she tossed her phone down as if it were a stick of dynamite. Marta couldn't press play on the voicemail, instead only reading the little transcript her phone provided. It killed her to think she might be upsetting Carol, but her fight or flight reflexes were strong. She'd fly the hell away from this as fast as she could.

In the end, she'd tell her brother it didn't work out and someone else had been selected for the award. Carol would have to eventually give up, and then Marta could hold on to the cobbled-together life she'd managed to make in the last two years. At night, when her head hit the pillow, she could swell with pride that they'd even considered her for such an award.

When the bell over the door jingled, Marta tucked her phone back in her pocket and stood up behind the register. The bookstore was mostly quiet this time of the morning on weekdays. People popped in before work and on lunch breaks, but now, at ten, she usually had the place to herself. She'd write, read, daydream, and reorganize the shelves. Being immersed in books—the sights, sounds, and smells of them—had been her childhood dream. She hadn't factored the subpar paycheck into the equation, but she found a way to make it work.

"Hi, welcome to The Sleepy Reader," Marta said with her best customer service voice. "Can I help you find something?"

The man who'd walked in was tall and dressed in a gorgeous bright blue suit. The pattern on his tie matched perfectly, as did the frame of his glasses. He had one hand tucked into his pocket, and the other dusted the flurries of snow off his shoulder. He wasn't wearing a coat and shivered a bit before righting himself.

"I don't know how anyone lives like this," he said, gesturing back outside. "That's not cold. That's freezing. I can't feel my hands."

Marta smiled. "You need gloves and a coat."

"It's not even winter. It's fall. Why is it snowing in fall?" He drew his hands up to his mouth and blew on them.

"Come stand by the fire," Marta insisted, gesturing toward the wall where the wood crackled and the stone was warm to the touch. "Do you want a coffee?"

"I'd love one," he said, rolling from his toes to his heels for a moment after he reached the fireplace. "Cream and sugar if you've got it."

"Sure," Marta called from the coffee station. "Do you just want to warm up, or do you need a book?"

"I always need books," the man said. She watched him lean toward a shelf and start skimming. "But warming up is a nice plus."

As she moved back toward him with the paper cup of coffee, she drew in the scent of his cologne. It was nice. Expensive. It was probably French and something she'd never smell again once he left, so she enjoyed it for an extra moment.

"Thank you for the coffee," he said, reaching his hand out for it. Marta was finally able to get a good look at him, and she blushed instantly. He was not just a well-dressed man who smelled good. His dark hazel eyes were rimmed with prominent lashes, and his mouth was curled into a mesmerizing smile.

This man was not just attractive. He was striking. "The coffee is terrible," she apologized as she tried to avert her gaze. Maybe he was used to being stared at. Perhaps he got paid to stand around and model that suit.

"It's fine," he said in a jovial tone as he took a sip. Wincing and gulping the coffee down, he cleared his throat. "Oh, you were right. That's pretty bad."

"We need a new coffee maker."

"Is it old?" He looked down into the paper cup and grimaced.

"I mean I'm the coffee maker, and I'm terrible at it. I either make it too weak or too strong."

"Yeah, this one is definitely not too weak. But at least you can fuel a jet engine with it later." He regretfully handed the cup back. "I appreciate it, though."

"I think it's a running joke around here. I've been working at this store for about a year, and people always ask who made the coffee before taking a cup. I swear I've tried. It's a lost cause." She emptied the cup, tossed it in the trash, and shrugged. "How can I make it up to you?"

She felt self-conscious instantly and blushed again. Marta didn't go out of her way to be coy and sexy with people. There was a time in her life when she'd hungered for attention, not discerning if it was good or bad attention, and usually ending up with the latter.

These days she found a solid footing of her own and didn't depend on chasing the spotlight someone else was shining. Still, she knew when this man walked out, she'd be sorry to see him go.

"I'm in the market for a book," he said, turning toward the closest shelf and scanning it. "Do you have any award-winning titles?"

"Of course," Marta sang happily. One of her favorite things to do was find just the right book for a customer. Something they'd never thought to pick up and try. Occasionally they'd come back into the store and rave about how much they liked her selection. "Tell me what you normally like to read."

"I prefer angsty, twisted tales that don't end perfectly happy." The man pulled a book from the shelf and flipped through its pages.

"Really?" Marta asked, trying to hide the surprise on her face.

"What would you have guessed I like?" He replaced the book on the shelf and turned toward her, tucking one hand thoughtfully into his pocket.

"Honestly?"

He shrugged and waved for her to go on.

"I'd have pointed you toward the business books in the corner," Marta suggested as she gestured toward the section. "Maybe travel. You don't strike me as someone who comes here to vacation."

"It's a charming town. I particularly like the mills."

"With all their history of child labor and environmental destruction? Or maybe you like how they bankrupted the town when they closed down and outsourced their work to other countries? Very charming."

"I meant it more from an aesthetic appreciation. I like to take photographs and they'd be a great backdrop."

"I have books on photography," she offered.

"I'm really looking for one book in particular," he said, keeping his gaze fixed on her. "Your book."

"Mine?" she asked, her cheeks tingling. "Who are you?"

"You cannot overact when I tell you who I am." He flashed a little smile and put his hands together as if he was praying for her to be understanding.

"Okay," she said, stretching the word out to show her skepticism.

"Promise?"

"I promise," she said, holding up a hand as if to make it official. "Who are you?"

"My name is Terrance. I work with Carol. She came out to see you a few weeks ago." His words were slow and chopped, as if he didn't want to spook her.

"Oh," Marta said, her heart thudding differently suddenly. It wasn't the excitement of chatting up a gorgeous man. Now it was wondering how to get rid of him kindly. "I'm sorry I haven't returned her calls. I've been—"

"Busy making jet fuel?" Terrance asked, gesturing with his chin toward the coffee pot.

Her hand flew up to her head, and she brushed her bangs away. "I really appreciate that you've both flown out here now to talk with me, but I am not going to accept the award."

Terrance looked flabbergasted. "I really didn't believe Carol when she told me you were turning it down. I didn't think anyone would ever do that. Hearing it for myself is just"—he shook his head— "wow."

"I'm not trying to be ungrateful. It probably seems that way. Trust me, I am honored."

"But?" Terrance stood expectantly as if she could just summarize it all in a sentence or two.

"It's not that easy to explain."

"I've read your book. Twice actually. It's brilliantly written. I think it's clear you have a way with words. You must be able to elaborate on why you'd ever turn down something that would be so life-changing."

Marta took a seat in one of the chairs near the fireplace and licked her suddenly dry lips. "Life-changing doesn't always mean a change for the better."

"In this case, it does," Terrance explained, sitting in the weathered, lopsided wingback chair across from her. "Look at all the previous recipients."

"Yes," Marta agreed. "Look at them. Not just after they got the award. Before. They were not in the same position I am in. They are actually nothing like me at all. In the last month, I took the time to go through every recipient since the first award forty-one years ago. They are all basically the same and nothing at all like me."

"And that's a positive?" Terrance stretched his leg out, exposing his black sock with bright blue embellishments.

He was so well put together it was rather mesmerizing. No detail had been overlooked. Well-tailored clothes with matching everything. If he was trying to be approachable to someone like Marta, he missed the mark.

"Terrance," Marta said quietly as she dropped her head down, "I'm not trying to be difficult. I don't mean to be rude. But I have my reasons. I'm just asking that you and Carol respect that. There must be hundreds of people who qualify for this award. Why is it a big deal that I turn it down?"

Terrance looked contemplative as he rubbed his cold hands together again. "We're not going to settle this here. Let's have dinner this evening."

Marta gulped, her mind flashing to the idea of sitting across from Terrance in a more intimate atmosphere. "I don't know."

"Marta," he said somberly, "this deserves at least a more in-depth conversation. I'm not going to try to strong-arm you into something you're truly not interested in. But to be honest, I answer to Carol. I can't very well fly back tonight without something of substance to tell her. Even if you're certain you won't change your mind, please just come to dinner with me so I can tell her I tried my best."

She felt ensnared by his expression: the subtle puppy dog eyes and the look of desperation. "Dinner?" she asked, still unsure this was all real.

"Yes, wherever you'd like. What's good around here?"

"Literally nothing." She waved her hand. "You're from California?"

"I am." He straightened up a bit. "But I like food from all over. There must be a regional specialty. I'm not picky. What's good in New Hampshire?"

Marta shook her head. "You're in Franklin Falls, New Hampshire. It's an old mill town that's basically fallen into ruin since the millwork dried up a generation ago. We're fifty miles north of anything decent. That goes for restaurants too. You must have noticed that driving in from the airport." Marta gestured out to the street.

"Well, I did notice it was quaint. Um, and very . . . How can I put this? It lacks a bit of diversity." Terrance lowered his voice and grinned.

"Yes, this town lacks just about everything. Resources, employment, culture, and a huge lack of diversity. If we can't even pick a decent restaurant for dinner, how exactly could you make a case for your award winner to call this home?" She raised a challenging brow at him, but Terrance didn't flinch.

"Going to dinner is more about the company you keep than the place you pick. I don't mind where we end up, as long as you and I can hash this out in some way. I promise not to steamroll you if you promise to be open with me." Terrance jutted his hand out and waited to make a deal.

"I'll have dinner with you," she said, reaching for his hand and trying her best not to turn bright red as she tingled with excitement. "But I hope you brought some casual clothes and a coat. We'll eat at The Down Easter. It's about as good as you can do around here. Are you staying close by?"

"I haven't found a hotel yet." Terrance stood and straightened his suit coat. "I looked online but—"

"But there are none besides a few run-down chains. A few towns over, there's a decent place. High end."

"I don't want to be that far. Really, I can stay anywhere." Terrance shrugged casually.

"Try Lakeview Cottages. They're clean and quiet. That's probably the best you'll do if you want to stay close by." Marta moved to the desk and jotted down the number. "Tell Lulu you're my friend, and I told you to stay there."

"We're friends now?" Terrance asked, lighting up at the idea.

"We're not, but trust me, Franklin Falls is the kind of place where you do better if you name drop. Walking around as a stranger can cause some problems."

"I don't exactly blend in here?" He blinked slowly and turned his lips up playfully.

Marta wasn't sure if he was talking about the fact that he was Black or that his suit probably cost more than most people's whole wardrobe in this town. Either way, the answer was sadly the same. She wrote her number down for him, though she assumed Carol had given it to him. "If you have any trouble, just call me. I'll be here until three and then around town if you need something. I feel responsible for you now that you're here."

"I can handle myself," Terrance promised, and she had no doubt he could. Now that he was standing again, she could sort out his height as over six feet, and with his arms bent, she could see his bicep stretching his suit jacket.

"Just call if you need something. Dinner at six thirty? Don't wear that suit."

"Perfect," Terrance said, his dimple deepening as his smile grew. "If nothing else, we get to have a nice meal together."

If nothing else . . .

His words lingered in her mind just as his cologne remained in the store after he left. She had phone calls to make. Heather would want the latest on this award saga. Ray would probably like to switch shifts to be tending bar while Marta was at dinner with this mystery man.

Nothing in her heart felt different about accepting the award. The sparkle in Terrance's eyes and the touch of his hand hadn't magically changed Marta's circumstances. She didn't believe there was anything he could say over dinner to make a difference either. But she'd made a deal with him, and she planned to keep her word. She'd listen. She'd be open. *And if nothing else*, it seemed as though she'd be in good company.

CHAPTER TWELVE

Carol

Breathing a sigh of relief, Carol felt grateful for the text messages from Terrance. As always, he was coming through for her. He'd already met with Marta and planned dinner. She wouldn't feel real relief until she knew they were both on a plane back to California.

The other challenge was pretending she could manage her routine without Terrance and his endless reminders and support. He kept her day moving at the right pace to get everything done just before she crashed into a wall of exhaustion. Today she'd only made it to lunch before she lost track of time and nearly missed a meeting. Luckily, she didn't have to go anywhere for it.

"Where is Terrance?" Robert asked, knocking gently

on her door. "Are you one of those nice bosses who give actual days off?"

"I am," Carol said, waving him into her office. The last time he was here, she was full of too much emotion and not nearly enough carbohydrates to think straight. She'd be sure to keep this middle-of-the-day meeting entirely professional. "But he's not on vacation today; he's on a secret mission."

Robert took a seat across from her desk. "Hopefully, he's restocking those snacks in his desk in case you get the spins again."

"Slightly more important than that." She slid the papers in front of her to the side. "But I'm more interested in what has you scheduling a meeting today."

Robert's smile slid away. "I've got an update on Eli. I've been trying to keep my ear to the ground since you tossed him out of the boardroom."

"I politely told him to leave," she corrected. "But I appreciate you trying to stay plugged in. What have you heard?"

"Eli is telling anyone who will listen that you're unfit for the job. It's a lot of his usual macho junk about you being too emotional and hormonal to keep a clear head."

"Wait," Carol howled, leaning back in her chair. "He says that? Like out loud? To people?"

"Yes, but that's not new. I've heard from a few investors that Eli was digging around trying to turn up some dirt on you. Any hints of insider trading or impropriety on your part."

"Insider trading? Does he think I'm a fool? That's about the fastest way to find yourself in handcuffs in this profession. He can dig all he wants for that. He won't find anything." Carol scoffed and rolled her eyes.

"I think he's come to that realization," Robert reported. "That's why he's moving on to some dirtier tactics. He's got blackmail on his mind. I've heard multiple people who know him well say that he's in a rage. I was hoping he'd have cooled down by now, but apparently not."

"There's nothing he can do to blackmail me. I've been an open book all my life. I couldn't have risen to this position if I had skeletons in my closet for someone like Eli to exploit."

"I almost wish you did have some dirty little secret."

"Really?" Carol asked, raising a brow at him.

"Then you could know what you're working with. I'm worried about what Eli will stoop to once he realizes there isn't anything he can do to hurt you. It's not as though he's just going to give up." Robert looked like he was pondering some kind of solution but coming up empty.

"I've been intentional over the years because of men like Eli. I don't plan to give him any ammunition to take me out. But if he decides he wants to create something out of thin air, I'll need to be able to prove he's a fraud." Carol tapped her pen on her desk. "I guess I just wait and see what he does."

"I'll keep trying to figure out what his next move is. I don't think he trusts me much, but the feeling is mutual. The good news is we travel in the same circles, and most people can't stand him. They'll tell me if they hear he's up to anything."

"I really appreciate this, Robert. You've been a great support for a long time now." Carol's expression softened as she looked him over again. He was a handsome man, and his most attractive feature was his integrity. Carol felt he was honest to the core with good intentions, and her radar was pretty solid.

"I'd still really like to have dinner with you." Robert shifted his posture to a more relaxed position. "I don't like the fact that we can't. It's so arbitrary and childish to think two adults have to be confined by social stigmas and perceived conflicts of interest."

"I could fill this room with arbitrary social stigmas that drive me mad. But at the end of the day, we don't get to decide what the world accepts and what they don't. Or at least not without suffering the consequences."

"We are two single adult people with a boatload of common interests and sparkling personalities who would have a smashing time out together."

"Smashing?"

"Don't you think?" he asked with a devilish grin. "Tell me the truth. If we were not in the positions we are, and I asked you out, would you say yes?"

"I would," Carol said without hesitation. "I wouldn't hold you to a smashing time, but I'd give you a shot."

"That's very gracious of you." He winked, and she didn't fight the flutter in her chest. It was unfortunate that they were beholden to what people would think. Robert was correct. They were two adults, and it was utterly plausible to believe that they could enjoy each other socially and still perform their respective roles. But that wasn't how the world worked. People would talk. Accusations of favoritism or bias would be laid at her feet. And she'd worked too hard to risk her reputation for the company of a man.

"I figured you'd turn me down again for dinner, so I brought you something." He grabbed his briefcase and put it on her desk as he flipped it open. "Have you ever tried the Dynamite Rolls from Zee Noodles on East Street?"

"I love Zee Noodles," Carol said, peeking her head over his briefcase. "I haven't tried the Dynamite Rolls. You brought some?"

"Just for you. I don't want to give the impression we're sharing a meal. Consider me a food delivery service. That can't possibly be a conflict of interest."

"I don't see how it could be," Carol said, excitedly waving for the food. She was hungry, and this was a complete surprise. She cooed as she saw him pull out not just a tray of food wrapped in foil but also silverware, sparkling water, and napkins. "You came prepared. I better tip well."

"Leave me a five-star review." When the food was in front of her, and the napkin across her lap, Robert stood to leave.

"You really aren't staying?" She pouted a bit and then scolded herself for the unprofessionalism. Robert was disarming, and she knew better than to lay down her weapons and shields just because he smiled warmly at her.

"We're keeping this on the up and up," Robert said, picking up his briefcase and tucking his other hand in his pocket. "I'll just smuggle you in little treats while we review the recent employee engagement survey results."

"We do that?" Carol asked, her face showing surprise. "I knew we had a survey, but I thought I just got a spreadsheet with the aggregated results."

Robert had his hand on her office door. "That's how it used to work. But you are meticulous and very invested in employee satisfaction. I am the liaison with shareholders on employee issues. We'll need to ensure the data is sound and we have a strategy for moving forward."

"I am meticulous, and I do care deeply about employee engagement surveys." Carol flushed with the excitement of their future meetings.

"Then I'll get on your calendar for next week. Lunchtime work?"

She gestured down to her food and beamed. "It's perfect."

He pulled open the door and turned back toward her. "Oh, and we meet your award recipient soon too. I'm looking forward to it. If you think she's special, I'm sure she is."

Carol sank down a few notches toward reality. Dinner between Marta and Terrance would be happening soon enough, and she was desperate for him to be successful. There was no backup plan. That was intentional. No one worked harder to stay on the tightrope than the person who didn't have a safety net.

"You'll see soon enough," Carol sang optimistically as Robert stepped out of her office and down the hall. She stood quickly and closed the door, watching him for a moment as he strode away. Turning back toward the food he'd brought, she couldn't help but smile. The anxiety still loomed. The pressure still clamped down tightly on her chest, but somehow, he'd managed to make her beam.

CHAPTER THIRTEEN

Marta

This felt a bit like a sting operation. Ray was working the bar, doing precisely what Marta had expected. Somehow, he'd managed to switch his shift and implant himself as the perfect spy and bodyguard. Not to be outdone, Heather had snagged a table in the corner. She wore a baseball cap and hid mostly behind her menu for far too long. Every few moments, she'd give Marta a little wave and then stare back at the door to see if Terrance had come in.

"She's very slick," Marta giggled to Ray, who brought her a glass of wine. "I think she could have a future with the CIA."

"We probably should have told her not to wave so

much," Ray said as he gave her a small wave back. "But she's adorable as hell."

"Good thing for that," Marta said, slinging her bag over the back of the barstool and taking a sip of her wine. "We'll eat here if that's all right. I don't think this will go too long."

"I want you right here," Ray said, patting the bar. "I'm glad they are pursuing you. I think you should give it all more consideration. But this guy sounds like a smooth talker. I'm going to have my eye on him."

"I feel very safe here with you and CIA Agent Heather. I can only imagine what she has packed in that enormous purse. Please tell me you took her taser away. She's more likely to shock herself with it at this rate."

"It was a battle, but I managed to talk her out of bringing it. I did not, however, deter her from packing the pocket knife, mace, and brass knuckles."

"Where did she get brass knuckles?"

"Okay, it's a piece of jewelry she bought, but it looks convincing enough. Just hope this guy doesn't give her a reason to take them out."

"We'll have a drink and a bite to eat, then he'll be on his way. She'll have to act fast if she wants to wrestle him to the ground."

"Is that him?" he asked, trying to gesture coolly with his chin toward the door. Marta nodded as Ray continued. "He's hot. Maybe you'll be the one to wrestle him to the ground."

"Shut your blabhole before I get the mace from

Heather," she said through gritted teeth as she stood to greet Terrance. She waved him over and drew in a deep breath. This was suddenly feeling like a bad idea. Marta had wanted the support of having her friends close by, but they had some serious potential to make this already awkward situation worse.

"Lovely place," Terrance said as he offered her a sweet nod. Not too intimate. Not too formal. He was wearing a light gray hooded sweatshirt and dark denim jeans. His shoes were more casual now but not sneakers. Some kind of slip-on fancy business type shoe that still shined under the bar lights. "How many of your friends do you have stashed in here as lookouts?"

Marta's face pinked. "Enough of them. Don't worry. They'll be easy to spot. They have exactly zero chill."

"Good, I'll be glad to meet them. Should we eat at the bar?" Terrance looked around for an empty table, but Ray chimed in.

"You should eat at the bar," Ray said as he jammed two menus into Terrance's hand and gave him an overexaggerated glare.

Marta rolled her eyes. "Zero chill."

"It's sweet," Terrance replied as Ray went on to serve another customer. "I like hometown places. Everyone knows everyone."

"This isn't my hometown," Marta corrected. "I'm not from here."

"Oh right," Terrance replied thoughtfully. "You're from Dreven or something like that."

"It's pronounced Dray-vin. Don't let anyone around here catch you saying it wrong. It's a whole thing. It's basically the same as this place. At one point because of the flow of the river and the value that had in factory work, it was booming. Now it's not. There's a lot unemployment, poverty and lack of opportunity. Don't bother asking why I moved to a place that's nearly the same. You wouldn't understand."

Terrance gestured kindly for Marta to sit, and when she was settled, he slipped off his coat and hung it on the back of his chair.

"You got a coat," Marta observed playfully. "Is that from the second-hand store or the hardware store?"

"Second-hand store," Terrance said, patting the coat proudly. "It came with a free pack of half-eaten crackers in the pocket."

"Jackpot," Marta teased. "Glinda, the woman who owns it, is sweet, but she's nearly eighty-five years old. I don't think she's able to keep up with rooting out all the pocket treasures anymore."

"Well, it works perfectly. I haven't seen a coat like this in ages. I'll wear it back west and everyone will be dying to know where I got it. Retro always gets people talking." He took a seat and flipped open the menu, looking entirely at ease.

It made Marta want to inspect him. To eye him closely and try to crawl in his mind to understand. Here was a man who'd never been here, knew no one, and stuck out as an outsider. Yet, he looked unbothered by all of those challenges. She envied his sureness.

"Don't ask what's good," she warned. "Nothing really is. But it's reliable. You know what to expect."

"Reliably disappointing isn't all bad. It's better than getting your hopes up and being disappointed." He shrugged and eyed the bottles of cheap liqueur behind the shelf. "Don't worry, I'm not some entitled jerk who's going to stick my nose up because they don't have fresh orange pulp for my drink. I have a great job now, thanks to Carol, but I didn't grow up with anything special."

"Definitely no orange pulp here. I'd stick with the basics. Vodka and tonic or something easy."

"Good deal," Terrance said coolly.

Ray took their drink order and shuffled slowly away, trying to eavesdrop a bit longer. "My friends are just curious. They mean well," Marta said apologetically.

"I don't blame them. It's not every day your friend wins an award like this. I'm sure they want to hear all about it."

"There isn't anything else to tell them," Marta replied quietly. "I told them the same thing I told you. I'm honored, but it's not the right thing for me."

"Fame, fortune? It doesn't suit you?" Terrance teased. "I doubt that. I can see you gliding across a ballroom floor in an elegant yet understated dress and every head turning your way."

"That's not me. But we can disagree on that. Tell me

more about you," Marta said, taking the drink Ray handed her and swirling the tiny straw in it. "You work for Carol?"

"I do," Terrance said, being agreeable enough to let her change the subject. She knew it would come back around to her and the award, but she would try to find some common ground with him for now. There must be some way to explain it so he could understand. "She's changed my life. I was basically entry-level at the company, and she saw something in me. I've had the opportunity to grow my career exponentially. That's because Carol sees potential in people and dedicates herself to making sure they reach it."

"That sounds lovely," Marta cooed. "I really enjoyed meeting her. I can tell she's a genuine person."

With that, Terrance lit up. She wasn't sure if it was because he thought he was making progress or if he cared deeply for Carol and truly agreed. Marta needed to probe. "You seem like you two are close. It's one thing to have a great boss, but she sounds like she means a lot to you." This was her way of laying a trap, and it seemed as though Terrance would walk right into it.

"We are close," Terrance reported happily. "She trusts me, and I trust her. Corporate life can be isolating, especially for someone at Carol's level. Everyone is out to take your place or get what they can from you. The fact that she knows I'm on her side means a lot to me."

"And you wouldn't let anyone do anything to interfere with her career. Or even worse, anything that might hurt her." Marta was doe-eyed and blinking slowly as she asked her leading questions.

Terrance's expression was severe, and his voice solid like cold steel. "I would do anything to protect Carol. That's the relationship we have. Carol is a strong woman. She can take care of herself, but I certainly wouldn't let anything bad happen to her on my watch."

His declaration was actually genuinely heartwarming. It made what Marta was about to say feel slimy and manipulative. But it was truly for the greater good. "If you really feel that way, then you need to talk Carol out of this. I am not a good fit for this award. I understand that she enjoyed the book, and I'll go so far as to accept the fact that maybe she sees some potential in my writing. That's not lost on me. But I pose a risk to Carol, and if you care what happens to her, you should protect her. From me."

She was glad to see he wasn't so quick to dismiss this warning. There was no lighthearted rebuttal or attempt to laugh it off. Terrance sat with the information for a long moment, taking a sip of his drink and then giving her a worried look. "What makes you a threat to Carol?"

"So many things," Marta sighed. "We're on the same team here. I understand the predicament you're in. Carol sent you here to convince me I'm worthy of this award. What you and I need to really do is show Carol why choosing me is a mistake. I'm sure it's not easy to go back to your boss and tell her she's wrong."

"I trust Carol." Terrance patted his hand to the bar

assertively. "She doesn't make decisions lightly. Why are you so convinced she's wrong?"

"Carol did a cursory look into who I am. There is no way she's dug deep enough to realize the liability I would be. What does she even know about me?"

Terrance shifted in his seat and looked uncomfortable for the first time. "She knows you wrote a book that people will fall in love with."

"Let's do some real talk," Marta pressed, folding her arms across her chest. "There's a file, right? There's some sort of write-up about me. What does it say?"

"The basics," Terrance replied with a shrug. "Where you grew up. Where you went to school. Your family information."

"Family information." Marta groaned. "What exactly would that entail? Two brothers. Mom. Dad. I'm guessing it doesn't go into detail. My mother is sick. She's been diagnosed with so many different variations of mental illness I can't even keep up. My brother Jonah and my father both died. Stories that won't exactly make for a good highlight reel at the award ceremony. Maybe you think you can PR your way out of this situation. You can't put lipstick on this pig."

"Excuse me?" Terrance chuckled.

"It's a saying from around this way. You can put lipstick on a pig, but it's still a pig. You're not going to be able to dress up my story. You can't spin it into something better. If you went to my hometown right now, there would be a line of people ready to tell you the dirt on me. Ready to tell anyone who would listen. And if I win this award, if I become a household name, there will be plenty of people who want to listen."

"Give me an example." Terrance sat back a bit and waited for her reply. He'd taken her by surprise with the simplicity of his request.

"I don't owe you an explanation." She could feel Ray inching closer and decided to relax her body language. If she kept looking this hostile, Heather would come over with her weapon of choice to knock Terrance over the head. "I'd rather not get into the sordid details of my life. I moved here to Franklin Falls because it was as far away as I could get with the money I had. I love writing. I want people to read my books. I'm just not ready for the giant spotlight you want to shine on my very screwed-up life."

"You don't owe me an example," Terrance said, leaning in, his dark eyes flickering with empathy. "But I'd still like to hear one. I'd like to know what has you this scared. I never in my life thought I would hear anyone turn down the chance at everything Carol is offering. I believe you when you say it's rough. I just want to know more."

Marta understood it wasn't fair to send Terrance back to Carol with nothing. He'd need to be able to make a case for exactly why he came back unsuccessful. She considered what layer of the onion she would peel back. She blurted out the safest one. "I didn't go to college."

"Carol knows that. Not everyone needs to go to college to be successful. Yes, sometimes we travel back to the recipient's university. But that's not imperative. People will connect with your story."

"I nearly failed high school." Marta pushed her hair off her shoulder and shook her head. "I was a delinquent in many ways. If you went back to talk to anyone in my town, they'd tell you."

"College isn't a big deal. The kind of student you were wouldn't matter either." Terrance was trying to be reassuring, but it was making her adrenaline pulse.

"It's not just that," Marta croaked out. "You don't get it. You won't. I'm barely put back together." Her eyes grew wet with tears. Something foreign to her in most situations. But this was intense. It felt like a tipping point. She needed Terrance to leave here tonight knowing she was a lost cause.

His face was stoic as he watched Marta fall over the edge of her feelings. When a tear streaked down her cheek, he looked pained for her. "Terrance," she whispered, "I've barely put myself back together. It takes everything I've got to just keep moving forward. There are so many things chasing me. If I slow down, if I look back, I'm gone. Everything I've done to just keep my head above water. It's gone."

"Marta," Terrance said, reaching out and touching her hand gently. "I'm so sorry. I didn't come here to dredge up painful things for you. I was just trying to understand. I thought you felt self-conscious about not growing up with money or not having a certain level of education. Those really are things that people could relate to and cheer you on about. But if there's something else—" He kept his eyes fixed on her. He wanted her to go on.

She brought her sleeve up to her eyes and dabbed. "There are so many other things. So many worse things."

"Okay," Terrance said with a reassuring nod. "You don't have to say anything else. Let's just change the subject. We can still have a nice dinner."

"Why are you crying?" Heather asked, practically crashing into the back of Terrance's chair. When Marta didn't answer immediately, she turned her angry energy toward Terrance. "Why is she crying? I have known this woman for two years, and the only time I've ever seen her cry is when she accidentally spilled a pitcher of margaritas on an eighty-six-year-old man in a wheelchair. And I don't see any margaritas or wheelchairs. What did you do?"

Terrance looked baffled. "I—" He turned to Marta for help.

She considered letting him feel Heather's wrath. "I'm fine, Heather. Really. We were just talking, and I got emotional. You don't have to use the brass knuckles."

Shifting again in his seat, Terrance looked suddenly worried. "Brass knuckles?" He put his hands up disarmingly. "I'm not here for trouble."

"Well, you found trouble, mister," Heather said, pointing her finger in his face. "Marta is the best person I know, and you're not going to come in here and make her feel bad. If she doesn't want your stupid award, you need to accept that and move on."

"Really?" Marta asked, the tears threatening to return. "You don't think I'm crazy for not taking it?"

"Of course, I think you're crazy," Heather cut back quickly. "But I'm your friend, and I get to say that. He doesn't. And he shouldn't be putting pressure on you."

Ray was hustling over toward them. "What's going on here?" He planted his hands on the bar and narrowed his eyes. "Are you and I gonna have some problems tonight, Terrance?"

To his credit, Terrance managed to keep a cool head. "I'm not here to cause trouble. I don't plan to pressure Marta into anything. We, at the foundation, just wanted the opportunity to talk with her. This is the chance of a lifetime, and we didn't want to let it pass by without more conversation."

"I appreciate that," Marta said, gulping back her emotion and steadying her breath. "I know you came all this way, and I'm not trying to be rude."

"It's all right," Terrance said earnestly. "You don't have to explain."

Heather nodded fiercely. "That's right, she doesn't. Maybe you should go."

"No," Marta said quickly. "We're having dinner. I'm really feeling better. I just got overwhelmed."

Heather turned her back on Terrance and leaned in close to Marta. "You never get overwhelmed. You never get emotional. What's going on?"

Marta considered brushing it off but could see Heather's concern was genuine and unwavering. "I don't know exactly. I just feel torn. It seems nuts to turn this down, but I can't see how I'll make it work. I can't."

Heather lowered her voice a little more. "He's so gorgeous. Maybe he's hypnotizing you with those freaking eyes. He looks like he just stepped off a magazine cover."

"I know," Marta said through a wry giggle. "But I don't want to make a rash decision."

"Maybe sleep on him," Heather laughed. "I mean sleep on it. No, I liked it better the first way."

Ray leaned in. "What's so funny? I thought you were crying?"

They were in this little huddle now and Marta felt silly. "I'm feeling better," she promised. "I just needed a pep talk." She put her hand on Heather's shoulder and squeezed.

"You're good?" Heather asked again.

Marta nodded, and her friends reluctantly backed away. "Just holler if you need us," Heather called over her shoulder as she went back to her table.

"I'm sorry," Marta sighed, turning back toward Terrance. "I'm sure you weren't expecting all of this." She waved as if that summed up the madness. "I seriously never cry. Well, unless I drop margaritas on elderly people."

Terrance laughed from his stomach. "You seriously did that?"

Marta covered her face. "It was awful."

"That man is definitely someone you wouldn't want on

your highlight reel at the ceremony." Terrance glanced down at the menu and then back at her.

"You know what, he was actually lovely about it. Once we cleaned off his wheelchair and gave him some free mozzarella sticks, he was all set."

"See, things have a way of working themselves out." Terrance smiled that mesmerizing smile and knocked her off-kilter for a second.

"That's what happy, shiny, well-adjusted people say because, for them, things normally do work out."

"I've been called worse." Terrance made a funny face. "Actually, I was called much worse by the guy who sells newspapers over by the secondhand store today."

"Oh, Joe. Yeah, he's not a nice guy. I meant to warn you about him." Marta felt her shoulders ease back to calm. They'd order some food. They'd chat. She'd stared at the magnificent bone structure of his cheeks and jaw. She couldn't figure out what was right or wrong with her decisions. But she could plainly see Terrance was a good-hearted man with the kind of eyes a girl could get lost in.

CHAPTER FOURTEEN

Terrance

Snatching up the check before Marta could reach for it, Terrance continued contemplating the problem. There was the apparent dilemma that the job he came here to do was far from complete. But a new trouble was looming even larger.

"You don't have to buy my meal," Marta protested, but he waved her off. "Especially since you didn't get what you came here for."

"I only came here to talk to you. I got that." Terrance pulled out his wallet and laid the company card down. It was laughable now to think of Carol's instructions. She insisted he live it up and expense whatever he wanted on this trip. She'd overestimated

Franklin Falls and what was available in the area. So far, he'd bought a nine-dollar used coat and a fifty-seven-dollar dinner at a bar that was pretending to be a restaurant. They'd have a laugh about this when he got back.

"I don't want you to get in trouble with Carol," Marta said soberly. "I will call her back and tell her you did everything right. I'll tell her it's not your fault."

Marta's heart was an interesting thing. Terrance had observed it to be tender but guarded. A kitten surrounded by barbed wire. Her offer was sweet, but his mind wasn't at that point right now. There was still hope as far as he was concerned.

"Can we go for a walk?" Terrance asked as he signed the slip Ray had just brought back. "I mean, is there anywhere around here to walk at night?"

"It's freezing," Marta explained. "Well, by your standards. And there aren't many places to sightsee around here."

"Oh," Terrance said, a rush of disappointment flooding him. Carol had been right about one thing: Marta was something special. The trait was fluid and hard to label. It wasn't something in particular she said or something special she did. It was just the way she made him feel. Noticeably different than other interactions he'd had. But he couldn't put his finger on what exactly made it unique. Perhaps he saw just what Carol had.

Marta took the last sip of her drink and slid the glass away toward where her bartender friend was wiping the counter. "We could go to the pond, I guess. If you think that coat will keep you warm enough."

"A pond?" Terrance twisted his face up in confusion.

"It's where everyone skates around here. It's usually quiet this time of night, but there are nice firepits."

"That sounds great." Terrance fought off the concern that he hadn't started a fire in twenty years. His apartment had a gas fireplace with a switch that he could flip to kick it on. But he wasn't ready for the night to end. "You want to say goodbye to your friends, or is Heather coming too?"

Marta smirked. "She'll want to."

"She's welcome," Terrance sang out, but Marta waved him off. She looked as though the idea of them being alone suited her just fine. He hadn't expected to like Marta this much. She had a sweet face and a cute disposition.

By the time they walked the half mile to the pond, Terrance was frozen to the bone. He'd spent all of his life in California, and besides a few ski trips, this was the coldest weather he'd been in. "How do people live like this?" he asked, shaking the chill out of his body.

"This is why everyone is so grumpy here," Marta explained. "We're out here chipping ice off our windshields and shoveling our way to our mailboxes. We don't have time for all that southern charm, and what's it called? Manners. We're tired. We're cold. We're in a hurry."

"I like it," Terrance said as they passed a few lit firepits, small groups gathered around each. It was a cool little hang-out spot. Beers cracking open, laughs spilling across the frigid night air. "Not the cold. I don't like that. But I like the bravado. This New England swagger is something I could get behind. It's right to the point."

"I better start a fire before you begin to pick up the accent and yell at these kids for playing their music too loud."

"I can start the fire," Terrance offered, praying he wasn't going to have to rub two sticks together.

"It's all right. There's a special way we do it here." The wood was already stacked in the homemade metal firepit. The sites were spread far enough apart that the next group sounded far off. Around the firepit, there were large logs for sitting.

"That's the special way you light fires?" Terrance asked as he watched Marta grab a lighter fluid bottle from behind the closest log and a large box of matches in a Ziploc bag.

"We grow up in the wilderness," Marta teased. "We're rustic and traditional." She squirted the stacked wood and threw in a match. Within a few seconds, the fire was blazing, and Terrance was glad for the heat.

"I love the vibe out here. The ice. The firepits. What a great idea." Terrance looked around before taking a seat on the log.

"This place might be considered cool by some, but when it's one of only three things to do in town, it gets old quick. We're here early enough, so it'll be fine. Once the real partying starts and the fights break out, it's lame." Marta sat by him on the log, and he was pleasantly surprised. There was another log on the other side of the fire she could have opted for.

"I've got to tell you something," Terrance began, knowing this might cut their night short if he didn't tread lightly. Honesty had always served him over the years, and he knew at a minimum Marta deserved that.

"Oh boy, I don't think anything good has ever come from a sentence that started that way." Marta leaned away to get a better look at his expression. The light from the fire flickered against her face, and he was again drawn into her magic.

"I don't understand you," he admitted as he kept his eyes on her. "But I believe you. I believe that whatever you're afraid of is bigger than whatever good might come your way. And that's a miserable realization." He dropped his head down and folded his hands. "I want to know. I want to know what's got you that scared. Not because you owe it to me or because I've got to report it back to Carol. I had a really nice evening with you. I've just seen in you exactly what Carol saw. And I want to know what's got you this afraid."

"Does it matter?" Marta asked quietly. She swept her hair up into a quick ponytail, and the more of her face he could see, the more beautiful she was.

"It doesn't matter for the foundation. It doesn't matter what I have to tell Carol. I'm just some guy who's going to get back on a plane, and you won't see me again."

"So then why do you want to know?" Marta asked, her voice so small now that he had to strain to hear her.

Terrance shifted on the log to face her. He wanted to reach out and take her hands in his, but he knew that wasn't right. "You're so close to the situation, Marta, that there's a chance you can't see a way past it. Maybe we can find the right shade of lipstick for that pig."

Marta chuckled reluctantly. "I don't think we can. It's a very ugly pig."

"And maybe you're right. But Carol has resources at her disposal, and that makes her powerful. I can't tell you how many things I've seen her navigate her way through. Things I thought were impossible."

"She does seem determined." Marta nibbled at her thumbnail and stared into the fire.

"I promise that anything you tell me; I won't share with anyone unless you want me to. That includes Carol."

"My friends," Marta began, "the ones at the bar. They don't even know. They want to. They're supportive and amazing. They swear there isn't anything I could tell them that would change their minds about me."

"But you don't believe them?" Terrance rubbed his hands together and held them up to warm them by the heat of the fire.

"I don't want to find out they're wrong. It might not look like much, but this is the best my life has ever been. I have my own place. I work at a bookstore, which is basically my dream come true. I have to pick up some other shifts and waitressing events to make ends meet, but it works. Heather and Ray are there for me. I know that I can count on them if I need them. I moved here because no one really knows my family or me. So, it's not fame and fortune, but it's safe. I'm safe here."

Terrance felt something swell in him. A knee-jerk reaction to step in front of whatever was racing toward Marta. He wanted to fight her fights and slay her dragons. It wasn't totally out of character for him. He tried to be one of the good guys, but he'd just met Marta. Her problems were not his, even if they were tangled up together in this decision she had to make.

"I'm not going to cry again," she promised. "That really isn't me. I have to admit that it's not easy for me to turn this down. I'm not doing it lightly."

"Let me try to help. I'll listen, and I'll be candid if I think there is no path forward. I'll get back on a plane, and you'll get to forget this ever happened." He was certain forgetting this encounter wasn't something he'd do so easily.

"I wouldn't even know where to start," she admitted, perking up just enough to give him hope that she might tell him something. "It's all so messy. Even before I met Carol, I've been trying to put it all back together. To figure out where it went so wrong and whose fault it was. I haven't found those answers."

"Maybe it'll help to say it out loud to someone objective. I'm not from here. I don't know anything about your family."

"At the end, you can tell me who sounds like the bad guy." Marta grinned, and then her face settled into grief. "I guess it doesn't work that way. We're probably all to blame. The whole family."

"Families are complicated." Terrance tried not to push. He didn't want Marta to think he was trying to capitalize on her pain. He truly just wanted to know what could hurt someone so badly they'd throw away a chance at a better life. He'd been the opposite. There had been nothing that would stop him from clawing his way toward something better. The distance he could put between who he was and who he wanted to be mattered—every inch of it.

"You know that my father and my brother both died?" She finally fixed her gaze back on him. "That's in my file, right?"

"Yes," he admitted, feeling apologetic for the voyeuristic nature of the process.

"What did it say about them?" Marta looked intense, anger flickering in her eyes. "How did it say they died?"

"Uh," Terrance hesitated, though he knew the answer well. "Your brother Jonah died in a car accident when he was twelve. Your father died in the hospital when you were nineteen. It didn't say how he died. An illness, I think."

Marta nodded and let out a humorless little laugh. "That's the whitewashed version of it. The part that Carol read and decided made me relatable. The poster child for loss and pain blooming into resilience. The story is a hell of a lot darker than that. There will be a line of people in my town ready to tell the real stories of how they died."

"What happened?" Terrance couldn't imagine the

depth of her loss, but clearly, there was more to it. Something sharper than just the blunt strike of grief.

"My brother Jonah was a sensitive kid. Middle child. A people pleaser. It's why my parents' divorce was so tough on him. It seemed to go on forever. People talk about divorce like it's nothing more than waiting for the papers to be filed in court. For my parents, it wasn't a life event. It was a lifestyle. They were in a perpetual state of divorce. It was never settled. We'd be in and out of court fighting about custody and child support. There were assault charges, threats, and anytime they were within a hundred feet of each other, there would be a scene."

"Selfish," Terrance said, shaking his head. "I don't understand how people can put their kids through that."

"They were kids themselves. No one showed them how to be married. No one showed them how to raise a family you could barely feed even though you worked yourself half to death. They couldn't survive it. They couldn't figure out how to stop being poor, how to stop being so damn tired. And they blamed each other for it until they couldn't tolerate the sight of one another." She'd always made these excuses for them. Now she wasn't sure if they held water at all.

"But to make a scene, to make it so public. That must have been awful for you."

"The cops knew us well. Hell, everyone in town knew our drama. They'd have to drag my father away from my brother Glenn's football games because it wasn't his week to come, and my mother wanted him thrown out. If we were five minutes late for my father to pick us up for his night with us, all hell would break loose. The day my brother died wasn't unique. It was awful, but it wasn't all that different than any of our other days for the previous three years." She sat with that truth for a long moment. How could something so horrible, be so normal to her. Wasn't that the root of all of this. The fact that so much had happened and in weathering it, she became weathered.

"I'm sorry," Terrance offered quietly. He was sorry she'd gone through it and apologetic for asking her to relive it. "You don't have to say anything else if you don't want."

"It's fine," she said softly as she waved him off. "It's probably better that you know. I don't think I'll ever be able to convince you I'm making the right choice other-wise. But the story you have of my brother's death, what you read, is not the truth. My mother's flavor-of-the-week boyfriend was fighting her battles for her that day. I don't blame the guy. He was like twenty-two years old, and my mother had convinced him that my father was the devil. He felt like he had to protect her, to protect all of us. But in reality, they were all equally dangerous. If they wanted to protect us, they only needed to stop what they were doing. All of them."

"Was there a fight?"

"My father came to pick us up. We weren't outside waiting like he expected us to be. My mom's boyfriend said it was too cold that day to wait outside, and my father was cruel to expect it. When my father pulled in and saw we were inside the house instead of outside, he lost it. He was screaming and kicked over the mailbox. My mom's boyfriend came out, and they started to fight. My mother got in the mix and caught an elbow in the stomach. She threw a fit on the ground, pulling at her hair and wailing. Glenn and I stood on the front steps with our weekend bags and just held our breath, waiting for it to be over. This was bad but not the worst we'd seen. I don't know why it set Jonah off. I don't know why he couldn't deal with it this time." Marta shook her head and pinched the bridge of her nose.

"A breaking point isn't always where we expect," Terrance said, his mind spinning through the sad possibilities of how the story might go. He was not prepared for how bad it was about to get.

"I guess he just couldn't take it anymore. He was tired of the fighting and the manipulation. Our parents wanted to win. I don't even know what winning would have looked like. I don't think they knew either. They were so caught up in hurting each other. Jonah pushed past them all. I thought he was just going to get in the car and wait." She stood up suddenly and waved her arms. "He was twelve. If any of us knew what he was going to do, we'd have stopped him. I would have stopped him."

"How old were you?" Terrance asked, layering his questions with absolution. A child couldn't be expected to fix something so out of their control.

"I was ten," Marta answered, dismissing his attempt at making her feel better. "But he listened to me. I could always get through to Jonah. He got in the driver's seat, threw the car into drive, and took off down the street. Mailboxes were crushed and a little white fence was bowled over. When he rounded the corner and disappeared, I actually laughed. Everyone was just standing there. Finally, they were silent. Jonah had wanted them all to stop, and for a moment they did. I think we expected him to turn around and come back, but he didn't. When he didn't return after a few minutes, my mother got into her car and had just started backing out when the first ambulance went by. A police car followed, and I think at that point we all knew."

"That's awful," Terrance croaked out. "I can't even imagine."

"You would think that would be enough. Your son hits a tree, flies through the windshield, and dies. You would think that would be the catalyst for them to change." Marta's hand was on her forehead, her eyes wide.

"It wasn't?"

"Things only got worse. The blame, making sure it was assigned to one of them, became the new fight. The funeral was a war zone. My mother broke mentally and never really went back together. Who caused Jonah's death was like the burning hot potato they tossed back and forth until the day my father died." Marta paced a bit, moving closer to the fire as a cold breeze blew.

"I can understand why you wouldn't want to relive all that." Terrance felt a pang of remorse fill his stomach. His presence was forcing Marta to experience it all again.

"And you can see why some file that Carol has on me doesn't really tell the story. Yes, my brother died in a car accident. The newspaper articles said he was joyriding. There was no joy in that ride. There was no joy in that day at all."

Terrance was cautious not to dismiss her pain. "People understand that some families are toxic. That some people come from broken homes where terrible things have happened. Why would something your parents did, their shameful failures, keep you from getting all you want in life? You don't deserve to pay that debt for the rest of your days. It's not yours to pay."

Marta sat back down on the log, this time a bit closer to him. "Do you think that's all?" She looked up at him earnestly, and he couldn't be sure if he was meant to answer the question.

"What do you mean?"

"That's not where it started, and it's not where it ended. I think people assume trauma is just the big events. Divorce. Accidents. Death. Custody battles. Courtrooms. Hurt feelings. Rumors. Lies. There aren't one or two things you could come in and explain away or fix. Yes, my brother died. It was horrific, avoidable, and traumatic. But you need to realize that isn't the hardest story for me to tell you tonight. Terrance, if you walked into my town today and brought up my family, you'd get it. Half would say my father killed my brother. The other half would say my crazy mother did. All of them would agree that I killed my father."

She fixed her eyes on him and was clearly searching for a reaction. A flinch. Shock. But he didn't waver. Her last statement was rattling, but she deserved his ability to absorb it without judgment. He sat silently and fought the urge to put his hand on her back to comfort her.

Marta's words continued coming in a steady flow. "Someone will see I was married and divorced. I was eighteen and desperate to get away. I couldn't do it on my own. It wouldn't take anyone long to find out how that went. They'll find the police reports and the restraining orders. The man I married to get away from my family was just as toxic. I was so desperate to create something better than I had. To scribble out the drawing that was my life and sketch a new one."

"People experience those things too. Hundreds of thousands of people, actually. Your audience isn't some monolith of perfection."

Her voice was suddenly cynical. "And I could be an inspiration to them. The domestic violence survivor who rose up from the ashes and faced her abuser."

"Well—"

She snapped her answer back quickly. "I never called Keith my abuser. I never stood up to him. I ran away. Literally, I filed for divorce and moved a week later. My family and the people in my life back then have absolutely no idea what I went through. I never dared to take him to court or press any charges. The restraining order was a favor a cop buddy of mine could push through. And only because he swore he wouldn't tell my brother."

"But you left," Terrance said, scraping to find some sort of hope to hold on to. He wanted that, not for himself, but for Marta.

"I don't want to be the spokesperson for this. I'm not ready for that. I left because I couldn't face it. I'm still afraid of what he would do to me. If I ever outed him . . . You don't understand."

"I don't," Terrance agreed. "I can't imagine what that must feel like. Any of it."

Marta went on, seeming as though she was still processing all of the possible repercussions. "He still lives there. About two miles from my brother Glenn. Do you know what it would do to my brother to find out what my marriage was really like? He'd be furious and embarrassed for not defending me sooner. The weight that he carries, the burden of keeping me safe all these years, would finally crush him. His job, his wife, their future kids would all be at risk because my secrets would come out. Glenn is a lot of great things, but he can't control his temper when it comes to protecting people he loves. Are you starting to get it now?"

This, Terrance could tell, she did want an answer to. "I hear you," was all he could muster at first. "I hear what you're saying."

"You can't dress this up and march it across that stage and pretend people won't notice. There are too many folks out there who have sold pills to my mother. Too many people who know my ex-husband and won't hesitate to stir that mess up. I can think of a dozen people who adored my father and will be clamoring to tell everyone how I caused his death. I am not the golden child of my town. They will not celebrate and honor me. I will be chum in the water, and they will be insatiable sharks. And you know what? I could deal with that. But my brother, Heather, Ray, Carol, they'll be the ones who really get hurt."

Terrance was angry. He was mad for Marta. For how she had to process the most exciting news in her life through a lens of unbearable pain and fear. "I want to fix this," Terrance admitted, knowing full well it was trite. "I don't know how. I just want to."

Marta's expression softened. She looked genuinely grateful for his sentiment. "I wish it was easier. But please don't put Carol in this position. I believe her intentions are good. She just doesn't know how bad it is. I don't think she could understand how merciless life can actually be."

"She's very optimistic," Terrance agreed. "And persistent. It won't be easy to explain this to her, but I will. If you really don't want to go forward with this, I'll respect that."

"It's not that I don't want to," Marta gulped, and he finally stopped fighting the urge. Terrance stretched his hand out and wrapped his arm over Marta's shoulder. "I want this. I just can't have it."

Leaning her head on his shoulder, Marta drew in a deep breath. She was tucked there beneath his arm. The fire crackled, and its heat warmed their cheeks.

"There's just no way, Terrance," Marta said quietly, and he could sense her waiting. She needed him to tell her there was some option. That something could set all this right and clear a path for her to embrace the potential her life held. "Right? It's too much to untangle."

"I'm not ready to give up unless you want me to," Terrance replied, his chin resting on the top of her head.

"It's hopeless," Marta sighed. "But maybe you'll figure something out."

He smiled and gave her a squeeze before letting her go. "You're supposed to come back to California with me in three days. Let's try to work it out by then. If we run out of time and ideas and I get on that plane by myself, at least we know we did all we could."

"Maybe someone will invent a time machine by then," Marta laughed as she straightened herself up and shifted herself on the log. "There's a lot I would change."

"You can't change too much. I think you're made up of the things that happened to you."

"Let's hope not, because then I'm mostly just a mix of bad luck and terrible choices."

"Marta," Terrance said thoughtfully, "you're a hell of a lot more than that."

CHAPTER FIFTEEN

Carol

The willpower it took not to blow up Terrance's phone all afternoon was substantial. She was desperate for an update. Marta had been such a tough person to read, and it was hard to know if Terrance would have better luck than Carol had. She hoped he did.

When the phone finally rang, she breathlessly answered.

"Tell me it went well," she pleaded.

"Well . . ." Terrance let his voice trail off.

"You mean it went well? Or well, I have some bad news?"

"Neither?" he offered in the form of a question.

"This is very cryptic," Carol said in a near scold. "Just

tell me the truth. We'll figure it all out. There's always a workaround."

"First," Terrance said confidently, "I can see what you mean. Marta is the real deal."

"Isn't she?" Carol sang. "I could practically feel her pain and passion when we spoke. It's all over the pages of her book, but it's in her expressions. Her words. Powerful."

"Yes," Terrance agreed. "We had a productive dinner, and we did a lot of talking."

"That's good. She's a beautiful girl too," Carol interjected slyly as if Terrance wouldn't have noticed how stunning Marta was.

"She is," he agreed through a smile she could hear over the phone. "But she's got some history. I don't want to rehash every detail, but it's some dark stuff. I know you gathered some cursory information on Marta's past, but it seems like that's the biggest barrier for her. Winning this award would cast a spotlight on her life, and she's worried about that scrutiny."

"Everyone worries about that. Was your Halloween costume in college not appropriate? Did you say something stupid that will come back to haunt you? You know how all of that works. Maybe it'll be a blip on the radar, but we do a great job of snuffing out those stories before they even take hold."

His silence was unsettling. Terrance never held back with Carol, which usually meant he was never at a loss for words.

"You're making me nervous," Carol pressed. "What is it?"

"I just need a few more days out here," he explained. "I know you have the meeting with the board coming up. The goal is to have Marta there. I'm going to be working on that."

"I don't want to cut it too close," Carol worried aloud. "If I walk into that meeting and it's a bust, I'll be eroding the confidence the board has in me. Judging by the last meeting, there are a few members who think I'm already on shaky ground."

"I'll do my best," Terrance promised. "How is everything going in the office? I like to pretend nothing runs right without me."

"No need to pretend," Carol laughed. "I'm a mess without you here. No one runs a schedule like you. All my meetings are running long, and I am never where I need to be when I need to be there."

"Did you eat?" Terrance asked, sounding concerned.

"Robert stopped by and brought some lunch, so luckily, I had something to hold me over."

"Robert?" Terrance asked cautiously. "Robert Riggens from the board of directors?"

Carol cleared her throat and tried to cover up. "We're discussing the employee engagement survey results. Making sure our staff is heard and appreciated is vital."

"It is," Terrance agreed, stretching the words out. "But I got the summarized results back two weeks ago. It's a glowing endorsement of your leadership at the company.

There was very little concern from employees. It was all very straightforward. Nothing you'd need a meeting about."

"Right," Carol hummed. "I forgot you screen those for me."

"So, Robert is just coming around and bringing you lunch and pretending there's some important data in those engagement surveys. I like it."

"It's not like that," Carol replied anxiously. "It would be highly inappropriate for me to socialize with any member of the board."

"Carol," Terrance said seriously, "you know I would never say anything to anyone. You're a whole person, not just the CEO, and if you want to have lunch with Robert, you should absolutely be able to. I'm the only one who gets the employee engagement results, and I always send them to Robert because he likes to stay up to date on them. The results don't go public to the rest of the company for another month. You should keep meeting with him about them."

"I hate how many rules there are," Carol sighed. "If we were two men meeting for lunch, a whisky, and a cigar, no one would even bat an eye. It's nothing romantic. But he supports me on the board, and I want to cultivate that relationship. I have a feeling I'm going to need whatever alliances I can get in the coming months."

"You don't owe me an explanation," Terrance reminded her. "It shouldn't be this hard. It'll all work out, and you'll have the entire board on your side by this time next year. The award ceremony is going to be the game changer you were hoping for."

"I guess that depends on how things go with Marta. Are you sure you can work this out?"

There was just a long enough pause for Carol to worry. "I'm working on it. I just have to figure out how to get ahead of all the things in Marta's past. You did look into her past, right?"

"I did," Carol said, thinking of the time she spent learning all she could about Marta and her childhood. "She's had quite a bit of heartache. I know they struggled financially. Her mother has mental illness. That's something I can deeply relate to." This was more than she'd ever shared with Terrance about her mother. She'd dropped hints and made a few jokes, but she hadn't called it exactly what it was. Illness.

"Your mother struggled with it?" Terrance asked gently. "You mentioned a few things, but I wasn't sure."

"I wouldn't say my mother struggled with it. She certainly didn't seem to struggle against it. There were days I think she loved it. But I know what that can do to a child. I also know what it can fuel. Creativity. Strength. You can do a lot with the energy it takes to try to overcome the madness."

"I've only really begun to talk with Marta about it, and I don't think she's in a place where she sees the silver lining of it all. It's pretty messy. I'm worried about the backlash."

"You're worried for the foundation?"

"No," Terrance admitted. "I'm worried about you, and

I'm worried about Marta. Just because someone is deserving of success and happiness doesn't mean the world will let them have it. Most people don't root for you, Carol."

Carol could tell how difficult it was for Terrance to state this fact. "I know they don't. Most root against me. I'd imagine it's the same for Marta. I want to change that."

"You're coming from two very different worlds. You've overcome your challenges, and you've worked hard to get where you are."

She could sense the "but" that he was hesitating to say. She did him a favor and filled in the blank. "But I've got a hell of a lot more resources than she has. I always have. I know that. I don't take it for granted. But her life doesn't disqualify her from being able to celebrate what she worked hard for. We can do this." Carol had been intentional about not sounding as though that were a question. There was no room for doubt in her mind. She'd leave that to everyone else.

"I better get to work then," Terrance said through a tired chuckle.

Carol could tell there was more he wanted to say. For the first time, she could sense him holding back. She wasn't sure if it was information about Marta or just a lack of confidence in what they were trying to do. "No matter what, Terrance, I know you're doing the best you can. I have faith in you."

CHAPTER SIXTEEN

Marta

Terrance called far too early in the morning for it to be a casual check-in. She considered letting it go to voicemail. The whole evening had been bizarre. At least by her standards. Her friends were hilariously protective. Terrance was good company. The strange part was not how they'd all acted but how she did. The idea of opening up to a stranger would usually send her head spinning and leave her stomach in knots. It had been the opposite. There was a sense of relief that came from telling someone just how bad it had all been. Some people in her life knew fragments, but she'd never blurted it all out like that before. Recounting it with Glenn or some cousin over the years was always some lighthearted jovial tale of the wild Leducs.

When she told Terrance, she expected to see horror on his face. That would have matched precisely what she felt. The way he absorbed it with a nonjudgmental expression was not expected. It was not funny. There was no explaining it all away as something in the past that should be left behind. It made answering his call seem urgent, even if it was early.

"I have an idea," Terrance said breathlessly. "And good morning. Are you doing all right?"

"Why wouldn't I be all right?" Marta asked, stepping out of her bed and pulling on her hooded sweatshirt. It was cold, but she'd been accustomed to leaving the thermostat just high enough to keep the pipes from freezing. Utility bills could easily climb if she wasn't careful.

"Don't minimize it," Terrance said gently. "It's obvious you're strong. I do not doubt that, but it couldn't have been easy to talk about all that last night. It must take its toll."

Marta fought the urge to deflect his empathy. She was coming to terms with how uncomfortable people's attention made her. "It wasn't easy," she admitted. "I don't feel like it changed anything."

"It did," Terrance said brightly. "It gave me an idea. Something I think can really work."

The excitement in his voice wasn't quite contagious, but it was at least making her curious. She'd given all her energy to this dilemma since the moment she'd spoken with Carol in the café. It was like she'd been running through a maze, and everywhere she turned was a dead end. If Terrance thought he'd found a way out, she wanted to hear it.

"It's just a start," he cautioned. "But I think we can make some progress. Before I started with Carol, I was in marketing. When we wanted to test out a new product or idea, we always brought in a small group of people. A focus group who would give feedback. We could see what it might look like to tell your story."

Marta snickered at the absurdity, but also felt instant dread at the idea of telling her story. "A focus group?"

"You trust your friends? They obviously care a lot about you. I think you should tell them what you're afraid might come out and see how they react."

"It'll change things," Marta sighed. "They'll look at me differently."

"Different isn't always bad. Do you really think it's sustainable to keep them completely in the dark about your past for the rest of your friendship? They already know something is up. Telling them can help flush out how it all might go down if you choose to tell your story to a broader audience."

Marta pressed the phone between her shoulder and her ear as she poured herself a glass of water. She thought it through. He was correct that it wasn't practical to think she could keep her past a secret from her friends forever. "I think maybe it's time."

"The more you talk about it, the better you'll be at shaping the story. The more questions they have, the better prepared you'll be to answer them. It's practice. And if nothing else, your friends get a clearer picture of who you really are."

"You say that like it's a good thing." She chuckled to herself. "I like the person I've pretended to be for the last two years. So do they. It's the uncomplicated version of me that they decided to be friends with. Should I really take that away from them?"

He answered quickly and simply. "Yes."

"I don't know how I'll even start to tell them. They're going to feel lied to." Marta thought instantly of Heather. "Heather is compassionate. She's going to have a million questions."

"What good practice you'll get," Terrance said, returning to his cheery tone. "I know this doesn't solve anything. But maybe it'll get us closer to a solution."

"It's a little bit like bailing out one bucket of water in a sinking ship," Marta countered.

"Well, maybe we'll end up with more people ready to bail water with us. What do you think?"

Begrudgingly, she closed her eyes and imagined how it would go. "I'll tell them. But you're coming. If this goes terribly wrong, I want to have someone to blame right away."

Terrance chuckled. "I make a great punching bag."

"I don't work at the bookstore today, and I can probably get Heather and Ray to meet us for lunch. They've been blowing up my phone trying to find out how last night went."

"Ask her not to bring so many weapons today. She doesn't need them. I'm harmless."

"I wasn't worried about you at all," Marta explained with a smile. "If I've learned anything in my life, it's how to spot trouble. You're not it."

"That's a high compliment coming from you." He hesitated, but she could tell he wasn't finished. "I know the circumstances of me being here are a little convoluted. But I want you to know that last night was actually pretty great."

"Yeah," she agreed coolly. "I haven't been out with anyone in a while. It was pretty good besides being a dramatic tear-filled therapy session. Just do me a favor, and the next time we have dinner, you do the crying."

"I'll turn the waterworks on if it means you'll come out with me again. But maybe this time we venture out a bit and find something new. Maybe tonight?"

"I was going to work a catering job at the veterans' hall, but I could get someone to cover for me." Someone covering her shift wasn't the same as someone covering the bills she'd need to pay, but Terrance was flying back to California soon. Something was telling her to take advantage of the time they had. She'd find a way to make up the lost work after he was gone. "I'll text you a place for lunch with Heather and Ray, and you find something good for dinner, okay?"

"Perfect," Terrance replied. "I'm determined to find something unique for dinner."

. . .

Marta spent the remainder of the morning writing. There was another book in her head, and she was anxious to give it life. If the publisher liked it, she could count on another five-thousand-dollar contract. That money could go toward fixing the unreliable clutch in her car.

There were a few dangerous moments that morning where Marta considered what might happen to her life if she accepted the award and all the things that came with it. What would it be like to not have to balance a checkbook perfectly to avoid bounced checks? What would she drive? What would she buy at the grocery store? By the time she'd mentally worked her way down the gourmet cheese aisle, she'd begun to realize how foolish she was being. It was a distraction she couldn't afford. Marta had looked at writing books the same way she'd looked at every other endeavor in her life. It would require immense work, but maybe she could create a new revenue stream from it. That was a realistic goal. The rest, all the promising accolades and life-changing moments, were just icy hills. Maybe she could climb up partway, but eventually, she'd come crashing down.

Heather and Ray were on the same side of the booth at the diner and looked perfectly cozy when she arrived. Marta almost felt guilty for interrupting their cute whispers and playful smiles.

"This is a very mysterious lunch," Heather sang, clapping her hands together excitedly. "What's the big news? You decided to take the award? You're about to be mega-famous?"

"No," Marta said through a forced smile. She'd underestimated how bad her nerves would be at this moment. Hurting Heather was a real possibility and one that made her stomach flip. "I've fallen madly in love with Terrance, and we're running away together," Marta teased, deflecting with humor always a safe bet.

"He's gorgeous," Heather cooed. "Sorry, babe, but he is." She looked apologetically at Ray.

With a shrug, he answered, "The man has a rugged build and gentle eyes. If you didn't think he was good-looking, I'd be worried about you."

Marta slid into the booth and checked her watch. Terrance would be there any moment, and she'd lose the opportunity to chicken out on telling them. When she saw his rental car pull into the parking lot, she felt compelled to get serious. "Promise me no matter what I tell you today, you'll try to understand. Keeping things from you these last two years wasn't about how much I trust you. It's about not trusting myself to relive it all."

Heather's face crumpled with worry. "Marta, you're freaking me out."

Ray reached his hand up and touched Heather's arm. "Nothing will change how we feel about you. Seriously. It's the three of us. We want to know so we can help."

"Right," Heather said, Ray's touch seeming to snap her out of her initial concern. "You can tell us anything. Are you sure you want Terrance here for this?"

"I told him everything last night." Marta said the words before she considered the implications. Heather wasn't one to hide her emotions, and she looked hurt by this. Marta tried to explain. "It's the reason he's here. Terrance needs me to go back to California with him and meet people at the foundation. Carol has a meeting planned, and I felt like I needed to explain exactly why I was turning the award down. Just like with you guys, it didn't make sense unless he could hear the whole story."

Terrance was in the diner now and making his way to them. If Heather was still upset, it would make this all the more awkward.

"It's fine," Heather said gently. "I get it. I'm just glad you want to tell us now."

There were brief introductions that were missed last night and a sense of unity at the table. This time they were all there for the same reason.

"I don't really know where to start," Marta said, fiddling with her menu. She ate the same things every time they came here, but suddenly, she let herself get lost in the list of side dishes.

"It all made sense last night," Terrance said as he pulled a menu from the table and started scanning. "It doesn't have to be perfect."

Ray agreed quickly. "Right, just start anywhere."

Marta hesitated as the waitress took their orders and disappeared into the kitchen. Then, just as she had last night, disjointed and blurting, she told the story. Marta knew it sounded more clinical today. She'd divorced herself from the emotion she'd felt last night. It was as if she was telling someone else's story now. She could eat her sandwich and explain her brother's death.

However, it didn't mean the morning was devoid of emotion, because Heather was feeling enough for all of them put together. She rose and fell with the heartache and grief Marta was holding back.

"How?" Heather finally gasped out. "How did all of that happen to one person?"

"It didn't," Marta replied flatly. "It happened to my whole family. And it's not all these isolated events. The tragedy didn't just keep befalling us. Some we brought on ourselves. It's all connected. I wouldn't have gone off and married the first person who asked me if I wasn't so desperate to get away from it all. My brother wouldn't have jumped in that car if he wasn't completely exhausted and terrified. It's this spider web of trauma, and you can try to unstick yourself and run away, but there's just so many damn spiders out to get you."

Ray put his arm around Heather as he spoke. "I'm sorry you had to deal with all of that. I can't imagine."

"I'm fine," Marta insisted. "The last two years living here have been great. I don't have all that stuff weighing on me like I used to. You have been the best friends. I have enough money to get by. I have an apartment. The book-store is a dream job for me."

Ray cleared his throat. "And you have written and published a book that has gotten the attention of some pretty important people."

"Yes," Heather sang out proudly. "That's a big deal. I

can completely understand why all this stuff you just told us would make you afraid to put yourself out there. But there has to be a way."

Terrance, who had been quiet through the telling of her story, finally spoke up. "What part of your past concerns you the most?"

Without overthinking it, Marta answered swiftly. "Keith. When I left him, it was a very volatile situation. I didn't take a thing with me. I gave him everything just so I didn't drag it out any longer than I had to."

"He won't hurt you again," Ray asserted, his hand balling into a fist. "No one is going to let that happen."

"It's not that I'm worried he'll hurt me again. Not physically. I don't want that part of my past coming out at all. I'm not looking to be a spokesperson for domestic abuse. I never confronted Keith unless I had no choice. I simply ran away. My family has no idea what I went through with him. But because there was a restraining order, people will find out. I may not have told anyone, and he certainly wouldn't have told anyone that he was abusive, but there is a paper trail for anyone who wants to dig."

Heather bit at her lip. "You could tell them, so they don't get blindsided if it comes out."

Marta thought instantly of her brother. "Glenn, my older brother, this would kill him. He and Keith cross paths all the time. It's one reason I never brought it up to begin with. I know my brother. He won't miss an opportunity to try to make it right."

Heather's face fell with sadness. "There is nothing anyone can do to make that right."

"True," Marta resigned. "But he will at least try to make it even. Glenn will go mad asking me for details. He'll want to know who else in town knew and why they didn't tell him. Some of the cops who helped me were his buddies. It'll be a nightmare. Glenn is a good man, but he tends to get obsessed with the idea of retribution. He sees right and wrong as two very separate things. There is no gray area as far as he's concerned."

Terrance shifted in the booth to face her. "There is no gray area here, Marta. If this guy, your ex, crossed that line, he is wrong. I don't blame your brother for wanting to get even. If anyone put their hands on my sister, I'd lose my mind."

"But you'd probably stop short of ruining your whole life over it. Maybe you would do something, but you'd plan it out and not just throw away everything you have in the name of some medieval justice. And it won't just be Keith. I'm telling you, Glenn will go off on anyone involved, or anyone who kept it a secret." Marta's leg began to shake nervously. Terrance reached under the table with ease and familiarity and touched her knee gently.

Marta didn't pull away. She only settled her leg and drew in a deep breath as Terrance spoke with an even and temperate tone. "We could talk to your brother. I don't think he should be hearing about it from some kind of third-hand information or leaked police report. Maybe if it was explained calmly, he could try to understand that lashing out at Keith would hurt you in the long run."

With a little giggle, Marta replied. "I don't know if that would help. It's not really how we operate. You're talking about thoughtful conversation delicately explained. We don't really do that."

Terrance smiled that unbelievably empathetic grin. "I get that. And who knows if he'll even be receptive to it. Maybe he won't. But just like this conversation, don't you think it's time he knew? Does it really feel right to keep it from him?"

Ray's brow creased deeply. "But only if that's what you want, Marta. I get that Terrance is invested in you. He's got a job to do. No offense, man, but you've got two days to convince Marta she should go to some big meeting. If she's not ready, she shouldn't do anything she doesn't want to do."

"Absolutely," Terrance said, holding his hands up disarmingly. "I know this is bigger than meeting with the board. It's bigger than the award. Marta should—"

Marta interjected, throwing a look at them. "I think I should not be talked about like I'm not sitting right here. That could be step one."

The two men cringed and then nodded. Terrance was the first to acknowledge his mistake. "Right. Sorry. You should be doing what you want. I'm not going to lie. I want you on that plane with me in a couple of days. I want you to walk across that stage next year and hold that award in your hand. The book deals will flood in. The sponsorships and the networking will change your life. I'm not going to pretend that's not part of my agenda. It is."

Heather cooed. "Oh my God, this guy." She pointed her thumb at Terrance and made a sappy face at Marta. "He's seriously adorable."

Marta shook her head but expected nothing less from her friend. "Aren't you glad you didn't mace him last night?"

"Mace," Heather said, bringing her hand to her heart dramatically. "Not that pretty face."

Ray sat up a little straighter and interrupted their jokes. "It sounds like we all want the same thing. We just have to figure out how to do it."

A lump grew in Marta's throat. No one besides Glenn had ever been this loyal to her. Her brother was always her cheerleader in his own gruff way. Now she suddenly had three new ones.

Heather snapped her fingers. "We need a fixer."

"A what?" Ray asked skeptically. "What's a fixer?"

"Oh," Heather said, leaning back as her eyes went wide. "It's this powerhouse woman in a sharp suit who swoops in and handles every scandal. There are payoffs, blackmail, really anything you can think of that would shut down the drama. Where can we get a fixer?" She looked at Terrance as though he would be able to offer some solution.

"I don't know if those people really exist," he reported regretfully. "Carol has resources that could help, though."

Heather leaned in toward Marta and put her hand to

the side of her mouth as though she were telling a secret. "That's code for money."

"I do love it when you translate for me, Heather," Marta replied, her hand next to her mouth too. "I don't think we'll find a fixer who could deal with all my garbage. If we did, we couldn't afford her."

Ray tapped his finger on the table. "Then it's the four of us." He looked around the table at each of them. "Maybe we can't sort everything out before the meeting. Maybe we won't fix all the things you're worried about, but we can try."

They nodded, exchanging glances of agreement. Ray seemed to rethink his words suddenly. "Well, three and a half people."

Marta glanced at each of them. "Who's the half?"

"Terrance," Ray said as though it was apparent. "We only half know him. I'm not convinced he's all in."

Terrance snapped his tongue in his mouth and looked insulted. "I'm all in. I don't do anything halfway."

"None of you need to do this," Marta groaned. "Seriously. I mean it when I say I'm happy here. These last two years have been great."

Heather reached across the table and took Marta's hand. "Does it feel good to have to pretend about who you are? To keep things from us? We want to know all of you."

"I mean," Marta shrugged and smirked. "When the real stuff isn't great, pretending works. I could have spun an outstanding story about my rockstar parents and my wild childhood on the road."

Heather squeezed her hand gently. "We love the real you. All the stuff you went through made you exactly who you are. And we're going to be your fixer. I have this amazing power suit I can wear."

"I don't get why you guys are doing this," Marta protested, dipping her head down and feeling wholly unworthy. "I'm nothing like any of you. I'm messy and banged up."

Terrance nudged her with his shoulder and waited until she looked at him before he explained. "You don't have to be the same to belong. It's hand-picked and intentional to belong somewhere. These two people care about you. It's pretty obvious. I wouldn't worry about how you're all different. I'd focus on the fact that you all want the same thing."

"We," Ray reminded him. "*We* all want the same thing." He pointed at each of them, including Terrance.

Marta felt compelled to jump in. "We met Terrance yesterday. I don't think we have to force him into the club."

"I need a club," Terrance admitted. "I've been so focused on work for the last couple of years that I've lost sight of a lot of things. It wasn't until I sat across from Marta last night that I realized I've had my blinders on lately. Like I said, I'm all in." His eyes were fixed on Marta.

"You say that like you have a plan," Marta exhaled, looking desperate for him to give some magic answer that would make her feel better.

"Dinner," Heather announced excitedly. "We should have your brother over to my house for dinner. Him, his wife, all of us. You can tell him what you need to, and he can see you're safe. Then he's three full hours away from home, and he can have plenty of time to cool off before being close to Keith."

"That's a great plan," Ray said, leaning in to kiss Heather. "You are a fixer. I can't wait to see that power suit."

"I like it," Terrance agreed. "Tomorrow?"

"I don't know if he'll come to dinner tomorrow," Marta said, pumping her hands to slow them all down. "I know you want me to go to California."

"You're going," Heather insisted. "None of us have been anywhere. You've got this great opportunity. No matter what happens in the next two days, you need to be planning to go to California. Period." She slapped her hand to the table.

"I agree." Terrance smiled wryly. "It can't hurt to take a free trip to California. It's not like any other place in the world."

Heather chuckled. "It's not like New Hampshire, and that's all that matters. She'll be on that plane. We might not have it all sorted out by then, but she's going."

Marta was on the inside seat of the booth. The wall was to her left and Terrance to her right. It would be easy to feel pinned in by all these people. Stuck. They had her locked in. But they didn't feel like handcuffs. They felt like shields.

CHAPTER SEVENTEEN

Carol

It was like an emergency hotline. She didn't dial that number unless she felt she absolutely had to. Nancy was busy. Carol knew it wasn't easy for her friend to sneak away and become a wine-pouring therapist. They'd grown apart, but their friendship was one of those. The kind that endured. Like a handprint pressed into cement. No matter how much time passed, Carol could come back and forever see she still fit perfectly with her friend.

They'd taken different paths. But unlike most of the other women who'd judged and been baffled by Carol's life choices, Nancy understood. She knew Carol. Not just socially or as a friend. There was a soul-deep under-standing between the two women. Nancy understood that, for Carol, fulfillment was tied tightly to accomplishment. It wasn't about being the most powerful in the room in order to dominate people. Carol didn't want to be the boss to be bossy. She wanted control. Rather than waiting for opportunities, she wanted to be responsible for doling them out.

Nancy had seen what the other people in Carol's life had not. Because their friendship was old, it carried shared pain. Joining each other for holidays meant a front-row seat to the dysfunction of their real lives. Not just their school lives or their work lives. Nancy had met Carol's mother. She'd heard the scorn and the vitriol. There were no cheerleaders in Carol's life. No fans cheering her on in the stands. Everything she'd worked for had been done quietly and without fanfare.

"I smell like spoiled milk." Nancy leaned in for a hug as she apologized. "Little MJ is the most colicky baby in the world, and apparently I'm the only one who can calm him. I think he enjoys projectile vomiting on me."

"You make an adorable grandma," Carol purred, clasping her hands together and tucking them for a moment under her chin. She was overjoyed to be in the presence of someone she loved. Someone who loved her. She'd almost forgotten how good it felt.

"I keep saying yes to babysitting when I mean no," Nancy groaned as she took a seat at the small table. They'd eaten there together before, but it had been years. This was Carol's go-to spot. Trendy atmosphere but not menu, Coral Bridge was everything she loved in a dining experience. The dim lights and eclectic art gave her tremendous energy, but the food wasn't so hip that it left her hungry. The staff knew her name, and she never felt out of place eating alone there. But tonight, she was grateful for the company.

"You always had a hard time telling people no. It's why you came out tonight even though you're exhausted. I'm sorry to call so last minute." Carol settled into her seat and saw her favorite waitress. With a smile and wave, Trinney lit up.

"Are you kidding me? I couldn't take another evening of rocking and fussing. I love my daughter, but she's got to get through this just like I did, on her own. This was exactly what I needed. I'm so glad you called. Let's split a bottle of wine and eat enough shrimp to feed a walrus."

"Do walruses eat shrimp?" Carol asked through a laugh.

"I have no clue, but we do."

Trinney presented two menus and her usual bright smile. "Hey Carol, glad to see you in tonight. We missed you the last couple of weeks."

"It's been madness at the office. I've been eating there most nights. But my oldest friend and I are going to forget all our troubles and enjoy a nice dinner."

Trinney cooed. "I love that. You deserve it. I tell everyone I want to be you when I grow up. I know it's not very professional of me, but sometimes when you have a meeting here, I listen in and do little air fist pumps when you just run the world."

Carol waved off the compliment. "I don't run the

world," she hummed. "I have no doubt you will someday. You're too kind to me, Trinney."

"I'm with Trinney." Nancy giggled. "You are a badass."

After taking their order and offering a few more shining compliments, Trinney stepped away.

"She's great," Nancy announced, jutting her thumb in Trinney's direction. "I need a hype woman like that in my life."

"You're right. She's a great girl. But I need more than someone hyping me up right now. Things are a little rocky at the moment." Carol pretended to be preoccupied, laying her napkin perfectly over her lap. She wasn't ready for Nancy to spot just how stressed she was.

Nancy leaned in. "Oh, honey, I'm sorry if things are tough right now. I thought that might be the case when you called. Do you want to talk about it?"

"I don't want to bore you with all the details. The last thing I want is for you to think the only time I call you is when I need you to talk me off a ledge."

"What are friends for?" Nancy reached over and patted Carol's hand gently. "You have an exciting and very fulfilling life. I love hearing about what's going on with you. It was hard for me to step away from my career all those years ago. Becoming a substitute teacher was not exactly how I planned to use my college degree. Leon and I have a beautiful family and tolerable marriage."

"It's more than just tolerable," Carol scolded. "You two lovebirds should be hosting a Ted Talk about marriage."

"I'm not saying I regret anything. I just enjoy listening

to you and how exciting your life is. I can't imagine running a company. I'm way over my head just running church bake sales. I want to hear what's going on. So tell me, am I listening or fixing?"

That had been a cornerstone of their friendship. That one simple question had set the tone for their relationship's longevity. When one of them was struggling or at a crossroads, the other would preemptively ask if they were meant to just listen or offer solutions. It seemed a small distinction, but it mattered greatly.

"Fixing. Analyzing. Slapping sense into me, please. You know me so well," Carol said earnestly. "I'd like you to give me your unvarnished opinions."

"Oh, I love giving my opinions. Lay it on me."

Carol waited while Trinney poured them each a glass of wine and brought them a basket of warm, freshly baked bread.

"I have two issues. One is in the form of a man with whom I have absolutely no business getting involved, and the other is a high-stakes decision I've made for the direction of the foundation."

"Start with the man," Nancy pleaded. "Leon is my high school sweetheart. It's lovely and all, but you get to be out there sampling all the desserts, and I'm still chomping on the same biscotti. Give me something."

"His name is Robert," Carol whispered even though there was no one in earshot. "He's divorced. A real gentleman. Charming. Thoughtful."

"Good-looking?"

"Remember Mr. Ellis, the principal of the school you subbed for," Carol asked in a hushed and excited tone.

"He was gorgeous," Nancy said, pretending to faint.

"Robert looks a bit like him but even better." Carol let a flash of Robert's face cross her mind before admonishing herself and remembering the problem. "He's a member of the board for the foundation. It's highly inappropriate for us to have any kind of contact on a personal level. There are some cases where that happens, but I'm new to the role. I'm completely shaking things up. The last thing I need is to create a scandal where there doesn't need to be one."

"But there is something between you?" Nancy asked, not looking deterred by the new information. "He likes you?"

"We're not children," Carol scoffed. "I didn't send him a note and ask him to circle yes or no."

"A woman knows if a man is interested in her. At least I think that's still true. I've been out of the game too long. He's sending you signals?"

"Egg rolls," Carol said with a shrug.

"Gosh, I don't know anything anymore. Is that like a dating site or something?"

"He snuck into my office under the guise of some fake meeting about something no one cares much about and brought me lunch. From what I can tell, he plans to do it again."

"Scandalous," Nancy said, looking utterly disappointed. "So nothing has actually happened between the two of you?"

"Nothing," Carol reported somberly. "And it can't. Even if we kept it extremely quiet, it would be dangerous."

"Oh, a precarious secret rendezvous with a handsome man must be so horrible." Nancy's voice was laced with playful sarcasm. "I can't tell you what to do there, but my advice is do not shut it down. You don't have to pursue it, just let it get some oxygen for at least a little while. See what happens."

Carol lifted her wine glass and swirled it around. "It might not be quite so challenging if I hadn't also taken some enormous risks in my new role."

Nancy nibbled on a crusty piece of bread and assumed her most comforting tone. "You told me how you are shaking things up there. I think that's great. There is no doubt things at the foundation were stagnant. Ratings were slipping. Donors moving on. You have to make bold choices. Not everyone is going to be supportive. I might not be a high-powered CEO, but I survived middle school with three kids. I know change is necessary but difficult."

"I've made ample adjustments to staff and the business model in general, but I'm staking everything on one new author."

"That's exciting," Nancy sang maternally. "I know how much energy you put into decisions."

Carol couldn't help but notice how Nancy could turn almost anything into a compliment. The idea that Carol put an abundance of energy into decision-making was code because the truth was, she obsessed over everything. She skipped meals. Stayed up brainstorming all night. Chased ideas until she couldn't see straight. But Nancy would never say that even if it was true. Her dear friend put soft edges around everything. The same way she childproofed her home all those years ago. Her words were now the squishy pads around the stone fireplace hearth, the gates at the bottom of the stairs.

"I did give this choice a lot of thought," Carol began as she nervously fiddled with her fork.

"But?" Nancy looked thoroughly concerned. "What happened?"

"She doesn't want to accept the award. I've literally built an entire strategy around her, and she's not interested. In a couple of days, I need to bring her before the board and show them how special she is." Carol pulled in her bottom lip and prayed her friend would have some sage advice.

"Why doesn't she want to accept the award?" Nancy asked, her brows crashing down with concern. "That's not normal, right?"

"It's not." Carol exhaled. "Apparently, there are things in her past she doesn't want to draw attention to. I sent Terrance out there to talk with her and hopefully get her to come back here. I don't know if he'll be able to. I have so very much riding on this."

Nancy shook her head. "You have time to move on. There must be hundreds of authors you could select. It might be late notice, but I am sure you have a plan B."

"Of course, there are other authors, but Marta is absolutely perfect for the vision I have for the foundation. She's the change we need. I can't—"

Nancy interrupted. "You can. You just don't want to. It's possible to select someone else, right? And if she's concerned about her past, then maybe you should be as well. I'm sensing a lot of red flags here. Like enough to make into a beautiful scarf you can wear in the unemployment line."

"It's not like that," Carol groaned, but in truth, she didn't know what exactly was keeping Marta from getting on that plane. "I think it's imposter syndrome and lack of confidence in her work. The book is stellar."

"I bet," Nancy said flatly. "And I have no doubt she's wonderful. You've gotten where you are because you have tenacity. But now that you're in the job you've always wanted, you need to be nimble. I say this with great love for you, but this is one of those moments where you have to let go."

"Let go?" Carol asked, closing her eyes for a long beat as if she was trying to decipher a long-forgotten language.

"I was there for the worst of it with your mother. I understand you're wired to think that letting go is the same as giving up. It's not. You can give something all you've got and still need to change direction. Your career is important to you, so preserve it."

"Right," Carol said, trying her best to open her mind to the idea that she may not be able to make this work.

"I knew it." A crass voice rattled her brain as a hand

came crashing down on their table. The silverware clanked, and the wine glasses nearly spilled over.

"Eli?" Carol asked, shock painting her face enough to alarm Nancy. The name would be familiar to her friend. She and Nancy had sat in this very restaurant commiserating about Eli and his uncouth behavior.

"Can we help you?" Nancy boomed in her teacher's voice. "We're in the middle of a conversation."

Eli smelled of expensive Scotch and old cigars. His eyes, always watery, were extra glazed over. Carol had had the displeasure of seeing him inebriated at plenty of events over the years. His sloppy speech always gave him away.

"I knew you were a lezbo," he announced in a raspy whisper as he pointed back and forth between Carol and Nancy. "No one can bust balls like a woman who never touches them."

Carol rolled her eyes. "I don't know if you're aware of this, Eli. Actually, I'm sure you're not, but calling someone gay isn't an insult. If you were trying to be offensive, besides the terrible language you used, you missed the mark."

"Don't get all human resources on me. You and your girlfriend are out in public. I can say what I want. If you don't like it, maybe you two can kiss, and she'll make it better."

Excuse me," Nancy said, shoving her seat back and standing to her full yet unintimidating height. "I don't know who you think you're speaking to that way."

"Oh, relax." Eli chuckled. That was always his go-to

response. The words he kept in the chamber to shoot at anyone who protested his filth. "I'm joking. At best, Carol goes both ways. That's how she got this far. You can't be picky when you're climbing the corporate ladder."

Nancy cut her hand through the air. "You will shut your mouth and leave this restaurant now before I call the police, you washed-up, has-been, power-hungry chauvinistic dinosaur." Her finger was pointing dangerously close to his face, and Carol sat stunned at the outburst. She was not surprised by Eli's behavior, but Nancy was ferocious and impressive.

"He's not worth it," Carol finally hummed out as she waved a hand dismissively in Eli's direction. The man hated being ignored and shelved like an old can of beans. "The trash will take itself out."

"You have no idea what is coming for you," Eli said, spit flying recklessly from his thin lips. "Just wait."

Carol plastered on a look of amusement. "You've already been digging around, Eli. There's no dirt on me. There's no storm coming my way." She fluttered her hands around and made her voice into a mock ghostly sound to show she was not afraid. "Things are changing. You're not needed nor, for that matter, wanted anymore. Deal with it."

"I don't need dirt on you," Eli laughed. "You aren't some powerful guy I can control with a few pictures of his mistress in an envelope. People already don't like you. They think you're a shrill, ball-busting banshee. I don't need a bulldozer to push you over the edge. Enough people want to see you fall. A light breeze will do it."

Nancy leaned back. "Can that light breeze not be from your mouth because I don't have a hazmat suit ready for that toxic waste. Men like you love to tell women like Carol that she's unlikable. Too loud. Too bossy. Guess what, we're not listening anymore. We're not waiting around for your permission to get things done. Drag your sloppy ass away from this table before I decide you're worth the trouble of breaking a nail over."

Carol laughed and covered her mouth for a second. "I wouldn't try her." She shooed Eli away from the table.

With an angry grunt, Eli took a step back. "You're done, Carol. It's over for you. Everything you think about yourself, all that doubt and uncertainty, you're right. I don't have to convince you this is all going to be over soon enough. You know it already. I'm going to set the dominos up, but you're the one who's going to put it all in motion. Watch your back. A woman like you needs a man like me to teach you a lesson. It's coming."

"Watch my back," Carol said, taking her napkin from her lap and finally standing up just as Nancy had. "Are you threatening me? I need to watch my back?"

Eli was gone before Carol could demand he answer for his words. Though the restaurant was quiet tonight, every pair of eyes in the room were fixed on them.

"Are you all right?" Nancy asked, reaching across the table and taking Carol's trembling hand. "That is the vilest, most disgusting man I have ever had the displeasure of encountering in my life."

"Yes," Carol agreed. She pulled her hand back so she could hide the tremble. "I'm fine. Really. He's just a creep."

"A creep? He threatened you. He intimidated and insulted you. That's not something you should shrug off. You need to report this."

"To who?" Carol laughed, hiding for a moment behind her wine glass as she took a long sip.

"The police. The board. Whoever will listen."

Carol considered her options, and she knew there were not many. "If I go to the board, Eli will slither his way out of this too. If I go to the police, it's his word against mine."

"No, it's not," Nancy declared. "I was here too. Plenty of other people heard what he said."

"It won't look good for me," Carol said in a hushed voice. "It will look like I can't handle myself. I can't afford to undermine people's confidence in me at the moment."

Nancy pressed her palms to the table. "I am utterly flabbergasted," she admitted. "I wanted to hit that man. I am not a violent woman."

"You were amazing." Carol smiled. "You really gave it to him."

With a slight blush, Nancy fanned her hand toward her warm cheeks. "I am so riled up right now. I don't like the idea of letting this go."

"I'm not letting it go," Carol said as she straightened her back. "The only way to get rid of a man like Eli is to give him enough rope to hang himself. I know how to do my job. It kills him that I'm in charge. The best thing I can do is keep excelling and watch him implode."

"Ugh," Nancy grimaced. "I say let's stop being the bigger people and just slash his tires already."

Carol let out her loud laugh and covered her face. "I'm playing the long game," she promised. "But if it doesn't work, that will be plan B."

CHAPTER EIGHTEEN

Carol

The hug goodbye was a little longer tonight. Carol knew the instant she was in her own car, she'd flood with emotion. The hug was the last thing anchoring her to some strength. As Nancy pulled away in her vehicle, Carol mustered a big smile and an overly animated wave goodbye.

Then the hair on the back of her neck stood up, and the knot in her stomach tightened. She moved quickly to her car and locked the door the second she had it closed. Logically, she believed Eli was not a clear and present threat to her physically. Or at least that's what she kept telling herself. The man had held an influential position at many large companies over the years. He was angry. He was drunk. But that didn't mean he'd be sitting in the back-seat of her car waiting for revenge. Telling herself that didn't keep her from checking the vehicle thoroughly just in case.

It was tedious to be a woman sometimes. The messages were endless and ominous. Hold your keys like weapons. Don't park in a dark area. Learn self-defense. There was this ever-present boogeyman and horror music theme song in the minds of women.

By the time she parked in her spot and made her way to the front door of her building, Carol's heart was thud-ding. Her palms were sweating. Did Eli know where she lived? Would he show up here? The next time this happened, would she be ready? What if she was alone? The questions barreled toward each other like out-of-control train cars.

When a hand touched her shoulder, it was as if the trains finally collided. Some strange yelp sprang from her mouth, and she jumped forward awkwardly.

"Carol," Robert said, catching her arm gently and righting her. "Are you all right?"

"Robert?" she asked, her hand flying to her heart. "What are you doing here?" They were just outside the lobby of her apartment building, and she couldn't think of a logical reason for him to be passing by.

"I wanted to make sure you were all right."

"She doesn't look all right," a young woman standing a foot behind Robert said. Her blonde hair was long and tied into a braid over her left shoulder. She was a fresh-faced beauty with long lashes and supple skin. Before Carol could wrangle the feeling, she formed a bit of jealousy. Robert was out on a date.

"I'm sorry," Carol said again, her hand upon her tired forehead now. "Why are you here?"

"I was having dinner around the corner, and I got a call from someone I used to work with. He said Eli had just made some big scene at a restaurant. Apparently, he was fighting with a couple of women."

"Oh dear," Carol said, wincing with embarrassment.

"My friend thought it might be you he was fighting with. I was going to call and make sure you were all right, but we were right around the corner, so we just came by."

"How do you know where I live?" Carol asked, trying to make sense of it all.

"You told me you lived in this building when we were at that art show last year. I wasn't completely certain you still lived here."

The young woman sighed. "I told you it was weird just showing up. You scared her half to death."

"I know, honey," Robert said, glancing at them both apologetically. "It just sounded like Eli really crossed the line, and I wanted to see you."

"I'm fine," Carol said, trying to sound convincing. "It was quite the scene, but I was out with a friend, and she certainly put Eli in his place. It's nothing."

"She's shaking," the young woman pointed out. "You don't seem like you're fine. Should we maybe go get a tea or something? I think there's a coffee shop not far from here."

Why this young woman was inviting Carol to be a third wheel on their date was baffling. But the girl was kind and had a charming smile.

"No, it's late," Carol sighed. "You two go back to whatever you were doing. I'll deal with the Eli thing tomorrow."

"Carol, I want to know exactly what he said," Robert insisted. "He does not get to show up somewhere and make a scene. You don't deserve that."

"Dad," the young woman said, placing her hand on Robert's shoulder. "We've intruded on her. We should go."

His daughter. This lovely young lady was not Robert's date, but rather his daughter. That shouldn't have changed anything, but it did. "You haven't intruded." Carol rushed the words out before Robert could agree to leave. "I don't think I want to go to the coffee shop but would you two like to come in for tea?"

"Sure," Robert's daughter said exuberantly. "I'm Tasha, by the way. Sorry my father didn't introduce me properly. He's been a wreck since he got that call. He was worried about you."

Robert croaked out a defense. "It's not that I thought you couldn't handle yourself. I know you can. I was just floored that Eli would pull something like that. The friend who called me didn't hear specifically, but he could tell it was not good."

Carol waved for them both to follow her through the lobby and up the elevator toward her sixth-floor apartment. The cleaning service had come earlier that day, so she wasn't worried about walking into a mess. Admittedly if

Robert had shown up alone, she would not have invited him up. Having his daughter join them made it all the more appropriate.

Carol unlocked her front door and showed them both to the sitting room. Her apartment was luxurious by most standards, but her mother would not have approved. Like most of Carol's choices, this place went against the vision of a proper woman's life, according to her mother. An apartment was not a home in her mother's eyes. But Carol felt happy here.

"I do appreciate you coming to check on me. I won't bother pretending it didn't faze me. It certainly caught me off guard and what he said was unsettling." Carol recounted the threats and the insults as she poured the tea and made a tray of accoutrements to share.

"What a pig," Tasha said, nodding politely as she took her teacup and saucer into her lap. "I am so sorry that happened to you. That generation of men has no idea what is going to happen to them. We are not tolerating that kind of behavior anymore."

Carol loved the fire in Tasha's words. She really hoped the women who came after her would have better experiences than she'd had over the years.

Robert took his tea and smiled at his daughter. "She's the reason I came to see you the day you tossed Eli out of the boardroom. I've been a bystander for far too many things in my life, trying to keep the peace and advance my career. But those days are done. If I was at a bar and heard a man speaking like that, I'd have him begging for mercy in the parking lot. The boardroom shouldn't be a place where they are suddenly exempt."

"Good job, Dad," Tasha said and offered him a little wink. "Carol, what do you want to do about Eli?"

"I told my friend earlier at dinner that the best thing to do with a man like Eli is let him take himself down. I'm going to keep doing my job and doing it well; he won't be able to stand that. What he's doing will catch up with him eventually."

Tasha sipped her tea, and then her face went slack with sadness. "Carol, I won't tell you what you should do in this situation, but if you want my opinion—"

"I'd love your opinion." Carol was perhaps only appeasing the girl, but she envied the energy all the same. This new generation was not settling for the same garbage she had, and if there was advice to be given, she'd be open to it.

"Eli threatened you. It was a poorly veiled threat intended to intimidate you. When someone says to watch your back, it's physical. He came into your space tonight. How did he know you were there? Did he follow you? Does he know where you live or what gym you go to? You can't underestimate what a man with a damaged ego and fading virility will do when losing power. You said it yourself. He doesn't have any dirt to dig up on you. He'll be desperate. You have to ask yourself if tonight was the end of something or just the start of it."

Perhaps it was the passion with which she spoke or the flash of possessed anger she'd seen in Eli's eyes, but Carol began to weep. She didn't blubber or gasp or whine, but tears rolled down her cheeks. "I doubt it's the end of something. I don't want to believe Eli is dangerous, but I can't ignore what he did or said tonight."

"And you shouldn't," Robert agreed. He and his daughter were sitting on the couch. Carol was perched on the end of her wingback chair. They were both looking expectantly at her as if Carol might formulate some plan or give some battle cry they could both rally behind. She had nothing.

"I'll have to sleep on it," she offered anticlimactically. "I don't know exactly what I'll do. Reporting things like this could undermine my authority in the office. It could make me look weak."

"Not anymore," Tasha replied proudly. "We've upended that crap. Now you're a hero if you speak your truth and hold people like Eli accountable. Likely there will be a long line of women sharing the same kinds of stories about him."

Tasha 's Pollyanna perspective was endearing, but Carol wasn't there yet. She'd smashed glass ceilings and made a space for herself in all sorts of places. But the idea of announcing Eli's bad behavior in some formal way still felt too lofty. Too dangerous. It was not a fear of Eli that kept her from speaking out. Speaking out would change how people saw her. Tasha was right. Things were changing, but had they changed enough?

Carol grew up in a generation where lousy behavior correlated directly with affection. It was familiar from the playground to the dorm room to hear, "he must really like you." That covered everything from a pulled pigtail to a persistent request for a date. Speaking out made you ungrateful, unlikable, and many times unemployable. Women of Carol's generation knew that even if you won the battle, you'd likely lose the war. The progress had been incredible. But she wasn't ready to test that water. Not unless she absolutely had to.

Blowing on her tea, Carol sipped it thoughtfully. "Thank you for the pep talk, Tasha. Tell me about yourself. Are you in school?"

"I'm taking the bar exam in a month," Tasha said, sounding pensive. "It's been brutal, but I'm in the home stretch."

"Law," Carol exclaimed. "I always wanted to go into that field, but I didn't have the discipline for the bar exam when I was younger. I applaud your perseverance."

Robert beamed with pride. "She's been arguing with me for the last twenty-six years. It started with potty training and never stopped."

"Dad," Tasha grumbled. "Can we make it through one conversation with anyone that doesn't come back to this?"

"You were a spirited child," Robert continued. "I started the lawyer narrative decades ago. I'd like some credit for your success."

"You get credit, Dad, and the tuition bill." Tasha grinned and rolled her eyes. "And I promise to have dinner with you after I win my first case."

"Win or lose," Robert said, patting Tasha's leg. "You can always come home for dinner."

Carol watched with delight at this new side of Robert. She'd seen him effectively run the boardroom and navigate social gatherings flawlessly. Seeing him as the doting dad was a new layer.

The next hour was a pleasant conversation that significantly ratcheted down Carol's raw nerves. They spoke about funny family vacations and corporate achievements. Silly stories and long-forgotten memories of encounters she and Robert had over the years.

"Dad," Tasha said, looking at her phone to check the time, "I'm going to order a rideshare and meet my friends."

"Is it that time already?" Robert asked in surprise as he checked his watch. "I'll go with you. I don't want you hopping in a car by yourself right now. Once you're with Cara and Molly, I'll be on my way."

Tasha shook her head. "Dad, you're usually asleep by now. You're not driving me thirty minutes to the bar and then driving back home. I can take a rideshare. I know how to be safe."

"I know you do," Robert said, already standing and pulling his keys out of his pocket. "But it's late, and I won't feel good until I know you're with your friends like you planned. And"—he glanced at Carol—"I don't go to bed this early."

"You do," Tasha laughed. "I don't want you driving back this late on your own."

Robert was about to dismiss her argument when Carol

stepped in. "You live like ten minutes from here, right Robert?"

He nodded, and his brows came together in confusion.

"I'll go along for the ride, keep him company on the way home, and then he's close to home when we get back." Carol rose to her feet and put her tea back on the tray.

"Are you sure?" Robert asked with a wide smile. "I don't want to trouble you. I've already barged in on your night."

"You can't ruin an already ruined night. It can only get better." Carol moved toward her coat. "I'm definitely still too worked up for bed. A ride will do me some good."

Tasha shot her father a funny look and then stifled a smile. "Then we have a plan."

As they made their way down to Robert's car, Carol fought the weight of the "rules" weighing down on her. She was always so cautious. So calculated. Was this appropriate? Should she be riding around this time of night with a board member and his daughter? How would it look?

At this point, as she hopped in the front seat of Robert's car, it was already too late to answer those questions. The night was dark. The car was warm. The laughter and conversation were easy. And soon, they'd be alone. His daughter, the buffer and safe chaperone, would step out of the car, squeal, and hug her friends. She'd leave behind two adults with similar interests and an apparent attraction who could not act on it.

That's when the real questions would need to be answered.

CHAPTER NINETEEN

Marta

Marta was impressed with the restaurant Terrance had found. It was thirty minutes outside of town and incredibly quaint, yet trendy. The old farmhouse had been converted into a restaurant and was run by a couple. Both were chefs. Young. Tattooed. Bouncing with energy. Marta loved it.

"This place is great. I didn't know it even existed. I always complain there is nowhere good to go." Marta straightened the silverware near her plate and pulled open the small menu.

"Sometimes you need a fresh set of eyes. Every town has some charm to it. You simply have to look harder in some places."

"Very hard here." Marta laughed. "But you were right. You found a great spot."

"Hopefully, I'll be right about more things. You just have to give me a chance." Terrance had a playful smile, and she found herself longing to see it more often. The appearance of that dimple was like the groundhog signaling something better. Something promising was coming.

"If I were to go to California with you"—she held up a finger to caution him—"a big *if*, I need to know what exactly this meeting with the board will be like. I'm picturing it like one of those fancy dog shows where they'll check my teeth and make me prance around."

Terrance choked out a laugh and banged his knee on the table accidentally. She liked the idea of getting a visceral response from him. Knocking him off his center.

"That's not at all what it would be like. You'd just come in and meet each board member, and they might have some questions for you about your book. By then, they will have all read it and I'm sure loved it."

"But what do they want me to be?" Marta asked, the silliness making way for her anxiety. "Believe it or not, I've never been in a boardroom. This is the nicest outfit I own, and I cut my own bangs. You and Carol might be kind enough to overlook all the things I'm not, but I don't think they will."

"If you want to, you can shop in California. You can get a new hairstyle or whatever you want."

"I don't want that," Marta replied quickly. "I hate the

idea of rags to riches. A fairy-tale transformation is not what I'm looking for. I'd like to maybe have something I feel comfortable wearing, but I don't want to completely change myself."

"You shouldn't," Terrance agreed. "You're perfect the way you are. Let your writing and your talent represent you. There are definitely some pretentious jerks on the board, but also some really great people. Carol won't let them push you around. You don't have to put on a show or do anything you don't want to do."

"Why do I feel like you're making promises you can't possibly keep? If you think Carol plans to let me, in this uncultured and unpolished form, waltz into her board-room, you're foolish." Marta pretended to scan the menu as she held her breath.

"I know Carol," Terrance asserted. "She's not like that. She doesn't care about manicures and trendy haircuts."

"She literally has both of those things." Marta raised a challenging brow. "Don't oversell this to me. I have a pretty good idea of what Carol wants from me. Maybe we should stop pretending."

"I don't follow," Terrance said, leaning back and looking defensive. "Carol is giving you an opportunity."

"Out of the goodness of her heart?" Marta sniped. "People don't do that. I've given a lot of thought to why Carol really wants me to take this award."

"Could you please stop saying it like she's offering you arsenic? It's a prestigious award given to just one person every year. She read your book and selected you."

"Why?"

"Because she found you to be a rising star in the industry. She sees your potential."

"I'm a means to an end," Marta explained, feeling a bit sorry for Terrance. Carol was clearly either his friend or his hero of some kind. She hated to diminish that with the truth. "Carol is new to her role, and she wants to make a name for herself. I'm the poor girl from the other side of the tracks who she can save and hold up as an example. A pet project. A moral token she can cash in."

"Where is this coming from?" Terrance asked, his brows crashing suddenly into each other as he set his jaw. "I've understood every bit of your apprehension about accepting the award so far, but this is way off base. Carol isn't treating you like a charity case. You're a stellar writer, and you deserve the opportunity. If you'd accept that as fact, you'd let this go."

Marta pondered that for a moment. But there was duplicity in the truth. "Maybe I am good enough to be selected, and maybe Carol sees a way to capitalize on that. But trust me, the second I say yes, she'll want to change me into something I am not to actually make this work."

"She's taking a big risk on you," Terrance argued.

"A big risk?" Marta chuckled. "I'm taking the risk. You heard everything I've put on the line. If this doesn't work out for Carol, what really happens?"

"She could lose her job," Terrance explained with a long exhale. "You don't think that's a big deal?"

"Do they take all her money? Do all her degrees go

away? She doesn't get another job? Ever?" Marta waved her hand as if magically making those things disappear. "I'm barely hanging on. If this doesn't work out, if just one of those things I've been running from catches up with me, it would break me. I'm the one taking a risk."

"A risk for success," Terrance said, this time more gently. "A risk for a better life."

Marta began trying to think through her escape plan. She could pull up her phone and take a rideshare back to her place. This restaurant was way too upscale to argue in. Her fight or flight response was sharp, and this was an easy choice. "I'm sure it's easy for you to assume how you would handle all of this."

Terrance nodded as Marta took out her phone. "You're right," he said thoughtfully. "I trust Carol, but it's not like I can just magically transfer that feeling over to you. You have to decide for yourself how you feel about her."

"What?" Marta asked, putting her phone down on the table for a moment. "What are you trying to do?" This felt like a trick or trap, and she was determined to be alert to either.

"I agree with you. We don't have the same lived experiences. I can't just insist you take my word for something. I was defensive about Carol because I care about her, and I want to believe that she wouldn't do what you're saying."

"I'm confused," Marta sputtered out. "We're fighting." She pointed back and forth between them and waited for him to explain.

"Fighting?" Terrance smirked playfully. "Disagreeing,

maybe. But then I took a second to try to see it from your point of view, and you're right. If Carol is saying you're qualified for this, then it would be wrong to try to change you to be more palatable for the board. You shouldn't need some movie montage transformation to be what the people in that room deem acceptable. I don't believe Carol would do that, but the most I can do is promise you that if she does, I'll be the first one in the room to speak up."

Marta felt her senses tingling. There had to be something wrong here. Some sucker punch coming. "What are you trying to do?"

"I don't follow," Terrance said, looking apologetic. "I'm talking. We're talking to each other."

"But we were fighting, and then you just got all calm and reasonable. Are you trying to trick me?" Marta nibbled on her lip as she scanned his face for some kind of tell.

"Trick you?" Terrance chuckled. "I took a beat and realized I was overreacting and not thinking about how you must feel. Then I stopped being so defensive."

"People do that?" Marta asked, crinkling up her nose as she thought it over. "I didn't realize that was actually a thing. My people, we just start arguing and fight our way out of it."

"What did you think was going to happen? Were we going to throw drinks in each other's faces?"

Marta lifted up her phone and flashed him the screen. "I was opening the app to try to order a ride out of here."

"Really?" Terrance asked, shock painting his face.

"Mostly because I figured this place was too nice to toss this drink in your face. So I'd just storm out instead."

"Well, please don't." Terrance leaned in across the table. "I'm sorry the idea of talking something out is so foreign to you. That must be a really stressful way to live. Don't get me wrong, I have fiery conversations, and I can get heated, but I always try to settle it."

"Interesting." Marta laughed.

"I'm not an anomaly, Marta. There is a whole world full of people who can deescalate rather than just ratchet it up. I hope you meet a lot of them."

"Ray is a bit like that, but not totally. Heather is super emotional, and it can be hard to calm her down if she's worked up. My family and most of the people I grew up with are all the same. Once the fuse is set, the explosion is guaranteed. It's what makes the prospect of talking to my brother tomorrow so scary. I can't see a single scenario where it doesn't blow up."

Terrance nodded thoughtfully as though he were trying to develop a solution. "Will that be how you decide if you come with me back to California? Are you waiting to see what your brother says?"

"No," Marta admitted. "Once my brother knows the truth about my ex-husband, there will be no unringing that bell. Whether I stay or go, I won't control how he reacts. And he wants me to go."

"He does?" Terrance beamed with optimism. "That's great."

"My brother is tired. He's working himself half to

death, and he wants one of us to have something better. He thinks I'm the one with the best shot at it."

"You are," Terrance agreed. "Do you think you'll come with me then?"

Marta drew her hand up to her forehead and swept her bangs away from her eyes. "I still don't know. I want to."

Terrance didn't push her any further. "Have you decided what you want for dinner?"

"Wait," Marta put her elbow on the table and rested her chin in her hand. "We just eat dinner now? The fight is over?"

"It can be," Terrance offered with a shrug. "Do you still want dinner?"

"I do," she replied through a wide smile. "It's just strange to me. I thought this would end a different way."

"It doesn't really have to end at all." Terrance blinked slowly at her, and she couldn't ignore the seduction in his voice. "I'm not going to blow up on you, Marta. We don't have to fight. I want you to succeed."

Those declarations should have been implied. It should have been completely normal to leave them unsaid. But hearing them out loud, watching the way his expression remained genuine, made her head spin. "Thanks," she croaked out awkwardly.

"I'm getting the sea bass, I think," Terrance replied casually. "Do you want some wine?"

"Always," Marta giggled. "What else are we going to talk about now?"

"Tell me about your next book."

Marta pulled the menu to her chest, leaned back in her chair, and basked in the interest and attention. She wanted to ask again if he was serious, but it would be redundant now. As frightening as it was to believe his intentions were good, she felt compelled to. There was still plenty of opportunity for things to all go wrong, but for tonight, over dinner, she'd pretend that wasn't the case.

CHAPTER TWENTY

Marta

The familiar sensation of dread wreaked havoc on Marta. There was a tingling in her scalp and a tightening vise in her stomach. The lump in her throat felt big enough to protrude, and her palms were slick and clammy. It was bizarre to realize this had been her default setting for most of her life. It wasn't until she moved away that she had some level of reprieve from the physical manifestation of fear. She was in no way cured of it. Fear reared its head plenty, but it wasn't her constant state of being anymore.

"Your brother just pulled up," Ray announced calmly as he nudged Marta's shoulder with his. "It'll be fine."

Marta couldn't decide if she envied their ignorance or pitied them for it. There was nothing fine about the situation. The best-case scenario was begging her brother not to throw his life away to make amends for what had happened. The odds were not in her favor.

Heather flitted around the kitchen, trying unsuccessfully to make the extra chairs at the table fit more naturally. They'd be squeezed in tight, but it didn't matter to her. When the emotional fireworks started, it wouldn't matter where they were sitting.

"Hey," Glenn said, fidgeting as he stepped into the living room. His wife was tucked in behind him, looking equally uncomfortable.

"Hi, Glenn." Heather beamed as she closed in on them like a lioness stalking its prey. "Come in, come in. It's Samantha, right?"

"Sammy," she corrected as she slipped out of her coat and handed it to Ray, who was waiting anxiously to take it. "Thank you for inviting us to dinner." It sounded as though she'd practiced, and it made Marta smile. She, too, rehearsed such things.

Heather waved off the idea that it was any trouble at all. "Thank you for coming all this way. I know it's a long ride for you guys. I hope our cooking makes it worthwhile."

"The hotel room didn't hurt either," Glenn joked. "You really didn't need to do that, kid." He jutted his chin out at Marta and winked.

Marta, who hadn't uttered a word yet, finally spoke. "You can't drive three hours home after dinner. Don't get too excited. It's not a great hotel."

"I'm staying there," Terrance said with a shrug. "It's not that bad. The people are nice."

"Introductions," Heather said, tapping her head as though she were absentminded. "I'm Heather. This is my boyfriend, Ray. We're Marta's best friends."

"I'm Terrance," he said, extending his hand for a shake. "I work for the foundation that has selected Marta for a prestigious award. I'm trying to convince her to leave for California in the morning so we can get the ball rolling. Maybe you can help me with that."

"She's going," Glenn said, releasing Terrance's hand and pointing at his sister. "You've got a shot to actually make something of yourself, and you aren't blowing that."

"Agreed," Ray said as he handed out drinks. "She's getting on that plane in the morning."

"So this is like a celebration dinner?" Sammy asked, still looking skeptical. It was customary in Marta's opinion to have some level of doubt when coming into a new situation. Some people sat forward and leaned into something new. Where Marta came from, it was much more common to sit back, fold your arms across your chest, and narrow your eyes, waiting for the bad news or the catch.

"Yes," Heather announced as she clapped her hands together. "We are celebrating tonight."

Sammy eyed Glenn. "Maybe we should tell them our good news too." She flashed her crooked smile, and her teased-up hair bounced as she giggled.

"Good news?" Marta asked, scanning her brother's

face for the familiar nuance she'd learned to map out. He looked cautiously happy, which was significant for him.

"Sure," he said, waving his hand and suggesting Sammy be the one to share with everyone.

"We found out yesterday; I'm pregnant," she sang, bringing her lacquered long fingernails up to her mouth.

Marta knew her family line would likely continue, but now that it was happening, she felt its weight. What traits would this child inherit from the damaged genes that plagued the Leducs? Could Glenn do it better? Would nurture win out over nature? She knew if she had all these worries, Glenn was likely experiencing them too.

As they did most of their lives, they exchanged a knowing look. This siblings' mind-reading occurred only when they were sure no one else in the room would be able to understand what they were feeling.

"That's amazing," Marta finally said, knowing everyone in the room would be expecting her to pull her brother and sister-in-law in for a hug. That would make sense—the social norm. But Glenn and Marta had only really hugged a few times as adults, and that was mostly when terrible things happened. The celebration of good news was fragile, and they grew up believing it was relatively easy to jinx your way out of good things.

"So no wine for me," Samantha said, handing the glass back to Ray. "I'll just take a soda if you have one."

"It looks like the Leduc kids have a lot to celebrate," Terrance said, sounding upbeat. "Congratulations."

"Dinner's ready," Heather said as the timer in the

kitchen started to beep. "I can't take any credit for it. Ray is the chef. But I cleaned up after him."

"Smells great," Glenn said, and Marta felt suddenly proud of her brother. They'd never done this. It was grown-up type business. Their socializing together in the last five years had been the occasional smoky bar post, a family funeral, or a holiday encounter where the Leduc brood descended on a relative's home with potluck dishes in hand and did their usual reminiscing and roasting each other. This was a dinner party. Friends. A decent meal. Good news.

When they settled in around the table, it was tight but balanced. The six of them looked like paired-off couples even though Marta and Terrance were certainly not. The conversation was easy, considering they knew hardly anything about each other. They talked about what they did for work and found common ground arguing about whose town was worse. Terrance was the odd man out, not talking much about California and only briefly discussing what he did for work. It was a smart choice considering he likely made in a year what the rest of them did in five.

Glenn finished his meal and slid the plate slightly away as he put his arm around Sammy. "I'm glad you decided to go to California," he said, nodding his head. "I would have never let you live it down if you hadn't."

"I haven't really said I was going yet," Marta admitted, and she rolled her eyes. A grumble of disagreement crossed the table at her.

"Don't start with that again," Glenn said, tossing his

napkin across the table at her. She caught it and gave him a look to behave.

"Well, I talked to you about why I'm worried about doing this," Marta began, and everyone around the table who knew what was about to happen fell silent. "But there is something else keeping me from going."

"Stupidity?" Glenn chuckled. He never minced words.

"Before I tell you," Marta began, holding up both her hands as if to tell him to stay put, "I need you to promise you won't overreact."

Glenn's face fell suddenly. "Has anything good ever come after that statement?"

Sammy lit up. "Are you pregnant too?"

"No," Marta cut back quickly.

Heather cut in with a wry smile. "It would be an immaculate conception. She's like a nun since she moved here."

"Good," Glenn said. "That's what every guy wants to hear about his baby sister."

"I haven't really dated anyone seriously since Keith," Marta said. She was looking for any bridge to lead her back to what she had to say. "And when I tell you why, I need you to please stay calm."

"Marta," Glenn barked, his face looking flushed. "Do we need to talk in private? What's going on?"

Marta pulled in her bottom lip and then released it. "You have a good job and clean record, Glenn," she began. "Now you have a child on the way. Please keep that in mind when I tell you why Keith and I divorced."

"He cheated?" Glenn asked, tilting his head to the side. "I figured maybe that was it. You hit the road so quickly after."

"There are going to be other people in town you're not going to be happy with," Marta said quietly. "Just don't overreact."

"Spit it out," Glenn demanded, his hand curling into a fist on the table. "You're freaking me out now."

"I had a restraining order against him," she blurted out. "We fought a lot, and sometimes it got to be too much. I knew I had to leave him, and if I stayed in town after they arrested him, he'd never leave me alone."

"He was arrested? Restraining order?" Glenn shook his head and dropped his arm down from Sammy's shoulder. "I didn't hear about any of this. What do you mean you fought a lot?"

"I asked Louis not to tell you. He was the one who arrested Keith the last time and helped me with the restraining order."

"Louis? Louis Magnus? My best friend since the third grade?"

"I know," Marta said, putting a hand on her hot cheek. "This is a lot of information, but I had my reasons for keeping it private. I knew if someone told you what was happening, you'd have beat the hell out of Keith."

"At a minimum," Glenn said, closing his eyes for a long beat. "Are you saying he hit you? Is that what happened? Specifically."

This was precisely how she assumed it would go.

Glenn wouldn't be pacified or distracted. He'd want the details because they would act as kindling to start the blaze he intended to set. He'd burn it all down.

"It doesn't matter," Marta said. "Keith is out of my life. I left him. You said it yourself last time we talked. It's been two years. I don't have to worry about him."

Sammy slapped her hand to the table. "He has to worry about us." There was a flash in her blue eyes. "That son of a—"

"You're pregnant," Heather said, looking baffled. "It's not like it makes sense to just go beat a guy up. What does that prove?"

"You wouldn't understand," Glenn said, pushing his chair back and standing. "Thank you for dinner. It was great. We have to go."

"Hang on," Terrance said, standing up quickly. "Marta is on the verge of something life-altering. Something a man like Keith would hate for her. The absolute best revenge she has is being a success despite what he did."

"You have a sister?" Glenn asked, reaching for his coat on the hook by the door.

Terrance hesitated as though this was a question that had caught him off guard. "I do."

"And you'd let this stand?" He raised a challenging brow and waited.

"I would listen to what my sister wanted because if I didn't, I wouldn't be any better than the guy who was hurting her. I know it's tempting to go be the hammer and make this guy the nail but, in the end, you'll be hurting Marta."

"How?" Sammy asked. Her expression made it obvious she was unconvinced.

Terrance continued, his voice calm and tempered. "There will be a spotlight on Marta. It's the downside of success. Right now, Keith is the bad guy. You can't go and muddy that water. It'll be bad enough for Marta if someone digs up the restraining order or confronts her about her marriage. If you suddenly have assault charges against the guy, it becomes his word against yours."

Glenn dropped his arm and tucked a hand into his pants pocket. "Are you saying I should let this go unchecked? He gets to hurt my sister and not answer for it?"

Ray cleared his throat. "He was arrested."

"And then what?" Glenn asked, turning toward Marta, already seeming to guess the answer. "He didn't go to court."

"I dropped the charges," she admitted, not letting her voice become small or apologetic. "You don't get to judge the choices I made to keep myself safe. If I had pursued the charges, Keith would have never left me alone."

Glenn's angry expression subsided for a moment and was replaced with sadness. "You should have told me. I could have handled it right then and there."

Terrance sidled up to Marta and let out a long breath. "If it were my sister, I'd find a way to get even with the guy that couldn't come back and hurt either of us. Something he never saw coming. Smashing his face in might feel good at the moment, but there are better ways to ruin a man."

Everyone was silent as they fixed their eyes on Terrance. "Damn," Ray said, breaking the quiet of the moment. "That's savage. I want to hear more."

"It takes time and planning," Terrance explained. "And it absolutely can't include anyone going after him. I don't care if you see him in the grocery store and want to knock his head off. If you want some lasting justice, that requires patience."

"What kind of justice?" Glenn asked, rubbing one hand over the knuckles of his other. "I like swift and painful justice."

Marta put her hand to her forehead and sighed. "I want him to pay. But I don't want it to cost us anything. Glenn, we've given enough of our lives to fighting and madness. I was so desperate to get away from our family that Keith seemed like the best solution. Some of this is on me."

Heather was like a mother, one of the good ones, ready to lift the car off her child with sheer will. She swept in and wagged her finger at Marta. "There is no circumstance, no choice, no nothing that makes what happened your fault. A marriage doesn't have to be perfect, but it has to be safe. I don't want to ever hear you talk like that again. Don't give him that kind of power over you anymore. You married Keith, and he hurt you. He's wrong. Hard stop."

"Thanks," Marta said, dipping her head down and trying desperately to try to believe what her friend was saying. It was hard. She'd seen enough people in her life walk straight into heartache and pain like they were magnetically drawn to it. There were signs very early on that Keith was not a healthy man. He was quick to call her out in front of people, not minding how much embarrassment it might cause her. There were rules right from the beginning about what he thought was the right way to do something. Inflexible and crass, Keith wasn't all that different from her own mother. There was something nostalgic about his temper, as twisted as that was to admit.

Glenn bounced from his heels to his toes, and he groaned. "That's why you got us a hotel room and had us come all this way? You wanted me to have time to cool down before I could get to Keith."

Marta moved in a bit. "I wanted you to meet my friends and have dinner with us. We never do stuff like this. I'm still trying to figure out what the hell to do with my life right now, and I wanted you here. I knew if you heard from someone else or the information was leaked somehow, you'd be blindsided, and that wouldn't be fair to you and Sammy."

Glenn pointed at Terrance. "I want to do something. I'll wait, but you better help come up with the idea that brings him down. I want him to pay. I'm not waiting long."

Terrance opened his mouth to speak, but Glenn cut him off. "And my sister is flying across the country with you in the morning. You'd better not screw this up. I might not be a polished guy. I'm not the smartest. But if you hurt her or upset her, I won't have the same patience with you as with Keith. It'll be quick, and it'll be painful. No schemes. No plans. Just retribution. Got it?"

"Loud and clear," Terrance said, holding his hands up disarmingly. "But Marta hasn't even agreed to use the plane ticket with her name on it."

"Marta," Glenn snapped. "You don't get to decide just for you anymore. You've got a niece or nephew on the way." He put his hand on Sammy's stomach. "I'm tired of this family having to lose all the time. I'm tired of us dying and failing. You have a shot. Take it."

"It might bring hellfire down on us," Marta warned, a knowing look spreading across her face. "Think of all the people in town who will want to tear us down and toss our dirty laundry out for the world to see. It'll be ugly."

"It'll be a fight," Glenn corrected. "And that's something we're good at."

Heather, Ray, and Terrance began clearing the table as Marta walked Sammy and Glenn to the door. "I'm really happy for you two," she said, gesturing awkwardly to Sammy's stomach. "You'll be great parents."

"Not likely," Sammy said, nibbling on her bottom lip. "But we're going to try harder than anyone tried for us."

"Bet your ass," Glenn agreed. "Kid," he said, lowering his voice and putting a hand on Marta's shoulder, "Mom's crazy. Dad and Jonah are dead. You're right. People are going to try to tear down your success. We'll worry about that later. Go to that meeting or whatever it is. Show them what it means to be a Leduc."

Marta laughed. "What the hell does it mean?" She raised a brow and rolled her eyes.

"You know exactly what that means. Maybe you've been hung up on all the bad stuff. Lord knows there was a ton of it. But get back to the place where you can remember what our family used to be all about." He pointed his finger at her as if to give an order. "But that's after this meeting. You're about to fly farther than any of us townie idiots have before. See the palm trees or whatever the hell they have out there. They picked you for a reason. Show them they were right."

Marta's eyes welled with tears. It was a strange time to cry. They'd long since given up this kind of show of emotion. At their father's funeral, neither of them shed a tear. They'd become numb to their mother's chaos and nonsense. No insult she hurled or guilt trip she tried impacted them anymore.

Now it felt different for some reason. Maybe it was because the house was full of ordinary people. The conversation she'd been so afraid to have for two years hadn't ended in disaster. Marta was faced with the reality that tomorrow she was getting on a plane and taking a risk she'd never imagined she was capable of. "I'm scared," she mouthed, catching and wiping a few of the tears before they could reach her chin.

Glenn looked rattled by the show of emotion, the declaration of fear and weakness. Sammy spoke for him. "Screw them," she hissed out. "You don't owe them anything. You go take that trip. And no matter what happens, you know you've got a fine life to come back to. It's better than it used to be, right?"

Marta nodded, pulling in a deep breath and patting her eyes completely dry. "Yeah," she agreed. "I am happy here."

Glenn cleared his throat. "You've got this," he asserted. "And don't take any crap from them. I meant what I said. I'll drive cross country and whoop people's asses if I have to."

Laughing, she put her hand to her forehead. "I know you would, but please don't."

Lowering his voice, he whispered, "It's going to be hard for me not to beat the hell out of Keith. You sure you don't want me to?"

"I'm positive," Marta whispered back. "I believe Terrance. If he says we can do it another way, we should give him a chance."

"You like him?" Glenn asked, and Marta could not believe how this night had altered their normal relationship. They were talking to each other in an entirely new way. This was a question he never would have asked, or at least not in a serious way.

"He seems like a good guy." Marta shrugged and looked down toward her shoes.

"Easy on the eyes too," Sammy joked. "I like him. He doesn't set off any of my red flag alarms."

"Well," Glenn joked, "neither did I, so I wouldn't trust your system too well."

"Good point," Sammy agreed as she slipped on her

coat and flipped her hair out over the hood. "Let's get to this hotel so we can actually have time to enjoy it."

"Night," Marta said, still contemplating how to say goodbye. Sammy put an end to her pondering when she pulled Marta in for a hug.

"You two are so weird about hugs."

"Right?" Heather called from the kitchen.

"Glad we could all agree on something tonight," Glenn said as he put his hand up for his sister to slap. A high five was their sarcastic answer to the huggers of the world. "Knock 'em dead, kid."

Marta nodded, and as her brother walked out, she felt something she hadn't in a long time.

Homesick.

CHAPTER TWENTY-ONE

Carol

The lack of control was stifling, like the sensation of nearly suffocating on an airless summer day. Carol was trying to find balance and fighting the urge to call Terrance. The flight would have landed an hour ago, and if all was going well, they'd be coming into her office at any moment.

That he'd been able to get her on the plane at all was a testament to Terrance's skills. They were far from the finish line, but they were still in the race. The spreadsheet on her computer was not nearly interesting enough to keep her from staring at her door. The anticipation was palpable. So much hinged on Marta. Likely too much. Carol understood the pressure she'd thrust upon this young woman, and she regretted that it had to be this way. But change was hard. To alter the fabric of something, you had to bust a few seams.

"Carol," Terrance asked, knocking lightly on her door, "is now a good time?"

There was the initial impulse to pretend to be busy or flustered, but she didn't have the patience for that act. All she wanted to do was jump up and hug Marta, praising her bravery. There would have to be some middle ground. So she stood, straightened the satin scarf around her neck, and smiled widely. "Now's a great time," she announced, sounding a bit too excited.

Terrance stepped into her office first, and Marta trailed in like a child preemptively apologizing for intruding in this very adult space. "Hi," she gulped out with a small wave. "Your office is beautiful."

Carol waved her off. "It's bland and unwelcoming, but I don't have any idea what I want to do with it. There is far too much space, and I don't have the patience to take time to fill it."

Marta only nodded as she stepped in a little farther. Terrance drove the conversation along.

"The flight was bumpy," he announced though no one had asked. "But we made it in one piece. I'm a little disappointed to know you survived without me the last few days."

"Survived maybe, but my email box is a mess, I burned myself making coffee, and I missed two meetings."

"You did?" Terrance asked, his mouth dropping open.

She put her hand to her head and blew out a long

breath. "Yes, but I covered pretty well and rescheduled them. I don't know how you keep up with all of this. It's a circus."

"I've always been good with animals," he teased. "The board meeting is at three. We have a couple of hours. Is there something you want to do prior?"

"Just talk," Carol said, gesturing for Marta to sit down. "Can I get you anything, Marta?"

"No, thank you," she said, whispering and then clearing her throat as she tried again. "No, thank you, I'm fine."

Terrance checked his beeping phone and headed for the office door. "I need to go put out any fires you started while I was gone. Just buzz if you need me."

"You're going?" Marta asked, looking like a child left at kindergarten for the first time. It made Carol swell with pride that Terrance had formed such a bond with Marta already.

"He's right outside that door," Carol explained. "And we'll need him about a hundred times before the meeting."

"Will he be in the meeting?" Marta asked, shifting her attention back to Carol as Terrance stepped out.

Carol took a seat and pondered the question. "Well, he doesn't normally sit in on a board meeting. Would you like him there?"

"Yes," Marta announced, speaking much more confidently this time. "I do want him in the meeting."

"That's no problem," Carol assured her and fluttered

her hand through the air to make it so. "Are you feeling anxious at all?"

"To be honest," Marta began, "I am not really sure how I ended up coming. I told you this was not going to happen. I'm a little shell shocked to be here."

"Is this your first time in California?" Carol asked gently, trying to ensure Marta knew this was nothing more than a friendly chat.

"It is. I flew to Florida once with my neighbors. It was their family vacation, but other than that, I've never been anywhere."

"I'd love to take you around to the sights and sounds of this magnificent city. San Diego is the kind of place you can fall in love with and never want to leave."

Marta only nodded. "The meeting," she stammered. "What are they going to want from me?"

"Well," Carol said, leaning back in her chair and tapping her pen to her chin. "They'll just want to meet you. They've all read the book. I expect they may have a few questions for you, but I would not worry about it being too personal. This is just a friendly meet and greet."

"What am I supposed to say?" Marta shifted in her chair, running her hands along the arms of it fretfully. "Can you tell me what to say to them?"

"Just be you, Marta. You're funny and charming. They'll adore you just as I did at our first meeting. You were so sweet at your book signing. I thoroughly enjoyed watching you engage with your readers. I know it's cliché but just be yourself."

"Myself?" Marta asked, drawing in her bottom lip and nibbling on it. "What if you're wrong? I could get in there, and they don't think it's all endearing that I'm some simple girl from a nowhere town with plenty of baggage who happened to write a book."

"That isn't who you are," Carol corrected. "You're an unpretentious woman who has honed her talent even when the resources of her environment did not foster such things. You've endured hardship and have channeled that adversity into a masterpiece."

Marta's eyes twinkled, and her lips curled up a fraction. "You're impressive. It's no surprise to me that you're in that chair."

"It's no surprise to me that you are in that chair," Carol replied in a cheery sing-song voice. "From this point on, we are in this together. My success is your success and vice versa. Even if you need me to tell you every minute of every day that you are not some damaged, unsalvageable creature but instead a hardy unstoppable force, I will remind you of that until you start to believe it."

"You're those things," Marta said, perking up a bit. "Look at this office. Everyone in this company answers to you. It's not much of a stretch to believe all that about yourself. You are a powerful woman. I'm not."

"I'm going to tell you something that brought me to this moment. To this office. To this place in my career. One day, when I was about your age, I stopped trying to be a beautiful flower. Everyone I knew, all the women in my life, were obsessed with being prim and perfect. Precious and fragile. There was this standard that everyone was trying to attain."

"Not you?" Marta asked, tilting her head to the side.

"I always knew it wasn't for me. Maybe it was because I couldn't live up to the standard. I'm not positive. But I knew I wasn't meant to be a decorative and wilting thing sitting in a vase."

"What are you then?" Marta leaned in. She waited breathlessly for the answer. The same answer Carol waited to hear when she was that age: Is there a place for people like me?

"We are weeds," Carol whispered. Her voice grew louder with every word. "Untilled soil. Direct sun. No sun. It doesn't matter. They pop up in the cracks of the sidewalk. They shoot out of fractured walls. They bust through asphalt. Weeds succeed anywhere and resist eradication. While everyone else is busy trying to be a dahlia or a lily, we're out here being stinging nettles."

Marta chuckled, "What is a stinging nettle?"

"They're a pain in the ass. Prolific and unstoppable. You can't get rid of them. Just like these people can't get rid of us." Carol stood and rounded her desk. "I'm not trying to wax poetic here. But when we first met, I said you and I were not so different. I know our lives have not exactly been similar, but in this, we are the same."

"I'm certainly not a flower," Marta agreed, a slight weight seeming to lift off her shoulders. "I don't think I've ever considered being called a weed a compliment before today. But I can see it now"—she narrowed her eyes and smirked—"I think. So, being a weed is a good thing?"

"Anywhere the weeds grow, there is life." Carol softened her expression. "When we get in that boardroom today, they'll have two of us to deal with."

Her desk phone rang, and she glanced over her shoulder at it as Terrance came back in with a large padded envelope in his hand. "This is marked urgent and doesn't have a return address. Should I leave it here for you?"

Carol reached her hand out and mindlessly began tearing it open. "Marta, what else would you like to do to prepare for the meeting? We should have a good lunch." When her hand slid into the envelope, she knew instantly something was wrong. There was an odor, and the sensation on her fingertips was all wrong. When she peered inside, she shrieked and threw the envelope to the ground.

"What?" Terrance asked, bursting into action and retrieving the envelope from the floor. "Son of a—"

Marta, looking ghost-white, stood, and moved away by another foot. "What is it?

Terrance was inspecting it more closely. "A dead rat," he explained, taking it out of the office and returning a moment later. "Are you all right? I should have opened it myself. I thought it might have been personal."

"It was," Carol crowed, running to her office bathroom to wash her hands thoroughly. She imagined no amount of soap would make her feel clean.

"Who would send you a dead rat in the mail?" Marta

asked, befuddled by it all. "This is some messed up stuff you'd find in my old neighborhood. Does this stuff happen here too?"

"Not usually," Terrance reported somberly. "We know who sent it, however. And I'll deal with him."

"No," Carol chirped as she stepped back out to join them. "He wants a reaction, and he's not getting one out of us."

Marta's tone was sharp and impatient. "Who sent you a dead rat?"

"A tiny man who is foolish enough to believe it would bother me." Carol tipped her chin up. "Let's forget this ever happened. Don't mention it outside of this room. He can sit and wonder if I even received it."

"Is he going to be in the board room?" Marta asked impatiently. "I'd like to know what exactly I'm walking into."

Terrance closed the door to the office and looked at Carol for a long beat. "He won't be in there because the last time he was, Carol asked him to leave. He's a piece of—"

"Work," Carol rushed to complete his sentence. "But he's not your problem. Eli doesn't like me because I replaced him. These little stunts are self-indulgent and performative. It's not worth our time to even worry about."

Marta shook her head. "Where I come from, if someone mails you a dead rat, they're trying to tell you something. And it's not good. I wouldn't be brushing this off."

"I agree," Terrance said firmly. "We should send it to security. Let them try to nail Eli for it."

Carol sank back into her chair, trying not to look flustered. "Just toss it out in the dumpster. We have to stay focused for today. You'll have to trust me on this, Marta. Eli is all talk and no action. He loves getting a rise out of people. We have nothing to be worried about. Now how do we want to spend the next couple of hours?"

"I lost my appetite," Marta admitted. "I don't think I'll want to eat before the meeting. But should I change?" She looked down at her clothes with disdain, and Carol felt the urge to rescue her. The offer of a shopping spree and a whole new wardrobe was tantalizing for Carol to suggest, but she held off.

"I think you look lovely, but if you'd like something to change into, we can arrange that as well."

"I don't have anything like what you're wearing," Marta apologized.

"Good," Carol cackled. "I'm an old woman trying to cover up everything that sagged and wrinkled. You don't need to wear anything like this suit. It's all smoke and mirrors. You would look perfect in anything you wanted to wear."

Twisting her mouth to the side, Marta seemed to give it some genuine thought. "I have no idea what I would wear, but I'd like to feel better in it than I do in this." She tugged at her too-long blouse. "I don't want to do some magic makeover; I just would like to have something that fits."

"We can do that." Carol shrugged, forcing herself to

sound casual. Never having a daughter of her own, something was titillating about the idea of shopping for Marta. "Do you have a color you prefer?"

"Not really," Marta replied. "I like pants. I don't wear skirts."

"I'll leave you two here to sort it out," Terrance said, backing up toward the door. "I'm going to go take care of the rat. Buzz me if you need anything."

When he was out of the room, Marta posed a question. "Do you think he means he's going to throw away the one in the envelope or go find the guy who sent it."

"I don't know," Carol hummed out worriedly. "I know he wants to help me, but with men like Eli, the best you can do is ignore them."

"I know," Marta answered soberly. "You just have to hope something shiny comes along and distracts them long enough for them to move on."

"Yes," Carol said, feeling truly seen in this moment. That was exactly what she'd need to do.

"But I always feel a little bad for the person they move on to. It makes you wonder if maybe you should have tried harder to stop them." Marta feigned a sudden interest in the business books lined on the shelf near her.

"Every time I think I have you figured out, Marta, you surprise me." Carol dipped her head down and looked at her shoes. "You're probably right. Waiting Eli out won't help the next person. Are you suggesting we take him on?"

Marta let out a breathy laugh. "I think I'm about to

have my hands full with people I need to take on. So what's one more?"

"That man mailed me a dead rat," Carol said through a clenched jaw.

"You have his address?" Marta asked, her face lighting with mischief. "You might know how to command a boardroom but I know how to finish the games he's playing."

With a nearly imperceptible nod and a coy smile, Carol agreed. Perhaps Marta was right. If he was going to play dirty, they might need to sling some mud of their own.

CHAPTER TWENTY-TWO

Marta

Emerald green. That was her favorite color. Or it was now that she saw herself wearing the lush pantsuit that fit her perfectly. It seemed laughable that she'd never in her life had a pair of pants that fell to the right spot at her ankle. Being five foot three inches meant everything off the rack was too long. But she'd just never known what to look for.

The sales woman was charming and forgiving of Marta's ignorance. Apparently, she needed a petite size designated as ankle length. She hadn't known her inseam measurement or even what style pants she preferred but somehow when she slid into these, she knew they were perfect. Cinched with a belt for fashion rather than function, the pants were a thick soft fabric. Her beige blouse was form-fitting, not bulky at all under the snug tailored jacket.

Marta had freshened her modest makeup and brushed her hair, willing it smooth with product. Though she was glad she stuck to her principles, a small part of her still daydreamed about the glamourous transformation Carol could have provided. But that would be disingenuous and the board had the right to see her for who she really was. Not some polished fake version.

"Great suit," Terrance said, giving her a thumbs up. "Are you happy with it?"

"I love it," Marta announced excitedly. "I'll be honest: they can keep the award and just let me have this suit."

"It looks great on you," he said in a slightly lower voice. "Do you have a minute for us to talk? I know the meeting is starting soon, but I need to follow up with you on something."

"Is it about the rat?" Marta whispered back as Terrance gestured for her to sit down and closed his office door. "I already talked Carol into letting me get back at that guy. I know how to play dirty for these kinds of things."

"No," Terrance said. The crease over his worried brow and the look of unease on his face made her panicky. As though he were searching for the right words, he gazed around and drew in a deep breath.

"Spit it out," she demanded. "I came all this way. I'm about to go in front of those strangers and suddenly you're acting strange. Out with it."

"I didn't want to bring this up back east mostly because I was afraid if I screwed up the conversation you might not come here. You mentioned something when we were talking at the pond. You said you killed your father."

Marta felt a wave of heat rush up from her toes to her scalp. "I said if you asked people that's how they believe it happened."

"It doesn't have to be right now, but at some point I think we should talk more about this. The more I know the more I can help. You said the thing you worried about most was Keith. We'll figure that out, but this seems pretty important too. I thought maybe you'd bring it up again but you haven't."

"Keith might be the most clear and present danger, but you're right, my father's death won't just fade away into the past either. I'll have to deal with that too, at some point."

"I'm sorry to spring this on you right before the meeting. It's been weighing on me and I didn't want to let it go any longer. You didn't kill your father, right?"

"The shades of gray on what causes someone's death are endless," Marta replied as she fidgeted with the button on her jacket. "There is a reason people blame me. I don't think they're wrong."

"But criminally," Terrance pressed. "There aren't as many shades of gray when we're talking about being criminally responsible."

"It's time," Carol sang in a chipper voice as she

knocked and peeked in the office. "Let's go show what kind of stinging nettles we are."

Marta plastered on a smile and straightened up. She could feel Terrance still staring at her. Still waiting for some kind of indication that she was not a murderer. Turning her back, she sidled up to Carol. "We need a better nickname," she teased.

"We'll have a whole year of working together to figure that out." Carol had a spring in her step as she led them toward the board room. "Just be yourself, Marta."

Terrance, still looking slightly trepidatious, caught up to them and held open the door as they filed in. The table was already full of people and only three seats remained empty for them. The chatter slowed to a stop as Carol rounded the large table and took her seat at the head. Terrance pulled out Marta's chair then took the seat beside her.

"Thank you all for making time in your schedules this morning," Carol announced in a voice Marta hadn't heard her use before. It wasn't all that different from the usual way Carol spoke but there was an umph to it that was new. "You all know Terrance and I'd like you to meet Marta Leduc, the next recipient of the Milton Cesar Breakout Writer Award."

There was a rise of niceties as everyone around the table greeted her, then it settled again to quiet before Carol continued. "I know you've all had a chance to read her book The Wild Wind Falls."

A man Carol introduced as Robert spoke up. He flattened his tie and leaned back in his chair. "Marta, you're a very compelling writer. It's been quite some time since I've read a book like yours."

"Thank you," Marta said, desperately trying to keep her voice steady. "I've always enjoyed writing. I'm honored to be selected for the award."

Larry, one of the men Carol had warned her about, cleared his throat. "You haven't had the *traditional* path toward releasing your first book. The publishing company" —he looked down at his paper and adjusted his glasses— "Glass Jar Publishing. I've not heard of them."

Marta worked hard not to skip a beat. "They're a small publishing house in Maine."

Larry hummed. "Did you not submit to the big five publishing companies?"

"I did," Marta kept her voice light and airy. "They rejected my book."

Carol cut in. "Just like many of the best sellers we've all fallen in love with over the years. How many authors do we know who have great success after dozens of rejections? As a matter of fact, it's well known that readers are drawn to books that don't fit the mold traditional publishers select. That's where you find the real gems. And we've done just that." Carol beamed with pride.

Larry didn't look finished as he scanned the papers again. "Where did you refine your writing skills? Last year's recipient had a masters in creative writing. You have . . .?"

Marta tipped her head back. "A computer and ideas.

That's what I have. Did you like the book, Larry?" She blinked slowly, waiting for his rebuttal.

"I've only skimmed it," Larry admitted, not looking embarrassed by being unprepared. "It seems promising."

Lori, the only female board member clicked her tongue. "Larry, if you didn't bother reading the book, you don't get to weigh in. I, on the other hand, shut myself in the house all weekend and couldn't put it down. Marta, I haven't read a story like this in ages. Do you know why it was so compelling?" Lori paused for effect as she glanced around the table. "Because you didn't sit in a classroom for eight years getting your masters learning all the rigid rules of writing. You broke quite a few of them." She paused again. "And I loved it. It was refreshing in all the best ways."

There were some rumbles of agreement around the table and Marta had to remind herself to breathe. This was just the first step of a staircase she was likely to tumble down.

Carol changed her posture, and with that subtle move retook control of the room. "This isn't a selection process. Marta is slated to be the recipient of the award. I wanted you all to have a chance to meet her. I understand that she, in some ways, deviates from prior recipients. That's to our advantage. The world is changing. We are ready to change with it. Over the coming weeks and months, the production team will be developing a new format for the video presentation at the award ceremony."

"What kind of change to the format?" Charles asked,

his overgrown brows waggling with concern. "People have been tuning in year after year to see what they love. We can't disrupt the natural order of things."

"The cornerstones of the Cesar Milton Foundation will remain intact." Carol leaned back in her chair and crossed her legs. "Marta is going to be the catalyst to change how our audience views us. As a matter of fact, I believe we will gain a broader and more inclusive audience."

Charles grimaced and looked more like a cranky Muppet than a man. "All that from one girl?"

"One woman," Carol corrected coolly. "And yes, change is coming. It starts here and now."

Terrance jotted down a few notes and Marta wondered if she was supposed to be doing the same. Before she could decide Carol was on her feet and gesturing for Marta to join her. "Rather than turn this into an interrogation, and a rather lowbrow one at that, Marta and I will make plans to meet with the production team. If you have any further questions feel free to request some time on my calendar. I'll leave you all to the rest of your monthly meeting."

Marta was on her feet and walking quickly to catch up with Carol who was already at the door. Terrance was close behind.

"I like it," Terrance whispered as they made their way back to Carol's office. "That should give them something to chatter about the rest of the day."

Not sure if that was a good thing or not, Marta shot

Terrance a look. "What happens now? I don't feel like that went very well."

"It went flawlessly," Carol said in a voice loud enough for anyone passing to hear. "We gave them just enough to hook them and now we focus on the next step. We'll put together a press release regarding our selection for the award. While those can be broadly distributed, most of the buzz won't start until much closer to the ceremony at the end of the year."

"That's the step that worries me the most," Marta confessed. "Once it's out there, I think my problems will really start."

When they reached her office, Carol turned to face Marta. "Your problems are my problems so we'll face them together. It'll take a bit of time for the press release to be put together. We'll work on things before then. Once it's out we'll begin designing the filming process. Today, you just have to see the legal department and go over the contracts."

"Contracts?" Marta asked, feeling suddenly blindsided. "The legal department? I didn't know we were doing that today." She suddenly felt like maybe she should have a lawyer there to help her. The only one she knew was her second cousin who was a divorce attorney. His reputation was abysmal and she was certain he wouldn't be able to help.

"It's all very standard," Carol promised, tilting her head to the side and flashing a benevolent smile. "Don't do anything with them today. Take the contracts and have them looked over if you like. We have time."

Marta nodded and had the urge to look over at Terrance but didn't until he finally spoke. "I've set up some time for you to meet with them today. I'll take you down to that department."

"Great," Carol said, clapping her hands quickly as though their work was done for now. "After that you two should call it a day. Take Marta around to see the city. Get dinner. I took a look at your expense report from your time in New Hampshire. You didn't exactly live it up."

"We ate at the best restaurant in town." Terrance shrugged. "I've got a lot to catch up on. I don't want to leave you in the lurch. Plus, I feel like we need to do something about that not-so-special delivery you got in the mail today."

Carol made a dismissive noise. "Forget it for now. You know where Marta's hotel is, right? Your job for the rest of the day is to make sure she settles in. I can take care of everything here at the office."

Terrance looked unconvinced.

Giving in, Carol conceded, "I can at least pretend to take care of it all for one more day. Go enjoy the city. Youth is wasted on the young. Before you both know it, you'll be relying on cholesterol medicine and wondering why you can't drive at night anymore. Do we still have hurdles? Yes. Plenty of them. Are we going to solve them tonight? No. San Diego is calling for you, Marta, don't miss your shot."

Marta's heart fluttered with the possibilities. There wasn't much of an argument to make. She was here now. Depending on how things went, there was a chance she'd never be back. It would be foolish to miss the opportunity. "I guess dinner would be nice."

Terrance looked instantly pleased. "I know the perfect place. We can probably catch the sunset if we plan it right."

"You two have fun. Put all of this out of your mind. Just enjoy." Carol was persistent as she shooed them to gather their things. "I have a few phone calls to make. Let's regroup in the morning. You see that she has everything she needs." She pointed to Terrance and gave him a threatening yet maternal look. As Carol left them, Marta felt those prickling nerves return. Terrance was not going to ignore the fact that she had avoided his question.

"We can grab the contracts and head out," Terrance suggested, picking up his bag and taking his keys out.

"Wait," she blurted, planting her feet. "I want to go with you and I'd like to see the city, but I don't want to keep rehashing every aspect of my life. I can't keep this pace. It's grueling and takes a significant toll. I need a break. A real break."

With some mild unease, Terrance agreed. "I understand that. Carol's right. Tonight should just be about the city and your opportunity to experience it for the first time. There's an energy here I think you'll love."

"I think I will too," Marta beamed. She'd never been one to compartmentalize. For her if there was something to worry about it didn't stay in a separate box in the back of her mind. It was more akin to a coating of mist clinging to the rest of her thoughts and feelings. Just enough to dampen them all. It would be out of character to give herself permission to experience something free of worry. To live only in the moment and soak it all in.

After they'd retrieved the contract from the legal department, Terrance led her toward his car. She didn't know what he had planned or where they would go. But as the sun warmed her cheeks and the breeze rustled the palms overhead, she didn't really care where they ended up. There would be nothing here that reminded her of home, and she found that abundantly appealing.

CHAPTER TWENTY-THREE

Terrance

This wasn't his first time showing someone around town, but for some reason the pressure was more palpable with Marta. Maybe it was because she'd admitted seeing so few places in her life. Or because keeping her in good spirits would help them all succeed. If he were being honest though, it was the simple fact that making Marta smile emboldened him.

Watching Marta drink things in was invigorating. It wasn't as if she painted on a doe-eyed tourist look or gasped every time she saw a tall building. Hers wasn't a look of awe but of introspection. Something deeper.

When she put her feet in the Pacific Ocean for the first time she didn't squeal with excitement. She raised one hand up to shield her eyes from the sun and stared out at the crashing waves. There was no reminiscing about beach trips she'd taken as a child or dreams she had of coming to California someday. He watched as the wind swept her hair wildly to the side and she grounded her feet against the push and pull of the tide.

"This is La Jolla Cove," he explained. "It's a very popular spot. People come to watch the sea lions play and picnic on the rocks."

"The sea lions?" Marta asked, keeping her face serious. "How do they carry their picnic baskets with those flippers."

"The people," Terrance corrected with a chuckle. "The people come and picnic. It was one of the first places I came when I moved to San Diego. I carried this little magazine photo of the place around in my pocket for years. I was determined to see it someday. To live nearby."

"Really?" Marta asked, turning her gaze from the sea back to him. He felt proud to be worthy enough to draw her attention back from something so compelling.

"Yes. I lived with my aunt and uncle most of my life. They had this tiny house in Yuma, Arizona. I absolutely hated everything about it."

"The house?"

"The house, the city, the heat, the people. Now, looking back I'm not sure if I truly didn't like it there or if I was just constantly comparing it to the life I thought I should have had with my parents. My aunt and uncle took me in when I was two years old. They're the only parents I ever knew and I had a massive chip on my shoulder about that for a long time. They took me in and instead of being grateful I held it against them."

"Normally I wouldn't ask, but since I've already spilled my guts to you about things, where were your parents?"

"I don't know," Terrance admitted, his gaze falling down to his bare feet in the sand. "My aunt and uncle didn't know either. One day I was a kid with two seemingly normal parents and the next, no one came to pick me up from daycare. Both of them just vanished. My mother's sister came and got me the following day from Child Protective Services and I lived with them after that. But I cut that picture of La Jolla beach out of a magazine when I was eleven and promised myself I'd move here."

"Why here?" Her eyes were fixed on him as she brushed her windswept hair away from her face.

"My family told me stories about my mother. She loved the ocean and she'd come here when she was young. I researched it one day and decided it's exactly where I wanted to be. It's good weather all year long. Yuma was one of the hottest places to try to survive in. Here, it's like this almost every day. San Diego has its problems just like any other city. But I've lived here for six years now and I've never been happier."

"How do you live with the not knowing? What could have possibly happened to your parents?"

"I don't know. There's a part of me that thinks no one has ever told me the whole story. But I don't focus on it. The older I get the more I realize how special my aunt and uncle were to take me in. She must have been terribly sad about losing her sister yet somehow she managed to raise me. You would think this would be the kind of thing that would come up all the time. But my family hardly ever discusses my parents."

"That's not hard to believe," Marta nodded. "It's the same thing in my family with Jonah. I've wanted to ask so many times for the details. For the parts of the story no one ever told me, but I learned pretty early on that if I brought it up, people would get upset or sad. They didn't talk about it, so I didn't either."

"Exactly," Terrance said, jutting his hand out toward her. "No one ever explicitly said we're not talking about this. I just knew after a while that I shouldn't bring it up."

"I'm sorry you went through that," Marta said, leaning in a little closer to him. "That must be very hard. Thank you for bringing me here to see this. It's stunning."

"So are you," Terrance uttered confidently before he could think better of it. "I've seen this beach a thousand times, but it's never looked this beautiful."

Marta's cheeks pinkened and she turned back to watch the waves. "I don't think that's what Carol meant when she told us to go have some fun. She wouldn't approve."

"How do you know?" He closed the gap between them as he moved to her side and watched the waves just as she was doing.

"Carol is a levelheaded woman. She's calculated. As benevolent and sweet as she's been to me, at the end of the day, she wants to be successful more than she wants to be altruistic."

Terrance opened his mouth to disagree but Marta's words plowed on.

"I'm not saying that as though it's a negative. I am not naïve; the only reason Carol made it to where she is today is because she's been willing to prioritize correctly."

"And what does that have to do with me calling you beautiful?" He folded his arms across his chest mostly to keep from reaching out and kissing her.

"This is a messy situation and any personal interest would only make it more complicated. There is far too much on the line for everyone involved to let any kind of meaningless attraction become a road block."

"Meaningless attraction?" he asked indignantly. "I don't know which of those two words I want to talk about first."

"Neither," she bit out quickly. "I say we just let it go. Nothing good can come from adding any more to this situation."

"So I shouldn't call you beautiful?"

"No."

"And I shouldn't take you to dinner tonight and ask you to dance when the jazz band I love starts playing?"

"You should not."

"And when I surprise you with a very special after-dinner plan that I lined up for us, you shouldn't be overcome with joy and hug me?"

"Trust me, no danger of that."

"And to be clear, when I take you back to your hotel tonight, full of decadent food, luscious wine, fresh memories of exciting outings, you should not invite me in?"

"I should not," Marta said, the corners of her mouth raising slightly. "And I won't. You can't possibly think any of those things would be a good idea."

"The distance between good idea and fun is immense," Terrance said coolly. "Sometimes fun wins out over logic."

"We shouldn't let it," Marta cautioned. "It would only make things tougher. We should just forget this ever happened."

"If I could forget how beautiful you are, I'd be worried. Something would definitely be wrong with me."

"You don't have to forget it, you just can't say it." Marta explained the small distinction.

"You have to admit, you and I would—"

"I don't."

"You're a strong woman, Marta," Terrance said, turning back toward the waves. "I don't think there is anything we could do that would create a hurdle you couldn't jump."

"Maybe you're right." Marta sighed, and for a second he thought there was a glimmer of hope. "But I'm tired of having to jump so high, so often. I don't expect things to be easy, but I don't plan to make them even harder. Not just because I meet a nice guy with a pretty face."

"Pretty," Terrance joked, pretending to be giddy about the compliment. After a long moment of teasing he dropped the act. "I can respect that, Marta. I'm not looking to make anything harder for you than it already is."

"But I still get the special after-dinner surprise, right?" She turned toward him with a playful smile.

"You do," he promised. "I'll try my best not to call you beautiful. Just stop standing in that sunset light and making those faces."

"What faces?"

"That dreamy far off look you get when you're in your head. It makes me want to know what's going on in there."

"It's scary in there, in my head."

"I don't scare easily," Terrance explained. "I'm not going anywhere."

He understood that promise meant more than any other he could make. Just being there in some reliable way, unshakably existing next to someone, mattered to people like Marta. It mattered to him too.

But the vibe changed quickly as the night rolled on. For all his optimism about what the evening would bring, the first three hours were mostly a bust. He'd rolled the dice on the restaurant, a top ten sushi place, to find out Marta didn't like sushi. The band he loved had canceled for the night because they were all sick. The stroll he'd planned to take through Balboa Park was interrupted by a closed path due to a movie being filmed. This last surprise felt as though it was destined to fail.

"It can't get worse." Terrance shrugged as he led Marta toward a metal gate.

"Never say that," she warned. "It can always get worse. Where are we?"

"The zoo. My friend works here and got us an exclusive after-hours tour."

"This zoo is like THE zoo. I saw a brochure at the airport. They do after hours tours?" Marta asked, looking leery of another disappointment. "Or maybe they decided last night was the last one and they'll turn us away?" She was teasing him now and he appreciated the levity.

"It's not technically a real tour," he explained sheepishly. "But my buddy said they do it all the time. A lot of the animals are sleeping but there is this one spot by the lions' den that apparently is amazing this time of night. They have a swing attached to this giant tree. If you swing high enough the view is supposed to be awesome."

"Oh Terrance," a voice said as the gate opened, "I'm so sorry, man. My boss is here tonight. They're doing like an audit." A young man with curly blond hair and a poor attempt at a beard stumbled out of the darkness toward them. "We'll have to reschedule."

Marta burst into a full belly laugh as she clutched Terrance's arm. The sting of the latest letdown was made slightly better by her touch.

"Ryan, are you serious? You can't imagine how many things have been screwed up for us tonight."

"Oh," Ryan said, waving bashfully at Marta. "I'm very sorry, ma'am. I am sure Terrance will find you something just as good for your date."

"Ma'am?" Marta choked out. "Date?"

"I've got to go," Ryan apologized again. "Text me, we'll try again a different night." The gate slammed shut and Terrance and Marta stood in the quiet dim parking lot just waiting for something else to happen. It didn't.

"Did he call me ma'am?" Marta finally asked. "And why are you friends with a kid who isn't old enough to grow more than peach fuzz on his face?"

"Okay," Terrance said soberly, "I'm friends with his mom. She's a waitress at a place where I hung out when I first moved here. She's really nice and I met Ryan when he'd come in to the place for dinner. They were always good to me. I can't believe how bad this night has gone. My date game is usually on point."

"Date? Again with that. This is not a date."

"Damn right it isn't," Terrance scoffed. "I don't want this on my record. This would go down as one of the worst in history."

"You didn't know I don't like sushi. And the walk was really nice until they kicked us out. This, well, it's the thought that counts. The swing sounds amazing. Maybe we should just call it a night." She yawned and tried to stifle it. "I'm still on East Coast time."

"Right," Terrance agreed. "The jet lag takes a bit to wear off. You'll be up before the sun until you adjust. I'll take you back to your hotel."

"Don't feel bad," she begged. "Really this is not even remotely close to the worst date I've been on. A guy last year took me fishing."

"That's not so bad."

"He didn't have fishing poles, a boat, bait—nothing. We just went to a pond and sat there. I didn't have the heart to ask him what he'd been thinking. We sat, barely talked, and went home. That was a bad one. And"—she held up one finger as if she'd just remembered something—"this is not even a date. So it can't be a bad date."

"Come on," Terrance said, leading her back to the car. "Let's get out of here before one of the animals breaks out and mauls us. That's basically where this is heading. Carol asked me to show you a good time tonight and make sure you had fun. This is not how it was supposed to be."

He took a few steps back toward the car before she tugged on his arm. Her tiny frame was stronger than he assumed. It wasn't enough to actually spin him back but after a beat he obliged. "I had fun. La Jolla was beautiful and I learned something about you that I didn't know. I don't like sushi but they threw tempura on some fish and fried that up."

"That was from the kid's menu," Terrance groaned.

"This isn't a date," Marta repeated. "But if it was, it would have been a great one. I'd have definitely kissed you goodnight."

Marta had her hand on his forearm, forcing his attention her way, though he didn't need to be compelled to turn to her. Her head was tipped up and her body was a mere six inches from his. He could easily pull her in, lean down, and kiss her. There was no doubt it would be as fiery as he imagined. But she'd been clear earlier in the night that was not what she wanted so he held himself upright and tried not to stare at her delicious lips.

"Well?" she whispered, her eyes wide and expectant.

"Well what?" he asked, bringing his arm up and brushing her bangs out of her face. It was exactly what he'd have done if he was about to kiss her, which he was not.

"I said I would definitely have kissed you good night."

"If this was a date," he replied, drawing the words out sarcastically.

"I'm not sure I can give you too many more signs, I'm basically air traffic control flashing those lights all around my face here." She rolled her eyes. "Aren't you going to kiss me?"

"You said—" he edged out just before she raised on her tiptoes and wrapped her arms around his neck.

"That was ages ago," Marta whispered, her lips an inch from his.

"It was three hours ago."

"A lot has changed."

"It has?" he asked, finally taking her hips in his hands and pulling her fully against him. "I don't want to make things more difficult for you."

"It's pretty difficult standing right here and not being kissed," she said coyly as she licked her lips subtly.

That was it. He couldn't take another second, and apparently neither could she. As he moved to close the gap between them so did she, and a frenzied urgent kiss began. In the back employee parking lot of the locked-up zoo, they stood by his car kissing with a passion he'd forgotten existed. Maybe it was because they knew it was foolish and taboo. Or because they'd already begun to share so many of the intimate details of their lives in this high-stakes situation. He couldn't explain exactly why kissing Marta was supremely intense. All he knew was that he never wanted it to stop.

When she pressed against his car the alarm began to sound, sending her jumping forward with a screech. He dug in his pocket for his keys and silenced the blaring noise.

Marta held one hand to her heart with the other clutching his arm. "That scared the hell out of me," she blurted out.

"Me too," Terrance replied breathlessly. He knew she meant the car alarm but he meant something entirely different. The way his senses were overwhelmed as their kiss began. The awareness of loss when she stepped out of his arms. That was truly frightening to him.

"Tomorrow," she said as she straightened her shirt and rounded the car, "we act like this never happened."

He nodded for lack of anything better to say and realized if he was capable of acting as though that kiss meant nothing, he'd have earned a shelf full of Oscars by now.

Terrance knew tomorrow would be interesting. There was still so much to figure out as it related to Marta's past. But right now, his mind wandered only to her future. He felt a swell of protective energy fill him at the thought of anyone in her life trying to ruin this for her. He was more convinced than ever that this was her destiny. She deserved to walk across that stage and receive her award. As he gripped the steering wheel and turned back onto the highway toward her hotel, he knew he'd do whatever it took to make that happen. No one would stand between Marta and what she deserved. Not anymore. Not while he was there.

"Don't be all quiet and weird now," Marta pleaded, nibbling nervously on her fingernail.

"There is nothing weird between us," Terrance promised as he ran his thumb over her cheek until she smiled. "There won't be. No matter what."

She turned toward him, trapping his hand between her cheek and the headrest of the car just long enough to plant a kiss on his palm. "I think we're headed for some hurt."

"I won't hurt you," he shot back quickly and earnestly.

Marta didn't answer. She didn't offer any scenario she feared or explanation for why she'd said it. Instead she turned toward the window and watched the world, one she'd never seen before, zip by.

"You're safe here, Marta. Trust me."

"I'm not fragile in the way you think, Terrance. I'm not afraid of goodbyes or endings. I can walk away from anything because of how many things I've had to give up and leave just to live. There is nothing in my life that makes me pause and stay around longer than I should. I don't keep trinkets or cover my walls with photographs of old memories. I am attached to hardly anything. I need almost nothing to survive."

"So what are you afraid of then?" Terrance asked,

placing a hand on her knee and praying she'd cover it with her own.

"I'm afraid something will come along and change that." She finally did cover his hand with hers and squeeze it gently.

The picture was far from clear, but he felt as though he could see the outlines and the shadows of what she meant. Marta wasn't afraid of him breaking her heart, she was terrified of what it might mean if she suddenly and unabashedly cared for him. Walking away was how she functioned. Having something she found hard to abandon abruptly would be daunting.

Terrance didn't have an answer. He didn't know how to make her fear subside. It was one thing to promise her he'd keep her safe from anything and anyone who wanted to hurt her. It was another thing entirely to promise he could keep her safe from herself.

They rode the rest of the way to her hotel in silence and he knew the right thing to do was let her go up to her room on her own. He had no business there tonight even if he desperately wanted to go with her. "You have your room key?" he asked, already seeing it in her hand as the doorman opened the lobby door for her.

Marta waved the key for Terrance to see. "You'll pick me up in the morning?"

"I'll be here," he promised as a thousand more things he wanted to say rose from his chest. But he bit at his cheek and kept them at bay. Tomorrow they'd start figuring out how to divorce Marta from her past so she could step into her future. Tomorrow they might not talk about the kiss. They might not touch at all.

Tomorrow seemed formidable in its great expansive unknown. Before Marta passed through the open lobby doors she turned quickly and ran toward him. She looped her arms around his neck again but this time did not wait for him to lean in. Kissing him with the same feverish exuberance as the last time, Terrance felt the familiar rush of connection flow through him.

When she pulled away she kept her eyes fixed on him. "We won't talk about it tomorrow," she reminded him. "So I thought I better get one more kiss tonight."

The same hollow absence overtook his arms as she finally stepped away and disappeared into the lobby.

"Tomorrow," he whispered to himself. It was half promise, half protest. He'd try his best to pretend this never happened. But he knew he'd fail. If Marta was afraid to fall for him, he'd just have to give her a soft place to land. "Tomorrow."

Continue the Story: Book 2: Anytime the Birds Fall

ALSO BY DANIELLE STEWART

Book 8: Defending Innocence

Book 9: Saving Love(includes excerpts from Betty's Journal)

Edenville Series – A Piper Anderson Spin Off:

Book 1: Flowers in the Snow

Book 2: Kiss in the Wind

Book 3: Stars in a Bottle

Book 4: Fire in the Heart

Piper Anderson Legacy Mystery Series:

Book 1: Three Seconds To Rush

Book 2: Just for a Heartbeat

Book 3: Not Just an Echo

Broken Mirror Series:

Book 1: The Way Down

Book 2: The Way Home

Book 3: The Way Back

The Clover Series:

Hearts of Clover - Novella & Book 2: (Half My Heart & Change My Heart)

Book 3: All My Heart

Over the Edge Series:

Book 1: Facing Home

Book 2: Crashing Down

Midnight Magic Series:

Amelia

Rough Waters Series:

Book 1: The Goodbye Storm

Book 2: The Runaway Storm

Book 3: The Rising Storm

Stand Alones:

Yours for the Taking

Love in a Paper Garden

****

Multi-Author Series including books by Danielle Stewart

All are stand alone reads and can be enjoyed in any order.

Indigo Bay Series:

A multi-author sweet romance series

Sweet Dreams - Stacy Claflin

Sweet Matchmaker - Jean Oram

Sweet Sunrise - Kay Correll

Sweet Illusions - Jeanette Lewis

Sweet Regrets - Jennifer Peel

Sweet Rendezvous - Danielle Stewart

Short Holiday Stories in Indigo Bay:

A multi-author sweet romance series

Sweet Holiday Wishes - Melissa McClone

Sweet Holiday Surprise - Jean Oram

Sweet Holiday Memories - Kay Correll

Sweet Holiday Traditions - Danielle Stewart

BOOKS IN THE BARRINGTON BILLIONAIRE SYNCHRONIZED WORLD

By Danielle Stewart:

Fierce Love

Wild Eyes

Crazy Nights

Loyal Hearts

Untamed Devotion

Stormy Attraction

Foolish Temptations

Surprising Destiny

Lovely Dreams

Perfect Homecoming

You can now download all the Barrington Billionaire books by Danielle Stewart in a "Sweet" version. Enjoy the clean and wholesome version, same story without the spice. If you prefer the hotter version be sure to download the original.

The Sweet version still contains adult situations and relationships.

Fierce Love - Sweet Version

Wild Eyes - Sweet Version

Crazy Nights - Sweet Version

Loyal Hearts - Sweet Version

Untamed Devotion - Sweet Version

Stormy Attraction - Sweet Version

Foolish Temptations - Sweet Version - Coming Soon

FOREIGN EDITIONS

The following books are currently available in foreign translations

German Translation:

Fierce Love

Ungezügelte Leidenschaft

Wild Eyes

Glühend heiße Blicke

Crazy Nights

Nächte, wild und unvergessen

Loyal Hearts

Herzen, treu und ehrlich: Die Welt der Barrington-Milliardäre

***

French Translation:

Flowers in the Snow

Fleurs Des Neiges

NEWSLETTER SIGN-UP

If you'd like to stay up to date on the latest Danielle Stewart news visit www.authordaniellestewart.com and sign up for my newsletter.

AUTHOR CONTACT INFORMATION

Website: AuthorDanielleStewart.com
Email: AuthorDanielleStewart@Gmail.com
Facebook: facebook.com/AuthorDanielleStewart
Twitter: @DStewartAuthor
Bookbub: https://www.bookbub.com/authors/danielle-stewart
Amazon: https://www.amazon.com/Danielle-Stewart/e/B00CCOYB3O